HOME IS WHERE THE HEART IS

Also by Joan Jonker

When One Door Closes
Man of the House

Victims of Violence

HOME IS WHERE THE HEART IS

Joan Jonker

HEADLINE

First published in 1993
by Print Origination (NW) Ltd

First published in this edition in 1995
by HEADLINE BOOK PUBLISHING

10 9 8 7 6 5 4 3 2

British Library Cataloguing in Publication Data

Jonker, Joan
   Home is Where the Heart is
   I. Title
   823.914 [F]

ISBN 0-7472-1180-9

Typeset by
Letterpart Limited, Reigate, Surrey

Printed and bound in Great Britain by
Mackays of Chatham PLC, Chatham, Kent

HEADLINE BOOK PUBLISHING
A division of Hodder Headline PLC
338 Euston Road
London NW1 3BH

Dedicated to my family and my friends
for their encouragement.

My gratitude to Mary Johnson,
without whose help and guidance
this trilogy of books would never have been written.

Chapter One

A spark from a hissing coal spurted from the fire and landed on the hearth rug by Eileen's feet. Quick as a flash her foot shot out and extinguished it before it had time to singe the rug. She glanced across at her husband who was sitting at the opposite side of the grate, but Bill was so absorbed in the evening paper he was oblivious to everything else. I dunno, Eileen muttered silently, once he's got his nose stuck in a paper, he wouldn't notice if the house burned down around him. If he had a mind like mine right now, he wouldn't be sitting there so càlmly. All the family were in bed and it was quiet in the small living room of the two-up-two-down terrace house, except for Eileen's heart, which was pounding so loudly she wondered that Bill couldn't hear it. Eileen sat back in the chair, her hands clasped tightly together. Go on, tell him, she urged herself. You've got to do it sometime, so the sooner you get it over with the better. But her mouth felt like a piece of emery paper with nerves and she didn't think she could speak even if she plucked up the courage.

Calm down, she told herself, taking a deep breath and exhaling slowly. Her gaze swept around the room, taking in the sideboard with a vase and ornament on top of the lace runner, the couch against the far wall and the dining table with its maroon plush tablecloth and four straight backed chairs standing neatly with their seats hidden beneath the table top. When her heart beat had slowed, Eileen licked her dry lips. It's now or never, so best get it over with.

'Bill, will yer put the paper down a minute. I've got something to tell yer.'

Bill Gillmoss lowered the *Echo* until his deep brown eyes were peering over the top. 'What's that, chick?'

'I'm havin' a baby.' Eileen was sitting on the edge of the couch,

1

her hands clasped between her knees. She pushed a wisp of mousey-coloured hair behind her ear as she waited anxiously for her husband's reaction.

Bill stared hard for a few seconds, then threw back his head and chuckled loudly. 'I nearly fell for that! How you can keep a straight face, I'll never know.'

'I'm not jokin', Bill. I went to see Doctor Greenfield today, and I'm nearly two months.'

The smile left Bill's face. 'You're having me on, aren't you, chick?'

Eileen shook her head. 'I wouldn't joke about a thing like that.'

The paper fell from Bill's hand, and for what seemed like an eternity to Eileen, the only sound in the room was the ticking of the clock on the mantelpiece. Then, in a voice thick with shock, he said, 'That's the last thing in the world I expected.'

'Well, I wasn't exactly plannin' on it meself!' Not for the world would Eileen show how frightened she was. It was twelve years since their Edna was born and that was a long time to go between children. 'It's happened, an' there's nowt we can do about it!'

'But we're too old to go through that again!' When Bill turned his eyes on her, Eileen could see he was bewildered. 'The children are all grown up now . . . Billy's nearly sixteen, Joan's leaving school in a couple of weeks, and Edna's twelve! I thought the days of having babies were well behind us!'

You can say that again! Eileen didn't voice her thoughts. As she'd said, it had happened and there was nothing she could do about it. It wasn't like buying a pair of shoes that you could take back if you found they didn't suit you. 'Bill, I'm forty-two, not a bloody hundred and two! An' if I'm pregnant then I can't be too old, can I? If it hadn't been for the war, an' you bein' away for six years, I'd 'ave probably had a few more children by now.' Eileen was close to tears. She'd been on pins all day, having to keep the news to herself until all the family were in bed and she had Bill on his own. She'd been hoping he'd be pleased, then she'd have felt a bit better. It wasn't that she didn't want a baby, she loved children. But the prospect of giving birth scared her stiff. 'It takes two to make a baby, Bill Gillmoss, so don't be lookin' at me as though I've committed a flippin' crime!'

'I know, chick.' Bill was trying to come to terms with the shock. he could see the disappointment on Eileen's face and tried to raise a

2

smile. 'What did Ma have to say?'

'I 'aven't told me mam. I wanted you to be the first to know, seein' as you 'ad a hand in it.'

'I wonder how she'll take it?' Bill reached for his cigarettes and matches. 'And the kids? It'll be a big shock to them.'

'Bill, I couldn't give a monkey's uncle about me mam and the kids! It's you who's my main concern, and yer actin' as though it's got nothin' to do with you! We, Bill . . . you an' me . . . are goin' to 'ave a baby whether yer like it or not!'

Out of the side of his eye, Bill gazed at his wife. He took in the droop of her shoulders and the troubled expression on her face. He quickly returned his cigarettes and matches to the mantelpiece and moved to kneel at the side of her chair. 'I'm sorry, chick!' He put an arm across her shoulders and pulled her towards him. 'It's come as a bit of a shock, so I need a little time to get used to the idea.' He kissed her lightly on the lips. 'That's what we get for playing mothers and fathers.' Eileen's arms went around his neck, a constant reminder of his days in the prisoner-of-war camp. She'd been able to fill out his skeletal frame and help him over his nightmares, but nothing could put back the dark brown hair he'd had before he'd joined the army. 'I'm worn out, Bill, an' I've got a splittin' headache. Me mind's been in a hell of a state all day. It's not that I don't want a baby, 'cos yer know I'm a sucker when it comes to babies. But it's been such a long time since I 'ad our Edna, I don't relish the thought of goin' through it all again.' She drew away to look into his eyes. 'But if I thought you were 'appy, Bill, then that would be half the battle.'

'Look, as long as you are all right, that's all I worry about, you know that. If you're happy, then I'll be happy.'

They were quiet for a while, wrapped in each other's arms. Then Bill asked softly, 'Have you thought about the upheaval this is going to cause? We'll have to move away from here, for a start. The house is too small as it is, we'd never manage with a baby as well.'

Eileen jerked up straight. 'I'm not leavin' this little house! I love it here!'

'Chick, be practical! Where would you put a cot? Your ma sleeps in the girls' room, and they can hardly move, and our Billy's feet are almost sticking out of the window in that little box room.'

'I'm not movin' away from 'ere!' Eileen persisted. 'I'd miss all me neighbours.'

Bill sighed. 'Okay, we've got plenty of time to talk about that. The first thing is to tell Ma and the children.'

'That's the part I'm dreadin'.' Eileen hunched her shoulders as her chubby face creased in a smile. 'I never told me mam when I was expectin' the other three, I just left it till she could see for 'erself.' Eileen started to rock back and forth and Bill could hear the springs in the chair creak in protest at the movement of her eighteen-stone body. 'Can yer believe it, I'm forty-two years old and frightened to tell me mam I'm 'aving a baby!'

'Five minutes is all it'll take to tell Ma, and the girls, and when it's over you'll wonder why you were ever worried,' Bill said confidently. 'You can leave Billy to me . . . I'll tell him.'

'Only five minutes, he says,' Eileen huffed. 'Yer can be hung, drawn and quartered in five minutes, Bill Gillmoss, an' that's what me mam will do to me . . . after she's laid a duck egg!'

'Is this one of your little jokes?' Maggie stood rubbing her chin, a look of doubt on her face. Her daughter was always pulling her leg, and Maggie never knew when to take her seriously. She was only half the size of Eileen, with a trim figure and an abundance of white hair which was always neatly waved. It was her face, with deep worry lines etched on her forehead and cheeks, that told of the sadness she'd suffered in her sixty-seven years. When her husband had died eighteen years previously, she'd come to live with Eileen and Bill, and never for one moment had she regretted it. They'd taken her into their home and surrounded her with love and laughter. They'd given her a reason for living.

'Mam, I know I clown around a lot, but I'd hardly make a joke about havin' a baby, now would I?' While Eileen's heart was thumping like mad, she told herself it was ridiculous to be so embarrassed. Having babies was natural when you were married. And it wasn't as though her mother had never had children of her own because she'd had her and their Rene. When Maggie didn't answer, Eileen leaned forward, so their faces were nearly touching. 'I know yer gobsmacked, Mam, but for 'eaven's sake say something.'

'That's the understatement of the year!' Maggie's mind was in a turmoil. She could see the pleading in Eileen's eyes, begging her to understand and be happy for her. And all Maggie ever wanted was her daughter's happiness. But while she willed herself to say the

4

words Eileen wanted to hear, Maggie couldn't suppress the fear she felt. She'd always worried that the weight her daughter carried round with her would one day put too big a strain on her heart. How was she going to cope with the extra burden of carrying a child?

'Come on, missus!' Making a fist of her hand, Eileen leaned on the table. 'Cat got yer tongue, 'as it?'

'You certainly know how to surprise people,' Maggie said, smoothing down the front of her floral wrap-around pinny. 'But this is one surprise I never expected!'

'I know what's worryin' yer,' Eileen smiled to ease the tension. 'It's the thought of another Easter egg yer'll 'ave to buy, an' another Christmas pressie.'

'What does Bill say?' Maggie asked. 'Is he pleased?'

'Pleased as punch, he is!' Eileen lied. 'When 'e went out of 'ere this mornin', he walked down the road with 'is shoulders back and his chest stuck out a mile. Real proud of 'imself, he is!'

'And do the children know?'

Eileen screwed up her face. 'Haven't told them yet. I'll tell them when they come in from school, so make yerself scarce, will yer, missus? I 'ad to take me courage in both 'ands to tell you, so God only knows 'ow I'm goin' to break it to them.'

'They'll take it in their stride,' Maggie said. 'As long as their tea's on the table, and they can go out and play with their mates, that's all they worry about.' She opened her arms wide and Eileen, blinking back the tears, walked into them. 'Congratulations, love.'

'Thanks, Mam.' Eileen grabbed her mother round the waist and lifted her off her feet. Swinging her round and round, she gasped, 'I always said yer were the best mam in the whole world.'

'Oh, you, Mam!' Joan's hand went to her mouth, her face the colour of beetroot. She was at the age now when sex was whispered about in the playground, and some of the girls in her class sneaked in copies of *True Confessions* magazine. The thought of her mam and dad doing what couples in the magazine did, horrified her. They were too old for that!

'What d'yer mean, "oh, you, Mam"!' Hundreds of butterflies were flying around inside Eileen's tummy, she was so embarrassed. It's worse than going to the flipping dentist, she told herself. 'I thought yer'd be please to 'ave a little brother or sister.'

5

'Well I'm not, so there!' Joan nodded her head to emphasise her words. 'I don't want it!'

'That's just tough on you, then, my girl, 'cos there's nowt yer can do about it.' Eileen raised her eyes to the ceiling. God give me the strength to keep my hands off her.

Edna had been standing with her mouth open, listening and taking in. Now she flew to put her arms around Eileen's waist. 'Ooh, I'm made up, Mam! I hope it's a little girl, and we can call her Susan . . . after that film star, Susan Hayward.'

Eileen patted her bottom, chuckling, 'An' if it's a boy, I suppose yer want it called Alan, after Alan Ladd?'

Edna's brows came together in concentration. She was two years younger than Joan, but they could pass for twins. Both had their mother's straggly, mousey-coloured hair and hazel eyes. And both were as thin as bean poles, as Eileen had been at their age. After a few seconds' consideration, Edna shook her head. 'No, if it's a boy, can we call it Randolph, after Randolph Scott?'

The rafters rang with Eileen's laughter. 'Some 'ope you've got! Can yez see me at the front door, shoutin', "Randolph, yer tea's ready"! I'd be the laughin' stock of the whole ruddy neighbour-hood!'

Joan spun on her heels. She didn't know what there was to laugh about. Fancy someone as old as her mother having a baby! It was a good job she was leaving school in a few weeks and wouldn't have to tell her friends. 'I'm going down to Dorothy's.'

'Don't go far,' Eileen called after her, 'yer tea won't be long.'

'Mam, will yer teach me how to knit?' Edna was moving from one foot to the other. 'Then I can make a matinee coat for the baby.'

'We'll see.' Eileen noticed the jerky movements and gave Edna a push. 'Down the yard to the lavvy, now! Yer always leave it till the last minute!'

Eileen, a smile on her face, watched through the window as Edna flew down the yard. 'At least I've made someone happy,' she said aloud. 'And the others will come round, given time.'

Bill threw the spent match in the fire grate, his eyes screwed up against the smoke drifting upwards from his cigarette. Last night, when Eileen had told him she was pregnant, it had hit him like a body blow, knocking the stuffing out of him. He'd been able to think of nothing else all day in work. But by dinner time, although he wasn't thrilled, he'd got used to the idea. And when he was clocking off, he told himself the eagerness he felt to get home was only because he wanted to make sure Eileen was all right. It was when he was stepping down from the bus, the truth hit him. He wanted this baby!

'Well, that's the last of the washin' in steep.' Eileen came through from the kitchen, rubbing her wet hands on the corner of her pinny. 'They'll be ready to mangle and put out on the line in the mornin'.' She turned one of the dining chairs to sit facing the fire and opened her legs wide to feel the heat from the glowing coals. 'Ooh, that's lovely! It's freezin' out there!'

'D'you feel like a cup of cocoa, to warm you up?' Bill asked. 'I'll make it.'

'Nah! Just give us five minutes to rest me weary bones, then I'll make us a sandwich.' Eileen kicked one of her shoes off and groaned with pleasure. 'That's better. Me feet are killin' me.'

'Will you sit still long enough for us to talk?' Bill asked. 'I've got something to tell you.'

Eileen closed her eyes and put her hand to her mouth, her fingers digging deep into the fleshy cheeks. Her huge tummy started to shake, and her words came out in a splutter. 'Yer not goin' to tell me yer in the family way, are yer, Bill Gillmoss?'

Bill had moved to the edge of his chair, thinking Eileen was upset and crying. Now he fell back, shaking his head. 'Aren't you ever serious?'

'Sometimes I'm dead serious, but nobody takes any notice of me, so why bother?' Eileen wasn't smiling now. 'This is not laughter yer hear, Bill, it's bloody hysterics! It's been quite a day for me, I can tell yer. First I 'ad to pluck up the nerve to tell me mam, then start again with our Joan and Edna. I wouldn't go through that again for a big clock.'

'I'm sorry! I should have been here so we could have told them together.'

Eileen tilted her head, gazing at him questioningly through lowered lids.

'What was it yer wanted to tell me?'

'That I'm ashamed and sorry about last night. I was a right bastard and no mistake.' Bill's eyes followed the path of his two fingers as they ran down the crease of his trousers. 'I was an unthinking, selfish swine, and I want you to know I'm sorry. I also

7

want you to know I'm happy about the baby. It'll be nice to have a little one in the house again.'

Eileen folded her arms and they disappeared from view beneath her enormous bust. With two fingers circling the deep dimples in her elbows, she said softly, 'Hearin' yer say that, Bill, has taken a load off me shoulders. Yer looked far from 'appy last night with a right miserable gob on yer!'

'I'm forgiven, then?' Bill smiled sheepishly.

'I'll forgive yer, but thousands wouldn't! I don't know about me mam an' our Joan, though! Me mam's not too 'appy, but that's understandable 'cos she's worried about me.' Eileen stretched her leg out and kicked Bill on the shin, a wicked glint in her eyes. 'But from the look of disgust on our Joan's face, I'd say she thinks yer just a dirty old man!'

'She's at an awkward age. Probably just learning about the birds and the bees, and she was embarrassed. It's romantic when you're sitting in the picture house and Clark Gable and Myrna Loy get in a clinch, but when it's your own mam and dad . . . well, that's different. But when I told our Billy, he was over the moon!'

'God bless 'im,' Eileen grinned. 'He thinks the world of you, an' anythin' you do is hunkey-dory with him.'

'I wonder what Cissie Maddox and the neighbours will think?' Bill mused. 'I bet they'll be surprised.'

'Sod Cissie Maddox and the neighbours! They don't keep us, so why worry what they think?' Eileen's round face beamed. 'Mary and Vera are comin' here tomorrow afternoon, an' I can't wait to see their faces. They'll be flabbergasted!'

'So, it's sod Cissie Maddox and the neighbours, eh?' Bill said. 'Only last night you said you'd never leave here because you'd miss them.'

'Well, so I would! Honest to God, Bill, yer can be as thick as two short planks, sometimes! I can fight like mad with Cissie one day, and be all matey with 'er the next. That's what neighbours are like. It doesn't mean because yer 'ave a difference of opinion with them over something that they're not good neighbours. There's not one in this street that I couldn't go to for help if I needed it, an' that's what bein' a good neighbour is all about. So, put that in yer pipe an' smoke it, Bill Gillmoss!'

Chapter Two

'I really enjoyed that.' Bill dropped his knife and fork on to the empty plate and pushed it away. Leaning back in the chair he undid the top button of his trousers and let out a long sigh. 'I've eaten that much I'm stored.'

'Yer eyes are bigger than yer belly.' Eileen started to gather up the empty plates. 'Sit by the fire, 'ave a ciggie an' relax.'

Bill scraped his chair back. 'Did you have a nice afternoon, chick?'

'Great! Mary and Vera were made up about the baby.'

All eyes turned when Joan stood up so quickly her chair banged into the sideboard and the table cloth dragged askew. 'I'm going out.'

Eileen watched her daughter disappear down the hall and heard the front door bang behind her. 'Oh, dear, someone's not too 'appy.' She shrugged her shoulders and pulled a face. 'Still, yer can't win 'em all.'

'Here, give me the dishes.' Maggie pushed Eileen aside. 'I'll do the washing up.'

'Ah, yer not a bad old stick, are yer, missus!' Eileen smiled fondly at her mother. 'Will yer cover our Billy's dinner with a plate for us, and put it on a pan of hot water to keep warm? He must be workin' overtime.'

'Shall I help me nan?' A few days ago Edna would have been out of the door like a streak of greased lightning to play with her mates. But not now. She'd made up her mind to help her mother all she could until the new baby arrived. 'Nan can wash and I'll dry.'

Eileen waited until she could hear the clink of dishes, then walked to the couch and flopped down. She was thoughtful for a while as her finger traced the pattern in the uncut moquette. Then she tilted her head sideways to gaze at her husband. 'Yer know what, Bill?

9

I've been that worried over the last few days, first about you, then me mam and the kids, I hadn't given a thought to the baby. It was only when Mary an' Vera were talkin' about it, that it slowly dawned on me.' Eileen ran a hand across her tummy, her happiness and excitement growing with each second that ticked by. 'In 'ere, Bill, is our baby! A tiny human being . . . our own flesh and blood. An' here's us talkin' about whether we want it or not. Of course we want it! An' when it comes, we'll give it all the love we've got to give, eh, Bill?'

Bill could feel the sting of tears behind his eyes and he blinked them away. 'Of course we will, chick! And we'll have more time to devote to it than we did with the other three, because they seemed to come so quickly, one after the other.'

'I'm gettin' real excited.' Eileen's chubby face beamed. 'Mary's gettin' Harry to bring 'er up on Saturday with some knittin' patterns for matinee coats. An' she's goin' to make me some baby blankets and pillow cases an' things. She was that thrilled, yer'd think it was her 'aving the baby.'

'The dishes are done, Mam!' Edna, her socks hanging round her ankles, sat on the arm of the couch. 'I heard yer tellin' me dad that Auntie Mary was comin' on Saturday. Are yer goin' to teach me to knit, like yer said?'

'Course I will.' Eileen's eyes twinkled. 'Tell yer dad what yer want to call the baby.'

Edna pursed her lips, her thin face serious. 'If it's a girl, I'd like to call it Susan, and Randolph if it's a boy.'

When Bill's jaw dropped in amazement, the room filled with Eileen's laughter.

And Maggie, putting the clean plates away in the kitchen cupboard, smiled. Everything's going to all right, she told herself. Then her eyes looked up, and she whispered, 'Please God.'

'I'll cast on for you, then you can take it from there.' Mary Sedgemoor's fingers moved rapidly, pausing now and then to pull a length of the white wool from the ball. 'It's a dead easy pattern once you get the hang of it.'

Edna sat beside Mary on the couch, her eyes taking in every movement, while Eileen's eyes were on Mary's bowed head. Pretty Mary, with her long, blonde, curly hair, vivid blue eyes, teeth like pearls and a figure as good as any film star. They'd been friends since the day Mary had started work in the munitions factory and Harry Sedgemoor, who was the supervisor in the shell department, had brought her along to work on the same machine as Eileen. She'd been Mary Bradshaw then, now she was Mary Sedgemoor. And she was Eileen's best mate.

'There you are, forty stitches,' Mary said. 'And you'll have to keep counting them in case you drop one.'

Eileen took the knitting needles in her chubby hands and groaned. 'It's years since I did any knittin', I don't know where to start.'

'Give yourself a chance! Look, watch me. In . . . over . . . through . . . off! See how easy it is?'

'Everythin's easy when yer know how, kid!' Eileen's hands were so chubby she couldn't keep the wool over her first finger. 'At this rate, the baby will be ready to start school before I've knitted its first matinee coat.'

'You've dropped a stitch already,' Mary tutted. 'Just take your time, Eileen, and you'll soon get into it.'

Edna's mouth was open, her tongue hanging out as she concentrated on knitting with some old wool Mary had brought. She finished a line and ran across to Mary to show off. 'I've done a row, Auntie Mary, aren't I clever?'

'That's very good.' Mary inspected the stitches. 'Just keep on with plain knitting until you get used to it, then I'll show you how to knit a line, purl a line.'

'Anybody home?'

When Eileen heard her sister's voice, a look of relief crossed her face. 'Come in, our kid!'

Rene walked in to see Eileen's huge body perched on the edge of a dining chair, the turban she had tied round her head slipped over one eye, and the knitting needles she was holding in her chubby hands pointing in every direction but the right one. 'I wish I had a camera with me,' Rene laughed. 'You should see yourself.'

'Go 'ed!' Eileen glared. ''Ave a good laugh! I feel a right bloody fool as it is, without you addin' yer twopenny worth.'

'I was only kidding.' Rene produced a parcel from behind her back. 'A little present for you.'

Eileen happily threw the knitting down, her face creased in a wide grin. 'What is it, kid?'

'Open it and see.'

11

Eileen tore the paper wrapping off, letting it fall to the floor in her eagerness. 'Oh, our Rene, they're lovely!' She stood up and spread the pram set on the table. There was a matching pair of leggings, a coat, bonnet and a pair of mitts, all in a pale shade of yellow. Eileen could feel her eyes fill with tears, and she brushed them away before facing her sister. 'Thanks, Sis, they're beautiful.'

'Not handknitted, I'm afraid, because I'm hopeless with a pair of knitting needles. But I'm glad you like them.'

'Honest, everyone's been so good I can't believe it.' Eileen sat down and motioned to Rene to pull one of the dining chairs out. 'The baby's goin' to be a proper swank.'

'And so it should be,' Mary said. 'Only the best is good enough for a Gillmoss.'

Rene had been eyeing Eileen, trying hard to keep a smile from her face. In the end she could keep it back no longer. 'Have a look at yourself in the mirror, Eileen. That turban is so cockeyed, it makes you look as though you've been out all night on the tiles.'

Eileen's hands moved to straighten the offending turban. 'D'yez know what? I've been wearin' one of these since the bloody war started an' I still haven't found the knack of tyin' it so it stays put.' She whipped it off in disgust. 'Don't know why I wear the bloody thing anyway.' She suddenly started to shake with laughter. 'Imagine me new baby, openin' its eyes for the first time an' seein' me in this! It would ask the doctor to put it back where it came from!'

Eileen put her backside to the old heavy mangle and pushed it back against the wall. 'Well, that's it for another few days, thank God!' She rubbed her wet hands down her pinny, then lifted the corner of it to wipe the sweat from her forehead. 'Will you see to the fire, Mam, while I go down to the lavvy? Then I'll make us a nice hot drink.'

Maggie knelt in front of the fire, carefully placing pieces of coal on the dying embers with the brass tongs. They'd been so busy with the washing, they'd forgotten the fire and now it was nearly out. She'd have to hold a sheet of newspaper in front and hope the draught would help the new coals catch fire. She heard the kitchen door open and called over her shoulder, 'There's not much heat from this, lass!'

When there was no reply, Maggie turned her head to see Eileen standing in the doorway, tears streaming down her screwed-up face.

12

'What is it, lass?' Maggie asked anxiously. 'What's happened?'

Eileen's body shook with sobs. 'Mam, I'm bleeding.'

'Oh, my God!' Maggie scrambled to her feet. 'Is it much, or just a few spots?'

'It's a big stain on me knickers,' Eileen gulped. 'I'm not goin' to lose the baby, am I, Mam?'

Maggie's tongue flicked over her lips as she looked into Eileen's distraught face. 'I don't know, lass.' She crossed the room and took hold of her daughter's elbow. 'Come and lay down on the couch.' As she eased the heavy legs sideways, Maggie's brain was racing. If only Bill was in, or even one of the children, they could have run for the doctor while she stayed with Eileen. But they wouldn't be home for hours and they couldn't afford to wait that long.

Eileen was sobbing and Maggie's heart went out to her. 'Does Cissie know about the baby, lass?'

Eileen nodded. 'Yer know what our Edna's like, Mam! The whole of flippin' Liverpool probably knows by now.'

'I'll nip down and see if she's in.' Maggie ran a hand through her hair. 'She can sit with you while I run for Doctor Greenfield.'

Cissie, her face full of concern, followed Maggie down the hall and into the living room. She took Eileen's hand in hers and patted it. 'You'll be all right, girl, don't worry.'

'Oh, Cissie!' Eileen looked into the eyes of the woman she'd had many a set-to with when their children were little. They matched each other in size ounce for ounce, and when there'd been a fight, neither would give way to the other. 'I'm frightened.'

'I've told yer, yer goin' to be all right!' Cissie turned to Maggie who was hovering near the door. 'Get goin', Maggie, I'll see to Eileen.'

Maggie ran as quickly as she could, and when she reached the surgery she was gasping for breath. The housekeeper who opened the door took one look at Maggie's distraught face and shouted for the doctor. Within minutes she was seated next to him in his car and they were on their way to Eileen.

Bill stepped down from the bus and his face showed surprise when he saw Edna waiting for him. 'This is a nice . . . .'

'Me Mam's sick.' The words poured from Edna's mouth. 'The doctor's been and me Mam's in bed.'

Bill could feel the hairs on the back of his neck stand up with fear.

'What's wrong?' He had Edna by the arm now and was almost dragging her along in his haste to get home. 'What happened?'

'I dunno! Me Mam was in bed when I got 'ome from school and Nan just said she was sick. Then she told me to meet yer at the bus stop an' tell yer to hurry.' Edna pulled her arm free. 'Let go, Dad, yer not 'alf hurtin' me!'

'I'll go on ahead, then.' Bill's long legs had never covered the ground so quickly and when he neared their house and saw Maggie at the door, wringing her hands, his blood ran cold. 'What is it, Ma?'

Maggie didn't speak until they were in the living room. She put a finger to her lips and jerked her head towards the ceiling as she closed the door. 'Doctor Greenfield thinks Eileen might be having a miscarriage.'

'Oh, no!' Bill banged his forehead with his open hand. 'No, Ma, not that!'

'It's not certain, son, so don't start getting upset.' Maggie touched his arm. 'And for heaven's sake don't let Eileen see you're worried! If she gets herself all worked up it'll only make things worse. The doctor said she's to stay in bed and not do a thing. He's coming back in the morning, but if we need him before, we've got to ring.' Maggie raised a smile. 'Go and cheer her up while I see to the dinner.'

Pulling on the banister rail, Bill took the stairs two at a time, his heart thudding. When he threw the bedroom door open, it was to see Joan and Edna sitting on one side of the bed, and Billy on the other. 'Hello, chick, how are you?'

Eileen waved her hand. 'Go downstairs now, kids, and let me an' yer Dad have a talk in private. I'll see yez later.'

Young Billy was reluctant to move. He wanted to know what was wrong with the mother he idolised, but his nan wouldn't tell him anything except she was sick. He wasn't a kid any more, he was sixteen now, and that was old enough to be told what was going on. So he hovered at the side of the bed. 'The doctor must 'ave said something, Mam!'

'He doesn't know 'imself yet, son! Perhaps when 'e comes tomorrer he'll know a bit more.' When Eileen looked at her son, it was like seeing Bill when she'd first met him. Billy had the same dark brown mop of hair and the same deep brown, velvety eyes. Eileen used to call them "come to bed eyes". But young Billy was a few inches taller than his dad had been, and he was still growing.

'Go down and 'elp yer nan, there's a good lad,' Eileen said softly. 'Yer can come up again later.'

Bill took over Billy's seat and reached for Eileen's hand. 'Confined to barracks, eh, love!'

'I'm scared stiff, Bill! I want this baby so much I don't know what I'll do if I lose it.'

Bill bent and gathered her warm, cuddly body close. 'Now come on, chick, who's always telling other people "don't trouble trouble, till trouble troubles you", eh? If you do as Doctor Greenfield tells you and stay in bed, you'll be all right, I know you will.'

'I'll stay in bed for the whole six months if need be.' Eileen's voice was choked. 'I'll do anythin' to keep the baby safe.'

'I'll take the day off tomorrow and I'll make sure you stay in bed. I'll see Billy out to work and the girls off to school, so don't you worry your head about anything.'

'I know I should argue with yer, Bill, but I'm not goin' to. I'd like yer to be here tomorrer when the doctor comes. Me mam's very good, an' yer know I love the bones of her, but it's you I need right now.'

Bill and Maggie sat either side of the fireplace, both deep in thought. The rest of the family were in bed and the house was still except for the occasional hissing from the coals and the ticking of the clock.

'I wonder what brought it on?' Bill wondered aloud. 'Eileen's been looking so well!'

'I know what brought it on,' Maggie said, her voice soft. 'It's that ruddy big mangle! I can't move it, and Eileen shouldn't . . . not in her condition, anyway. I'll bet me bottom dollar that's the cause of it.'

'She shifted that mangle on her own?'

'Well, there's nobody else to do it, Bill, so don't start blaming Eileen for what's happened.' Maggie was quick to defend her daughter. 'The damned thing has to be pulled out to turn the handle, and the kitchen is too small to leave it out all the time. You can't swing a cat round out there, never mind having that ruddy thing stuck in the middle.'

'I'm not blaming Eileen, Ma, I'm blaming meself!' Bill scratched his head. 'Me own common sense should have asked me how she was coping with the washing.' His fist came down heavily on the arm of his chair. 'I've tried to talk her into moving to a bigger house, but every time I mention it she pooh-poohs the idea. But this has put the top hat on it. If she comes through this all right, I don't care what she says, we're moving to a place where she'll have more room to move around . . . a house like Mary's, where there's a wash house with a boiler and running water.'

Chapter Three

Dr Greenfield snapped his bag shut. 'You can come in now, Mr Gillmoss.'

He'd barely finished speaking before Bill was in the room. 'What's the news, Doctor?' Bill's eyes flitted anxiously from Eileen to the doctor. 'Is she going to be okay?'

'It's far too early to say. The bleeding has slowed down, but until it's stopped I can't give Eileen an internal.' John Greenfield swung his bag from the tallboy and moved to the side of the bed. 'I can't promise anything, all I can do is advise you to stay in bed, have complete rest. If you do that then there's a chance you may keep the baby. But you must do as you're told, Eileen, do you understand?' He waited for Eileen's nod before continuing. 'You mustn't attempt to go downstairs, and no lifting anything.'

'I'll be as good as gold, Doctor,' Eileen answered tearfully. She had known John Greenfield for years and he didn't seem to have aged at all in those years, even though he'd seen service at the battle front when the war was at its height. He was as slim as ever, still had that boyish, lopsided grin and the fine baby hair that had a mind of its own and kept falling on to his forehead. 'I'll do everythin' yer say, honest.'

'I'll make sure she does,' Bill said, 'otherwise she'll have me to answer to.' He scratched his head. 'What about visitors? We've got a full house downstairs.'

'Uh, uh! Not for a few days.' John squeezed Eileen's hand. 'Best to take no chances because we don't want to lose this baby . . .' he started to chuckle, 'although I'm not sure whether the world is ready for another Eileen Gillmoss.'

'Thanks, Doctor.' Eileen wrapped her fingers around his hand, remembering the times she'd gone to him with her troubles, and everybody else's for that matter. And he'd never let her down. 'I'll

17

do everythin' yer said, scout's honour. Yer know I've got every faith in you, always 'ave.'

'I'll be on my way then.' At the door John turned. 'I'll call in tomorrow and I expect you to have behaved yourself till then, okay?'

'Haven't got much bloody option, 'ave I?' Eileen sounded more like her old self, and the two men smiled at each other. 'Even if Cary Grant walked in that door now, I wouldn't move a muscle.' It was too dark in the room to be sure, but John would swear she had a twinkle in her eye when she added, 'On second thoughts, though, for Cary Grant I might just make the effort.'

'I'll see the doctor out, chick, then explain to our visitors. I'll be back in a couple of minutes.'

Eileen heard Bill running up the stairs and turned her head on the pillow when the door opened. 'D'yer want a little bit of useless information, Bill? Well, there's a hundred and twenty-seven flippin' roses on the paper on that wall.'

Bill grinned. 'Aren't you glad you don't have to water them?'

'Have the visitors all gone?'

Bill sat down gently on the side of the bed. 'Your Rene's gone. She's got to pick Victoria up from school at twelve. But Mary and Vera are still here with the children.' He took Eileen's hand and squeezed it. 'Ma's been busy making cups of tea for the last two hours.'

'I could murder a cuppa, right now. Me mouth's that dry with nerves.' Eileen stroked a finger over Bill's hand. 'What d'yer think, Bill? Did the doctor tell yer anything when yer were seein' him out?'

'Only what he told you. He's not going to commit himself and get the blame if he's wrong.' Bill removed his hand and stroked the hair back from her forehead. 'But I've got a feeling in me bones that everything's going to be all right.'

'I hope so, Bill.' Eileen closed her eyes and prayed. I know I'm no angel, God, and I only come to you when I want something. But I'm in real trouble this time and I really need your help. Please don't let me down, and I promise I'll be good from now on.

'What's wrong with me mam?' Edna was sprawled on the couch, her thin legs stuck out in front of her. 'She doesn't look sick to me.'

Bill's finger made a groove in the plush of the tablecloth as he sought the right words to explain. He could feel Edna's eyes on him

18

as she waited for an answer, and knew that Joan, who was standing by the sideboard with her back to him, was also all ears. 'Your mam's not really sick, as such,' Bill said. 'She hasn't got a cold or pains, or anything like that.' Oh, lord, he thought, how do I get round this? Then he decided it was best to tell the truth. If things didn't go right, they'd have to be told anyway. Best to do it now and get it over with. 'It's the baby, you see. Your mam might lose it.'

Edna shot up straight, her heels banging against the front of the couch. A choking sound left her mouth as her eyes widened with horror. 'Lose the baby?' She ran to stand in front of her father. 'What d'yer mean, Dad? How can me mam lose the baby?'

Joan didn't turn round as she waited for her father to answer. There was no look of horror on her face, just a faint smile. She didn't want anything to happen to her mam because she loved her. But as long as she was all right, then Joan would be quite happy if the baby didn't come along.

'I'm not saying she is going to lose it, pet. The doctor said if she stays in bed then everything might be all right.' Bill ran a hand across his forehead as he sighed. 'So you've both got to help me look after her so she gets better. And when you go to bed tonight I want you to say a few prayers, will you do that?'

Edna nodded, her eyes filled with tears. 'I'll say six Hail Mary's and six Our Father's,' she gulped, as a stray tear trickled down her cheek. 'And I'll pray to Saint Anthony as well.'

Bill turned his head. 'You're very quiet, Joan.'

'I never get a word in edgeways when our Edna's around,' Joan said, her voice kept deliberately low. 'I'll help, Dad. And I'll say me prayers every night.'

'You're both to muck in with the housework,' Bill told them. 'I can't stay off work and we can't expect your nan to do everything.'

'I'll help with the washin' up,' Edna said. 'An' I'll run all the messages for 'er, Dad, I promise.' She sniffed up and wiped a tear away with the back of her hand, leaving a dirty streak across her thin face. 'Can I go up and see me mam now?'

'Well, Eileen, and how are you today?'

Oh, my God, Eileen muttered under her breath as she struggled to sit up when she heard Father Murphy's lilting Irish brogue. Wouldn't you think someone would have warned her the priest was here. 'I'm feelin' all right, Father.'

'Well now, isn't that good to hear?' Father Murphy drew the small wooden chair nearer the bed, his rosy cheeks beaming. 'I've been having a cup of tea and a little chat with your dear mother. She tells me you're expecting the doctor this morning, is that right now?'

'Yes, Father.' Eileen's eyes darted round the room. Thank goodness her mother had been up earlier and tidied around. 'He should be here soon.'

The priest was carrying a square black box in his hand, and before sitting down he placed it carefully on the floor, followed by his black, round-crowned hat. He rubbed his hands together before leaning forward and resting his elbows on his knees. 'With every hour that passes, Eileen, hope grows a bit stronger. So don't look so down in the mouth, for that's not like you at all.'

'I can't say I feel like me, Father. I'm so frightened, me sense of humour 'as deserted me.'

'Now, now, Eileen! Put your faith and trust in the good Lord. Isn't He up there now, looking down on all His children?'

Eileen looked into the face that shone with goodness and compassion, and nodded. 'I know, father. And although I've been naughty sometimes, I've never done anything really bad in me whole life.'

'D'you think I don't know that, Eileen? For sure, you haven't got a wicked bone in your whole body.' Father Murphy looked at his watch. 'I know you can't come to church, so I'll hear your Confession and give you Holy Communion now.' He pushed his chair back and moved to the window to draw the curtains. 'I'm sure you'll feel better after . . . more at peace with yourself.'

Eileen pulled the sheet up to her neck. 'Thank you, Father. Yer an angel.'

'Not yet, Eileen, but sure now, aren't I living in hopes?'

Eileen had been in bed for two weeks, the longest two weeks of her whole life. Apart from the family, the only visitors she'd been allowed by Bill were their Rene, and Mary and Vera. She was sick of looking at the ceiling and the four walls, but not for all the tea in China would she have ventured out of that bed. Not until the doctor said it was safe for her to get up. He was due this morning and she'd been praying he would tell her the danger had now passed. She'd given herself a good wash down and put on her best nightie, the blue one with lace trimming on the neck and sleeves. Her mam had taken her dinkie curlers out and combed the hair that was lifeless and greasy after not being washed for two weeks.

Eileen looked at the alarm clock on the small wooden-topped table at the side of the bed. 'Come on, Doc,' she said aloud. 'If yer don't come soon I'll be a nervous wreck.' Her eyes swept round the four walls. 'Three hundred and fifty-seven flowers on this paper. I used to like flowers, but now I'm sick of the sight of them. Wouldn't care if I didn't see another one for the rest of me life.' Her eyes travelled to the ceiling. 'See, God, all that and not one swear word. I'm bein' good, like I promised.' The sound of the front door knocker reached her and Eileen's tummy started to turn over. She crossed her fingers on both hands, raised her eyes again and whispered, 'Please, please, please.'

'And how is my favourite patient today?' John Greenfield breezed into the room, a smile lighting up his face. 'Fed up to the teeth being in bed, eh?'

'Can't say I'd fancy much more of it,' Eileen answered truthfully. 'But if it's done the trick, then it's been worth it.'

John placed his bag on the tallboy. 'Your mother is bringing me a bowl of hot water up, then I'll give you a good examination.' He saw Eileen's eyes widen, and grinned. 'No need to be embarrassed, I see women like you every day.'

Maggie pushed the door open with her elbow, a bowl of hot water in her hands, a towel draped over her arm. 'Mind the water's not too hot, Doctor.'

'That's fine, thank you.' John slipped his coat off and draped it over the back of a chair. 'I'll give you a call when I've finished.'

Eileen stayed flat on her back, her eyes following the doctor as he walked towards the bowl of water. 'Well?'

John dipped his hands in the water, the corners of his mouth curved upwards into a smile. He was always glad when he had good news to give a patient, but this time it was extra special because it was Eileen. He reached for the towel and turned to face the bed. 'Mother and baby fine, I'm glad to say.'

Eileen shot up in bed. She joined her chubby hands together, 'Oh, thank you, God, thank you.'

'Been saying your prayers, have you?' John asked.

'To tell yer the truth, Doctor, I think God is makin' everythin' come right 'cos he's fed up listenin' to me and me mam! She's been goin' to Church every day, an' I've said more prayers in the last two weeks than I've said in me whole life.'

'It seems to have paid off.'

'I've been lucky havin' Him, and you, on my side.' Eileen felt weak with relief and happiness. 'Yez make a good winning team.'

'I'm not in the same league, Eileen, but thank you. Now, you can go downstairs today, but only to lie on the couch. You're to do nothing at all until I call again, understand?'

John had moved to the side of the bed, and before he knew what was happening he was being pulled down and clasped in Eileen's big arms. 'Oh, you lovely man.' Eileen kissed his cheek, squeezing him so tight he had to fight for his breath. 'I'll never forget yer for this, honest I won't.'

Trying to regain his balance, John stammered, 'Eileen, I haven't done anything! Any doctor would have told you to do what I did.'

'Ah, but yer not any old doctor, are yer?' Eileen bent her head and straightened the front of her nightdress. 'Yer've been more like a mate to me, over the years.'

'And can I say I couldn't have a better friend?' John held his hand out, winced at Eileen's tight grip, then said briskly, 'But right now I'm back to being your doctor. For the next few weeks you take it easy. No thinking, well it won't do any harm to wash the dishes or rinse a few things through. If you do anything foolish, Eileen, I won't be responsible for the consequences.'

'I won't take any chances, Doctor, don't worry. I've learned my lesson the hard way.' Eileen flung the bedclothes back. 'I'll go down and give me mam a surprise.'

'Take it slowly,' John warned. 'You'll be weak after being in bed for so long.'

'How about yer givin' me a piggy back?' Eileen asked, her face straight.

John looked at the size of the big woman and burst out laughing.

'Would you come and visit me in hospital?'

'Yeah!' Eileen's tummy started to shake. 'I'll bring the baby in with me.'

Edna was the first in from school, and when she saw Eileen on the couch, a pillow behind her head and the quilt from her bed covering her, the surprise on her face brought a chuckle from Eileen. 'It is me, sunshine, not a flippin' ghost.'

'Mam!' Edna flung herself at her mother. 'Are yer better now?'

'I've got to take it easy for a few weeks, but yeah, I'm better now, thank God.'

'An' yer haven't lost the baby?'

'No, sunshine, I haven't lost the baby.' Eileen turned her head to see Joan standing in the doorway. 'I didn't hear a knock.'

'The front door was open.' Joan had come in just after Edna and had heard the exchange between her sister and mother. She felt so disappointed it took her all her time to hide it. 'You all right now, then?'

Eileen's eyes narrowed. She knew her daughters inside out, and this one didn't look too happy. Still, she thought, like Bill said, she was at an awkward age and was probably embarrassed.

'Give yer nan a hand and set the table, will yez?'

Edna rushed to the sideboard to get the tablecloth as Joan turned towards the door. 'I've got to go down to Dorothy's to get a book off her. I won't be long.'   ·

'Ay, skinnymalinks,' Eileen shouted after her. 'If yer not back in five minutes, I'll flatten yer, d'yer 'ear?'

'She'll be halfway down the street by now.' Maggie came in from the kitchen wiping her hands on a towel. 'Anyway, she's neither use nor ornament when she's here! Me and Edna will manage, won't we, love?'

Eileen leaned back on the pillow, muttering under her breath. 'Kids, who'd 'ave 'em?'

'I could get used to this, yer know.' Eileen grinned as she steadied the plate on her lap. 'I always said I was born to be a lady and get waited on hand and foot.'

Bill turned his head and grinned back. If only he could tell her how good it was to see her downstairs again. He was so happy he felt like a young boy again. When the rest of the family were in bed, he'd tell her how he felt and how much he loved her.

When Maggie saw the look exchanged between Bill and her daughter, an idea entered her head. She looked from Joan to Edna. 'If you hurry up and eat your dinner, I'll mug you to the pictures.' Maggie didn't really feel like going out, but it would give man and wife the chance to be alone. 'Abbot and Costello are on at the Walton Vale.'

Edna's face lit up and her movements quickened, the fork

ramming the food into her mouth. 'I'm nearly finished, Nan.'

'Don't speak with your mouth full,' Bill warned. 'How many times do I have to tell you?'

Joan didn't speak, but she was secretly pleased. None of her friends had seen the Abbot and Costello film so she'd be able to swank about it tomorrow.

'I'm ready, Nan,' Edna said.

'Me too!' Joan reached for her sister's empty plate. 'I'll take these out.'

'Leave the dishes,' Bill told her, 'I'll wash them.'

Bill followed them to the door where he pressed a ten-bob note into Maggie's hand. 'Thanks, Ma! Buy them an ice cream in the interval.'

He walked back into the room and took Eileen's plate from her knee. 'I'll see to the dishes before I sit down. Once I get comfortable I won't feel like budging.'

Eileen listened to the clattering of the pots and pans, thinking it was wrong for Bill to have to do the washing up after working all day. Still, it wouldn't be for long.

Bill stood in the doorway, a look of relief and happiness on his face. 'Chick, you'll never know how good it is to see you sitting on that couch. The last two weeks have seemed an eternity.'

'Yer can say that again, Bill Gillmoss,' Eileen said. 'I thought it was never goin' to end. But right now I feel so happy I could sing me 'ead off.'

Bill swung one of the dining chairs round and set it next to the couch. He took hold of Eileen's hand and kissed it. 'I love you, Eileen Gillmoss.'

Eileen fluttered her eyelashes. 'Ooh, yer sound dead romantic! Tell me more, I'm all ears.'

'Well, I haven't got a voice like Issy Bon, but I'll have a go.' Bill cleared his throat, threw back his head and started singing a very passable rendition of the popular singer's "I Don't Want To Set The World On Fire". When he'd finished he bent forward to kiss Eileen on the cheek. 'How was that?'

'Yer sing better than Issy Bon,' Eileen chuckled, 'and yer better lookin' than 'im too.'

'That shows what good taste you've got.'

It was so unusual for Bill to act the goat, Eileen knew he was feeling as happy and as thankful as she herself was. 'Aren't we lucky, Bill?'

'We can certainly count our blessings,' Bill answered. 'We've got each other, the children, Ma, and now a new baby. There's not many as fortunate as us.' Bill clasped his hands between his knees, his thumbs circling each other. Was it the right time to bring up the subject, he asked himself, or should he leave it until Eileen was on her feet? She might start getting upset and he didn't want that. He'd have to be careful and choose the right words.

Bill cocked his head and looked into Eileen's eyes. 'There's only one blot on the horizon, chick, and I think we should talk about it.'

Eileen's brow furrowed. 'What's that?'

'Now don't start getting all het up,' Bill said. 'I wasn't going to mention it until you were on your feet, but time isn't on our side.'

Eileen knew immediately what he was getting at. 'Yer mean about us movin' to another 'ouse?' When Bill nodded, Eileen groaned, 'Oh, not that again, Bill! Yer know 'ow I feel about this house! We came 'ere the day we got married, remember? We didn't 'ave a honeymoon because we couldn't wait to get in our own little 'ouse.'

'Yes, but there were only the two of us then,' Bill reminded her, his voice soft. 'When the baby comes, there'll be seven. It's only a two-up two-down, Eileen, not meant for so many. We had to divide one of the bedrooms into two when the girls came along, and you can't swing a cat round in them. You certainly couldn't put a baby's cot in either of them.'

'I thought we could 'ave the cot in our room.' When Eileen saw the frown on Bill's face, she went on quickly. 'It wouldn't be for all that long. Our Billy's growin' up an' he'll probably get married in a few years.'

'He's only just turned sixteen.' Bill closed his eyes, his fingers pinching at his bottom lip. After a moment's thought, he asked, 'You do love me, don't you?'

'What a daft question! Yer know I love the bones of yer!'

'That means we both love each other. And what do two people do when they're in love? Have you thought about that, chick? With a growing child in our room, there wouldn't be much loving going on, would there?'

Eileen pursed her lips. She hadn't thought about that.

Bill saw the wavering and took advantage. 'Unless you want me to go out and find myself another woman.'

'Over my dead body, Bill Gillmoss!'

25

'Then think about it, will you, for my sake? And while you're about it, think of the girls and our Billy, too! When they start courting, where will they go to entertain their friends? They certainly wouldn't have any privacy here.'

Eileen's face was a study. None of these things had entered her mind. And the more she thought of it, the more she saw that Bill was right. But she loved this little house so much, she'd never be happy anywhere else. Bill could see Eileen's brain ticking over. 'We'll have to make up our minds soon, Eileen. It could be months before we find a house we like.'

'Let me sleep on it, will yer, Bill? It's not a thing to decide on in a hurry.'

Bill could see the tiredness on Eileen's face and took her hand in both of his. 'It's time you were going back to bed. You've been up long enough for your first day.' He pulled her gently to her feet. 'I'll come and tuck you in.'

Bill drew the covers up to Eileen's chin. 'I'll be as quiet as I can when I come up, so as not to wake you. So have a good night's sleep. And don't worry about moving, for heaven's sake. If you're dead set on staying here, then here we'll stay. I only want what's best for you.'

'I know you do, love.' Eileen felt drowsy as soon as her head touched the pillow. It had been a long day. She turned on her side and curled up. 'I will think about it, Bill, honest . . .' Her voice trailed off as she drifted into a deep sleep.

Bill stood looking down at her. He loved her very much and couldn't bear the thought of anything happening to her. That's why he had to get her away from here, to make life easier for her when the baby came.

Chapter Four

'Ay, ay, Mam!' Joan's voice was high with indignation as she stood before her mother. 'I can't go for an interview in me school socks! I'd be a laughin' stock and I wouldn't get the job.'

'I'm not made of money,' Eileen answered. 'I've already bought yer a new blouse an' skirt, what more d'yer want?'

'A pair of long stockings.' Joan turned to Maggie, her pale face flushed, her eyes pleading for support. 'Tell her, Nan, please? You must see how stupid I'd look in me short socks.'

Maggie looked up from the pram pillow case she was embroidering. She usually refused to be drawn into any argument between Eileen and the children, but this time she could see Joan's point of view. 'She's right, lass. First impressions are always important.'

Eileen sighed. 'Oh, all right. But yez'll have me in the workhouse one of these days with wantin' this, that an' the other.' She reached down to the side of the couch and took her purse from her bag. 'How much d'yer want?'

'Only a shilling.' Joan looked down at her feet. She and her friend Dorothy were going for interviews at Vernon's Pools in Aintree on Monday and Dorothy had been swanking about what her mother had bought her to wear for the big day. And Joan wasn't going to be outdone by her friend if she could help it. 'Can I 'ave a suspender belt as well, to keep the stockings up?'

'What's the matter with a pair of garters?' Eileen asked.

'Mam, they're old fashioned! I can't go for an interview with pieces of elastic keepin' me stockings up.'

'An' who the 'ell is goin' to see up yer clothes, might I ask?' Eileen looked up to the pleading in her daughter's eyes and relented. 'Oh, all right, you win. Run down to County Road and see what they've got.'

'Dorothy got hers from T.J. Hughes.' Joan's heart was beginning

27

to feel lighter. 'She said they're cheaper there.'

'I'm not goin' into town with yer, sunshine. It gets too packed, especially on a Saturday.' Eileen was four months pregnant now, and after the scare last month she avoided buses like the plague. 'Besides, yer dad and Billy will be 'ome from work about one o'clock an' they'll expect their dinner on the table.'

'I'll nip into Liverpool with her,' Maggie offered. 'Go and get yourself ready, Joan.'

'Ooh, thanks, Nan!' Joan kissed Maggie's cheek in a rare show of affection before running up the stairs singing a tuneless song at the top of her voice.

'I don't know,' Eileen tutted. 'Fourteen an' wantin' a suspender belt. When I was 'er age it was either garters or a knot in the top of yer stocking.'

'Children seem to be growing up quicker these days,' Maggie said. 'I think the war had a lot to do with it. All the men in the army and most women working, there was no discipline. The old saying, "spare the rod and spoil the child" is true, and we'll find out to our cost. They're like old men and women now before they've left school.'

'I ain't goin' to argue with yer on that, missus! A clip round the ear 'ole is what some of them need.' Eileen rummaged through the silver in her scruffy purse, then stretched her hand out, three half-crowns lying the palm. 'There should be enough 'ere for 'er stockings and those thingamajigs. It's only a couple of coppers on the bus, so there might be enough to go mad an' mug yerselves to a cup of tea in the cafeteria in T.J.'s.'

Young Billy put a cushion behind Eileen's back, his face creased in a grin. 'You take it easy, Mam, I'll help me dad with the dishes.'

Eileen's eyes were tender as she watched him walk to the kitchen. He was a good lad, was Billy. He was nearly as bad as his dad for fussing over her. When they were home, neither of them would let her lift a finger.

'Put me mam's and our Joan's dinner in the oven with plates over them,' Eileen called. 'They shouldn't be long now.'

A knock on the front door brought Eileen to the edge of the couch. But before she had time to stand up, Bill appeared, a tea towel in his hand. 'Stay where you are, chick, I'll get it.'

Eileen cocked her ear for the sound of voices, and when she heard

28

Mary's laugh, followed by Harry's, her face lit up. 'Hi-ya, kid!'

Eileen's arms went across her tummy as two young bodies threw themselves at her. 'Hey! Let me breathe, will yez?'

'Come away at once.' Mary had to drag the struggling children from their favourite auntie. 'Behave yourselves or we'll go home.'

'Hello, Auntie Eileen.' The two young voices spoke in unison.

'Are you better now?' asked five-year-old Emma. With her blonde curls and bright blue eyes, she was as pretty as a picture and the spitting image of Mary. 'I missed you.'

Tony, a year younger, pushed his sister aside. He was as dark as she was fair, a miniature version of his handsome father. 'I missed you too, Auntie Eileen. Mummy wouldn't let us come to see you.'

'Well, yer see,' Eileen put an arm round each of them and pulled them towards her, 'I haven't been very well. But I'm all right now.'

Eileen looked up at Mary and noticed her eyes were twinkling with excitement. 'You're lookin' very pleased with yerself. Have yez come up on the pools?' Then a frown creased Eileen's forehead. 'Where's Harry?'

'Talking to Bill in the hall.'

'What the 'ell are they standin' out there for?' Eileen raised her voice. 'Hey, you two, get in 'ere! Don't be whisperin' behind our backs.'

She heard Harry's loud guffaw before he marched into the room, stood to attention in front of her, clicked his heels and saluted. 'Reporting for duty, Sir!'

'I'll just finish the dishes,' Bill said, 'I won't be a tick.'

'Eileen looked from Harry to Mary, her eyes like slits. 'What 'ave you two been up to? Yez look as though yer've lost sixpence and found half-a-crown.'

'All will be revealed in good time.' Harry flopped down next to Eileen on the couch. 'Where is everybody?'

'Billy's in the kitchen, me mam an' Joan 'ave gone to town, and our Edna's out playin' somewhere.' Eileen pulled a face at him. 'What d'yer want to know for?'

'Just idle curiosity.' Harry drew Tony on his knee. 'Shall we go and look for Edna and she can take you for some sweets?'

Tony's deep brown eyes looked from Eileen to his father. He wanted to stay with this big woman he adored because she always made them laugh. But a bag of sweets was very tempting. 'Yes, Daddy.'

'Come on, then.' Harry took the small hand in one of his and held the other out to Emma. 'Let's go and look for Edna.'

There's something going on here, Eileen thought. But they'll tell me in good time. 'Give a knock next door, I think she's playin' in their yard.'

Liverpool were playing at home and Billy had gone off to the match with his mates, his red and white scarf worn with pride. Edna was playing hopscotch in the street with Emma and Tony, and Maggie's and Joan's dinners were still in the oven awaiting their return.

'Well?' Eileen asked. 'Whatever it is that's got you two on edge, spit it out before I die of curiosity.'

Mary looked at Bill. 'Shall I tell her?'

Bill nodded, keeping his fingers crossed. Please God let Eileen be as pleased as I am.

'D'you know Mrs Kenny, who lives next door but one?' Mary asked. 'You know, the old lady who lives on her own.'

'Of course I know Mrs Kenny!' Eileen was more confused than ever. 'But what's Mrs Kenny got to do with us?'

'I was talking to her the other day,' Mary told her, 'and she said the house was getting too much for her and she was thinking of looking for a smaller place.'

Puzzled, Eileen asked, 'So what?'

Bill couldn't contain himself any longer and he spoke before Mary had time to answer. 'Chick, she might do an exchange with us if the landlords don't object.'

While his wife was digesting his words, Bill carried on. 'Just think, a nice house and right by Mary and Harry.'

'But, but . . . she might not want to come here,' Eileen stuttered. 'She's not goin' to move from a posh neighbourhood to here.'

Harry leaned forward, his elbows resting on his knees. 'It's worth a try, Eileen. If you don't ask, you'll never get.'

'And we'd be able to see each other every day,' Mary said. 'I'd be able to help you when the baby comes.'

'It's the chance of a lifetime, we'll never get another one like it.' Bill ran his fingers through his mop of white hair. He'd been to see several houses but Eileen always found an excuse for not going with him. Either she didn't like the area or it was too far from Edna's school. He knew if it was left to her, they'd never move. 'We'd be fools if we didn't try. I know I'd move heaven and earth to get it if it was left to me.'

Eileen's eyes travelled from Harry to Mary, then on to Bill. They were all waiting anxiously for her answer. It was the pleading in Bill's eyes that finally broke her. 'If that's what yer want, love, then go an' see what yer can do.'

Bill shot up straight in his chair as a sigh of relief left his lips. 'You mean it, chick?'

When Eileen nodded, Mary clapped her hands in glee while Harry dropped back in the chair as the tension left his body. 'Thank God for that!'

Bill stood in front of Eileen, cupped her face in his hands and gave her a noisy kiss. 'That's my girl.' He turned to Harry. 'What do we do now?'

'I think the first thing is to ask Mrs Kenny to come and see this house and ask her to let you look over hers. I don't think there'd be any problem with the two landlords,' Harry raised his bushy eyebrows, 'as long as you've got a clear rent book.'

'Go way, yer cheeky sod! Of course we've got a clear rent book!' Eileen placed her two hands on her hips. 'For two pennies I'd crack yer one, Harry Sedgemoor.'

'That's more like it,' Harry grinned. 'I was beginning to think you'd lost your spunk.'

'Aye, well, yer know what thought did, don't yer? Followed a muck cart and thought it was a weddin'. And any more cracks like that out of you, Harry Sedgemoor, an' I'll be throwin' you on the back of a muck cart.'

'Oh, aye, you and whose army?'

'I don't need an army,' Eileen fluttered her lashes, 'not when I've got my feller to protect me.'

Bill closed his eyes. It was like music to his ears to hear Eileen back to her old bubbly self. And if the house came off, he wouldn't call the queen his aunt.

When there was a knock on the door, Bill cursed as he walked down the hall. The last thing they wanted now was visitors. 'Hello, Vera! And how's my little girlfriend?' Bill looked down at Carol, Vera Jackson's nine-year-old mongol daughter, who had her arms wrapped around his waist. He stroked the fair hair as the large, round eyes smiled up at him.

'Come on in and see Auntie Eileen.'

'Well, look what the wind's blown in!' Eileen held her arms out to Carol and crushed her in a bear-like grip. 'Who's a little smasher, then, eh?'

'Me, Auntie Eileen.' Carol rained kisses on Eileen's face before making a bee-line for Harry and Mary.

Eileen eyed Vera up and down. 'Yer lookin' very well, Mrs Jackson. Gettin' used to bein' on yer own, now, are yer?'

'Well, it's a damn sight better than when Danny was there. At least I'm not living in fear all the time, worrying about him coming in drunk.' Vera slipped out of her coat and held an arm out. 'Look, Eileen, not a bruise in sight! Makes a change, doesn't it?'

'I wonder if he knocks 'is Dutch lady friend around? I bet she won't put up with 'is shenanigans the way you did.'

Vera shrugged her shoulders. 'I couldn't care less, as long as me, the boys and Carol aren't getting it.'

'Well, park yer carcass.' Eileen motioned for Bill to pull one of the dining chairs out. 'We've got some news for yer . . . at least we might 'ave some news for yer, it's not definite yet.'

Vera listened, wide eyed. She was an attractive woman with a slim figure and lovely, long auburn hair. Her eyes changed colour with the light, from pale brown to green.

'Wouldn't it be lovely if you could get it?' Then a thought struck Vera and she began to chuckle. 'Moving in with the snobs, eh? Remember how you used to pull Mary's leg about being stuck up?'

'Ay, don't be puttin' the mockers on it, Vera, we 'aven't got the flamin' 'ouse yet.'

Harry stood up, and straightening the crease in his trousers, said, 'I think Mary should come because she knows Mrs Kenny better than I do. If you'd keep an eye on the children, the three of us could be there and back in an hour.'

'I'll watch out for the children,' Vera said. 'Wild horses wouldn't move me till I know how you get on.'

Eileen clicked her tongue. 'Some people aren't 'alf nosy, aren't they?' She jerked her head at Bill. 'Go on, love, I know yer on pins. Hurry back and let's know what the score is.'

'The children are having the time of their lives out there. Your Edna is teaching Carol how to skip.' Vera crossed to look in the mirror over the mantelpiece and ran a hand over her long, smooth hair. 'Bill's a long time, isn't he?'

32

'An hour and a half.' Eileen glanced at the clock for the umpteenth time. 'They should've been well back by now.'

'Give them a chance,' Maggie said. She and Joan had been back an hour, had their dinner and washed up. Now they sat waiting. Joan had come in flushed with excitement over her first pair of long stockings and suspender belt, but when she heard the news her purchases quickly took second place in her train of thought. Just fancy, they might be going to live in a posh house like their Auntie Mary's! Now that would really be something to brag about to her friend Dorothy.

The sound of a car braking outside turned all heads towards the door.

'They're here!' Joan was out of the room like a streak of greased lightning, and they could hear her call, 'Are we goin' to live in Orrell Park, Dad?'

'Oh, my God!' Eileen cringed. 'I'll flatten 'er when I get me hands on 'er. Talk about a mouth like the Mersey tunnel, the whole flamin' street will know by now.'

'Eileen, the neighbours probably knew an hour ago,' Maggie said dryly. 'Joan might have a big mouth, but she's not in the meg specks with your Edna around. I'll bet that little madam's been knocking on doors and stopping people in the street.'

Bill was first through the door, his face aglow with excitement. 'Mrs Kenny is coming in the morning. Harry's bringing her in the car.'

Amid the gasps of pleasure and surprise, and the questions being thrown at Bill from all sides, Eileen sat quietly, her heart pounding. This is it, she thought. All the talking about moving to another house had now become a reality and her feelings were not of pleasure, but sadness. Nobody understood how much she loved this little house, how much it would grieve her to leave. 'You're very quiet, chick.' Bill bent to look in Eileen's face. 'You haven't said a word.'

'With this lot jabberin', I couldn't get a word in edgeways.' Eileen forced a smile to her face. Bill looked so happy she didn't have the heart to spoil things for him. 'Is Mrs Kenny really interested?'

Harry came to stand beside Bill and flung an arm across his shoulder. 'She is very interested. And before you say it,' Harry grinned, 'she knows this area very well. In fact, she was born only a few streets from here.'

Edna appeared in the doorway flanked by Emma and Tony, with Carol bringing up the rear. Never one to mince words, Edna asked, 'Did yer get this 'ouse, Dad?'

Mary, who had taken a seat next to Eileen on the couch, turned to look at the group framed in the doorway. 'Good grief,' she groaned, 'will you look at the state of them! Their clothes are filthy!'

'Holy sufferin' ducks!' Eileen's eyes went to the ceiling. 'Didn't you ever get dirty when you were a kid?'

'We've been playing ollies,' Tony said proudly. 'And I beat Edna, didn't I, Edna?'

Harry's loud chuckle filled the room. 'Good for you, son! I'll have to have a game with you, and see if you can beat me.'

Mary shook her head in despair as she searched in her pocket for some loose change. She couldn't bear to see the children dirty. Oh, she knew she was too fussy and was frightened of the wind blowing on them, but she couldn't help the way she was. 'Here's sixpence. Go to the corner shop with Edna and get yourselves an ice cream while we have a talk with Auntie Eileen.' Edna's mouth opened in protest. 'But I want to know . . .'

'Do as you're told, Edna.' The tone of Bill's voice was enough to silence his daughter, and when she reached for the sixpence, Bill put a finger to his lips and said sternly, 'And keep that mouth of yours closed, d'you hear?' Edna, not looking too pleased, nodded as she steered the children out to the street.

'What's Mrs Kenny's house like?' Eileen asked. 'Is it exactly the same as yours, Mary?'

'The house is the same,' Mary answered, 'but it's not in the same condition as ours was when we got it. Remember, ours was nicely decorated and everything. All we had to do was move in.'

Harry sat on the arm of the couch next to Eileen, and with a finger under her chin, turned her face towards him. 'Mrs Kenny is an old lady and her house hasn't been decorated since the year dot. She hasn't been able to do it herself and couldn't afford to have a man in. But there's nothing that can't be put right with a bit of elbow grease. Me and Bill could have that place like a palace in a few weeks. And I'm sure Arthur Kennedy will be more than happy to give a hand.'

'It sounds lovely, Eileen.' Vera clapped her hands in pleasure. 'You won't know you're born with an inside toilet and a wash-house.'

34

'Ooh, I hope we get it.' Joan rubbed her tummy. She was dying to go to the lavvy but was frightened of missing something. 'If we do get it, and I get the job in Vernons, I can get the train from Orrell Park station to the Old Roan. It's only two stops.'

'Don't count your chickens before they're hatched,' Maggie warned. 'There's many a slip twixt cup and lip.'

'Well, we haven't got long to find out.' Bill was trying to keep calm but his nerves were as taut as a violin string. 'Harry's picking Mrs Kenny up after church in the morning, so she should be here about eleven.'

'That means all hands on deck 'ere for eight o'clock, and we'll go through this 'ouse like a dose of salts.' Eileen pinched at the fat on her elbows, her forehead creased in concentration. 'We'll take a room each so we don't get under each other's feet.'

'To hear you talk, anyone would think the house never got cleaned!' Maggie's face was red with indignation. 'I gave the three bedrooms a good do on Thursday and they're as clean as a whistle.'

'Okay, Mam, don't get off yer bike!' Eileen smiled and her chubby cheeks moved upwards to cover her eyes. 'I'm always tellin' yer that yer the best maid I ever 'ad.'

'Huh!' Maggie grunted as she smoothed down the front of her pinny. 'Half an hour to tidy up and this place will look like a little palace.'

'Listen, I'm not runnin' round like a blue-arsed fly five minutes before Mrs Kenny's due, so yez are all up by eight o'clock . . . Okay?'

Not a voice was raised in protest and Eileen nodded, her layer of chins rippling with the movement. 'Right, that's that sorted out.'

The cleft in Harry's chin deepened as he threw back his head and roared with laughter. 'I'd give anything to be here in the morning. It'll be like a Laurel and Hardy slapstick comedy.' Tears of laughter were shining in his eyes, and his laughter was so infectious there were smiles on everyone's faces. 'Or better still,' Harry was holding his tummy now as his laugh grew louder, 'one of those Keystone Cop films where everyone runs round in double quick motion.'

Eileen reached behind her for a cushion, screwed up her eyes till she had the target in sight, then aimed at Harry. It hit him full in the face with such force he had to gasp for breath.

'Bull's-eye!' Eileen chuckled. 'That'll teach yer, clever clogs!'

35

Chapter Five

'You what?' Eileen's mouth gaped. 'We're movin' house tomorrer an' you want me to do a disappearing act? Have yer lost the run of yer senses, Bill Gillmoss?'

'No, chick, I haven't.' Bill stood in front of her, feet spaced apart. The sleeves of his blue and white striped shirt were rolled up to the elbows, there were streaks of dirt across the front and a ragged tear where a pearl button had been ripped off when he'd tried to lift a bedstead on his own. 'I want you out of the way while everything is moved from here and taken to the new house. I'll have me work cut out without worrying about you.'

'I think yer've flipped yer lid!' Eileen snorted. 'Who d'yer think is goin' to make sure everythin' is put in the right place?'

'Don't argue,' Bill said firmly. 'I know where all the furniture has to go and I'm not having you lugging things around in your condition. I've got our Billy and Arthur to help me, and there'll be two men with the removal van. We'll have everything in place by the time you get back.'

'I've never 'eard anythin' so daft in all me life.' Eileen lifted her hands in disgust. Her gaze went around the room, resting for a while on the large tea chests containing all the bedding and pans, and the smaller cardboard boxes where crockery and ornaments were packed, each item wrapped in a piece of newspaper to prevent breakages. 'Who's goin' to tell yer where all those things go?'

Bill sighed wearily. He'd been on the go since he'd got in from work and he was dead tired. Not that he'd done it all himself, because Harry, Mary, Arthur and Vera had been there all night and they'd worked alongside him to make sure everything was ready for the van which was coming at nine in the morning.

Bill ran a hand across his forehead. 'Your ma and Mary will be there to unpack all the boxes, and if they don't put them where you

37

want them it's not the end of the world. You'll have plenty of time to sort them out later.' He put a hand under her chin and lifted her face. 'Do this to please me, will you, chick? I'll have enough on me plate without worrying about you.' When Eileen opened her mouth to protest, Bill put a finger across her lips. 'It's no good saying you'll just stand by and watch, because I know you too well. If I took my eyes off you for a second you'd be moving this, that and the other, and I'm not taking any chances.'

Eileen folded her arms and rested them on her swollen tummy. 'I don't know,' she grumbled, 'the day we move house, I go on a ruddy picnic?'

Bill held his hand out. 'Come on, chick, let's hit the hay. I'm so tired I could fall asleep standing up. But this time tomorrow night we'll be all settled in our new home.'

Eileen averted her eyes as Bill pulled her up from the couch. She didn't want him to know that inside she was crying. This was the last night they'd be sleeping in the house that had been their home since the day they were married. But no one seemed sorry. They were so full of the nice new posh house, it was as if they'd already forgotten this little place with all the memories it held.

'This is the most cockeyed bloody idea I've ever 'eard of,' Eileen gasped as she struggled out of the front passenger seat of Harry's car. 'Half past nine in the mornin', an' we're takin' a ferry trip across the Mersey.' As she lowered her feet to the pavement her dress rumpled up to reveal pieces of knotted elastic keeping her stockings up. 'I must be stark ravin' mad to 'ave let Bill talk me into this.'

'It's for your own good, Eileen, so don't be hard on Bill.' Harry bit hard on the inside of his cheek, but it was no good, he couldn't keep the laughter back. 'I'm sorry, Eileen, but you should see your face.'

'An' I'm sorry, 'cos it's the only bloody face I've got.' Eileen glared at him for a few seconds, then her body started to shake. 'I suppose I might as well see the funny side, seein' as 'ow I can't do nowt about it.' She held her tummy as the laughter erupted. 'I 'aven't been on a ferry for years, an' I 'ave to pick a day when there's a bloody gale force wind blowin'.' She wiped a tear away with the back of her hand. 'On top of that, I haven't a clue what number bus to get back to me new 'ouse!'

Harry bowed, waving his hand towards the car. 'No problem, madam. Your car will be here to pick you up at two o'clock.'

Harry helped Vera and the girls from the back seat and slammed the car doors. 'I'll have to move, I'm blocking the traffic. See you later.'

Eileen stood by the rails as the ferry ploughed its way through the choppy waters of the Mersey. Her head thrown back, she breathed in the sea air. 'Yer know, it wasn't such a bad idea after all. I'm really enjoying this. The wind's blowin' all the cobwebs away.'

'Mam, the water looks all frothy.' Edna was hanging over the rail fascinated by the surf made by the ferry breaking the waves. 'It looks like your dolly tub does when you've put Persil in the water.'

Vera, her hand tightly gripping Carol, was pointing out the flock of seagulls that were following the ferry boat. 'Look, darling, see all the birds?'

Carol's eyes were wide as she watched the seagulls swoop and soar, a sight she'd never seen before. She struggled to free herself from Vera's grip so she could join Edna at the rails, but Vera held on tight. 'Mummy will lift you up, otherwise you might fall in the river.'

Eileen turned her back to the rail to watch the receding waterfront of Liverpool. 'Yer can't beat old Liverpool, can yer?' Her eyes rested briefly on the two Liver birds perched proudly on top of the Liver Building, then she turned to Vera. 'I wonder 'ow they're gettin' on? I should be there, yer know.'

'Eileen, they'll manage much better without you, you'd only be in the way. Now, for heaven's sake stop worrying and enjoy yourself.'

Because it was early on a Saturday morning, there weren't many people making the crossing, so there was no pushing and shoving when the ferry tied up at the landing stage in Seacombe. Having been warned by Bill not to let Eileen overdo things, Vera kept the pace leisurely as they strolled in the direction of New Brighton. They'd been walking for about twenty minutes when they came to a small cafe. 'How about a cuppa?' Eileen asked. 'With me feet swellin', these shoes are pinchin' and me feet are givin' me gyp.'

The smell of home-made scones pervaded the air and Eileen took a deep breath. 'Smells just like our kitchen when me mam's bakin'.'

They ordered tea and scones for four, and when the homely waitress had set the table, Eileen smiled with satisfaction. With the plate of scones came a dish of butter and a bowl of strawberry jam. 'You can be mother, Vera, and pour the tea.'

Carol's eyes were like saucers. She watched carefully what Edna did, then followed suit. It was the first time she'd ever been in a cafe and the excitement and pleasure was there on her face for all to see. 'She's a little love,' Eileen said.

At that moment Carol misjudged the thickness of the scone and ended up with a blob of jam on her nose. She couldn't understand why everyone started laughing but she joined in and her infectious laugh filled the room. Even the waitress, standing by the counter hoping for more customers, had a wide smile on her face.

When they came out of the cafe the wind had dropped and the sun was making a brave attempt to push its way between the clouds. The foursome continued towards New Brighton, stopping on the way to watch a Punch and Judy show while licking their way through ice cream cornets. And when Edna saw some children paddling, she was over the railings and running across the sand before Eileen could stop her. 'She'll get 'er death of cold, the silly nit.'

'Look, there's a bench here, you sit down while I take Carol for a paddle. She's never been to the seaside before . . . Danny never took her anywhere, and on the money he gave me, I couldn't afford to.' Vera waited till Eileen was seated. 'She may as well enjoy herself while she can, like all the other kids.'

Eileen watched Vera run across the sand, her long hair bouncing on her shoulders, and heard her laugh ring out when Carol screamed with delight. She's a changed woman, Eileen thought. Pity Danny didn't leave her years ago.

With Vera holding their shoes and socks, and their dresses tucked into their knickers, Edna and Carol ran into the water. 'Ow! It's freezing.' Edna ran back, dragging Carol with her. 'It's like ice.'

'You wouldn't be told,' Vera said. 'I've got a cloth here, come and dry your feet.'

Edna eyed the other children splashing about happily. If they could do it, so could she. 'No, I'll 'ave another go.'

Carol picked up a handful of sand and her eyes filled with wonder as it trickled through her fingers. 'Sand, Mummy. Carol likes sand.'

Eileen waited with growing impatience. 'I wish I 'ad me watch with me,' she said aloud. 'It must be gettin' on now.' Ignoring the curious glances of the people walking by, she kept up her one-sided conversation. 'I bet they're wishin' I was there to tell them where everythin' goes.'

Eileen had slipped her shoes off to relieve the pain, and was completely unaware of the sight she made. An eighteen-stone woman, heavily pregnant and shoeless, was enough to cause people to stare. One couple passed, stopped a short way from Eileen, then turned and came back. 'Are you all right, dear,' a man asked kindly, 'do you need some help?'

Eileen looked at him blankly. 'I don't need any 'elp, thank you.'

The man raised his trilby. 'My wife thought we should ask in case you needed assistance. Happily you do not, so we'll wish you a very good morning.'

Vera came back with the children, their faces glowing, their hair windswept. 'Who was that you were talking to?'

'Some feller tryin' to click,' Eileen said, passing it off. 'Anyway, what time is it, Vera? It must be nearly time to make our way back to Seacombe.'

'Eileen, we've got two hours yet!'

'In that case, I'm goin' for somethin' to eat.' Eileen's face did contortions as she squeezed her feet into the shoes. 'There's a smell of chips comin' from somewhere, so let's follow the smell.'

'Eggs, chips and mushy peas, please.' Eileen smiled at the waitress. 'Two adults' and two children's portions.'

When the order came, Eileen covered her chips with Daddies tomato sauce and tucked in with gusto. The plate of bread and butter disappeared quickly, with Eileen using the last piece to mop up her plate. When she'd finished she patted her tummy. 'I needed that. The sea air's given me an appetite.' She scraped her chair back. 'Now, let's get crackin', or we'll miss the half one ferry.'

Everyone was talking at once as Harry helped them into the car. Edna and Carol were telling him what they'd done and seen, while Eileen was firing questions at him. Did the van turn up on time? Did they manage to get everything away in one go? They hadn't left anything behind, had they? Harry shook his head as he drove up Dale Street and turned into Byrom Street. He took his eyes off the road for a fraction of a second and patted Eileen's hand. 'Everything is under control, so don't worry.'

'It's all right for you,' Eileen muttered darkly. 'You wouldn't worry if yer backside was on fire.'

Harry grinned but was too busy concentrating on the road to answer. It was always busy on a Saturday down Scotland Road and County Road, with women getting their week-end shopping in, and his eyes were wary for the absent-minded pedestrians who stepped off the kerb without looking to see if the road was clear. There were Mary-Ellens on the corner of every side street down County Road, their barrows laden down with potatoes, vegetables, fruit and flowers. They were a familiar sight, with their long black skirts and hand-knitted, fringed black shawls draped around their shoulders. Their sing-song voices could be heard over the roar of the traffic, inviting passers-by to inspect their wares and promising to return their money if they could buy cheaper anywhere in Liverpool.

Vera tapped Harry on the shoulder. 'You can drop me and Carol off anywhere here. We can cut through the side streets and be home in five minutes.'

'I'll run you there.'

'You've got enough to do.' Vera pulled a hankie from her pocket, licked it with her tongue and rubbed at the remnants of tomato sauce and ice cream which had hardened around Carol's mouth. 'Anyway, I want a couple of things from the shops.'

Eileen twisted in her seat as Harry pulled in to the kerb. 'Thanks, Vera, yer a pal! Bring Carol down on Monday to see me new 'ouse. We should be straight by then, please God.'

Vera was walking away swinging Carol's arm when Harry wound the window down. 'I almost forgot, Vera, Arthur said to tell you if it wasn't too late when we finished today, he'd call in and see you. Otherwise he'd try and make it tomorrow.'

Vera's face flamed as she jerked her head in reply and walked briskly away.

Harry faced Eileen, his eyebrows raised. 'What's going to happen there, d'you think?'

'The Lord knows.' Eileen turned to look out of the window. 'You never saw 'is wife, Harry, so yer don't know the 'alf of it. I couldn't believe me eyes the day I went up there. Right brazen bitch she is, with 'er dyed 'air an' thick make-up. An' the 'ouse was filthy . . . God, I'll never forget the smell of bugs. An' that's what Arthur came 'ome to. Prisoner of war for five years an' he comes 'ome to find 'is wife's turned into a prostitute.'

Harry turned his head both ways before crossing the busy road over Breeze Hill. 'Apparently she hasn't changed, either.'

'No, she 'asn't changed.' Eileen watched the stream of visitors to Walton Hospital turn into the gates. 'I think that's why Arthur an' Vera are drawn to each other, they're both in the same boat. Married the wrong partners.'

'But Vera could get a divorce from Danny on the grounds of desertion, surely?'

They were crossing the awkward humpback bridge at Orrell Park station and Eileen waited till they were clear before answering. 'She probably will, given time. But what other feller is goin' to take 'er on with Carol?'

'Every man is not like Danny Jackson, Eileen.'

'No, I know. An' Arthur Kennedy's one of them.'

'Don't go matchmaking, Eileen, you'll get your fingers burned.'

'I've already been told not to interfere by Bill,' Eileen told him. 'So I just say me prayers every night for two good friends.'

Edna was out of the car before it stopped and disappeared into the darkness of the hall. But Eileen stood for a while weighing up the house that was to be her new home. She turned her head to look up and down the deserted road. No neighbours standing at doors chatting, no girls playing skipping or hop-scotch, no boys swinging from a lamppost by a piece of rope or kneeling in the gutter playing ollies.

Harry put his hand under Eileen's elbow and urged her forward. 'Welcome to your new home, Mrs Gillmoss.'

'My God, it's like Casey's court!' Eileen tried to squeeze past a tea chest in the hallway, but gave up after a few attempts. She could hear shouting, banging, and furniture being dragged across floors. 'It reminds me of one of Stan Laurel's "another fine mess".'

'Hang on a minute and I'll get someone to help me move this.' Harry put a hand on top of the chest and vaulted over. 'Won't be a tick.'

'Hi-ya, Mam!' Young Billy came down the stairs carrying a cardboard box. 'This has got stuff in for the kitchen.'

The door of the front parlour was closed and Eileen eyed it for a second. This was to be her mam's bed-sitting room. They didn't have enough furniture to put in it, but next week they were going to Hartley's auction rooms in Moss Street to see what they had. You could get some good bargains at Hartley's if you were lucky.

43

Eileen was getting impatient waiting for Harry. 'Where the 'ell's he got to?'

In the end she opened the parlour door which was the only one she could reach, and poked her head in.

'Watch it, our kid!'

Eileen held her breath when she saw her sister perched on top of a ladder hanging curtains at the bay window. 'I'll hold the ladder for yer.'

'I'm finished now.' Rene tilted her head to make sure the gathers in the curtains were uniform. 'I'm afraid they're not nearly long enough, but they'll do for now. At least me mam won't have to go to bed with nothing covering the windows.' Rene, half the size of Eileen, stepped gingerly down the ladder. 'That's all the windows done now . . . not bad, eh, kid?'

Maggie's bed had been set against a side wall and was already made up with her hand-crocheted counterpane covering bedclothes and pillows. The only other thing in the room was a small rug placed in front of the tiled fireplace. 'The room looks bare,' Eileen said, 'but when we get some furniture, me mam should be very comfortable in here.'

'She'll be as snug as a bug in a rug.' Rene gave her sister a quick hug. 'Me and Alan are going to buy her a new sideboard as an early birthday present. And we've got a little table she can have for her bedside, so all she needs is a couple of easy chairs or a settee.'

'Yer mean couch, don't yer?' Eileen stuck her tongue out. 'Settee, indeed! We want none of yer fancy posh Old Roan talk 'ere.'

Eileen felt two arms circle her waist and her eyes slid sideways to meet Bill's. 'Did yer 'ear that, Bill? That thing we've been callin' a couch for years, isn't a couch . . . it's a ruddy settee!'

Rene laughed good-naturedly. 'What would you do with her?'

'Right now I'm going to give her a tour of inspection.' Bill turned Eileen round and reached for her hand. 'Come on, Mrs Woman.'

Eileen's head was reeling when she finally sat down. She couldn't take it all in. Couldn't believe so much had been achieved in such a short time. They didn't have nearly enough furniture for such a big house, but what they did have had been placed just where she would have put it herself. The men had done all the heavy work, while Rene had seen to the curtains and Maggie and Mary had sorted the kitchen out. All pans and crockery had been put away in the kitchen cupboards and drawers lined with bright wallpaper. Pictures and mirrors had been hung, photographs lined the top of the sideboard, and in the middle of the dining table stood a vase filled with carnations and roses.

Eileen rubbed two fingers against her temple to relieve the tension. 'I don't know what to say. For the first time in me life, I'm lost for words.'

In front of her, forming a semicircle, were Bill, young Billy, Harry, Arthur, Rene, Mary and her neighbour, Doris, and Maggie. Her eyes moving from one to the other, Eileen shrugged her shoulders. 'Yez know I'm no good at makin' pretty speeches, so I'll just say yer the best mates anyone could 'ave and I love all of yez.'

'I wouldn't thank us until you get our bill,' Harry said, catching Arthur's eye and winking. 'How much did we say, Arthur? Half-a-crown an hour, was it?'

'Yer can sod off, Harry Sedgemoor,' Eileen huffed. Then she straightened her back, thrusting her enormous bust forward. Half closing her eyes, her nose pointing to the ceiling, she put on her posh accent. 'Hi'll give you sixpence to go to the children's matinee at the Carlton next Saturday, to see Tom Mix. Hand you should have henough hover to buy yourself ha quarter of Basset's liquorice hallsorts.'

'I can't wait.' Harry rubbed his hands together. 'Tom Mix is me favourite cowboy.'

Mary gave him a gentle dig in the ribs. 'Let's make a move and leave them in peace.'

'Yes, I'd better go too,' Doris said, 'If Jim's tea's not on the table at five o'clock, he'll give me my marching orders.'

'Have a cup of tea before you go,' Maggie coaxed. 'God knows, you all deserve one.'

'No thanks, we'll have one when we get home,' Mary laughed. 'It's only two doors away.' She waved her hand over Harry's shoulder. 'See you tomorrow, Eileen.'

'Okay, kid! Ta-ra!'

'I'll see them out,' Bill said, 'I won't be a tick.'

'Mam, can I go and get meself ready now?' Billy asked. 'Me an' Jacko are going to a dance at the Holy Name in Fazakerley.'

'Hopin' for a click, are yer, son? Well, with your good looks, yer should get the pick of the crop.' Eileen gave him a broad wink. 'Go 'ed, son, an' get yerself all dolled up. Oh, an' while yer upstairs, see what our Edna's doin', will yer? She's been up there for hours.'

'She's putting her clothes away in the drawers,' Maggie said dryly. 'She's bagged the top two before Joan gets home.'

Eileen groaned. 'There'll be skin and 'air flyin' up there tonight. Still, me an' our Rene were the same when we were young.'

Arthur pulled a chair from the table and sat down. 'How does your Joan like working at Vernon's?'

'She loves it, but 'ow long the novelty will last I don't know because they 'ave to work till nearly ten on a Saturday night markin' the coupons.' Eileen chuckled. 'Yer should see 'er! Thinks she's the whole cheese now she's workin'. Savin' up to get 'er 'air permed, if yer don't mind.'

'I'll stick the kettle on,' Maggie said. 'Me mouth's that dry it feels like emery paper.'

'I'll give you a hand,' Rene said quickly. 'You've done enough for one day. I think you forget you're not a spring chicken any more.'

Left alone now with Arthur, Eileen asked softly, 'How's things with you, Arthur?'

Arthur rolled his sleeves down and dipped into his trouser pocket for his cuff links before meeting Eileen's eyes. 'I was going to say they were just the same, like I always do. But they're not the same, and I'm not going to lie to you.' He fiddled and cursed under his breath while struggling to get one of the cuff links through the two holes in his cuff. In the end Eileen became exasperated.

'For God's same come 'ere an' let me do it for yer. Bloody 'elpless men are, just like babies.'

Eileen held on to Arthur's arm when she'd successfully fastened his cuff links. 'What's wrong . . . is it Sylvia?'

'She's ill, Eileen, but won't go to see a doctor. You wouldn't know her if you saw her, she's lost that much weight. She's got a terrible cough and her skin's a yellow colour.'

'Call the doctor in,' Eileen told him. 'She can't do much about it if he walks in on her.'

'I'll have to do something.' Arthur heard Bill close the front door and knew he didn't have much time. 'How was Vera?'

Bill would go mad if he knew she was interfering, but Eileen felt so sorry for Arthur and Vera. They both deserved better out of life. She glanced at the clock. 'If yer left now, yer'd 'ave time to call in an' see her, an' still be 'ome for the boys before it gets too dark.'

Bill came in rubbing his hands and calling through the kitchen, 'How about that cup of tea?'

'I won't stay.' Arthur made up his mind quickly. He hated lying to a friend, and Bill was a true friend. And there shouldn't be any need to lie, because God knows, he and Vera did nothing wrong. But Arthur knew instinctively that Bill didn't approve. 'I'll get home, have a bath and listen to the wireless with the boys.'

'Are you coming up, chick?' Bill asked. 'I'm that dead beat I could sleep on a clothes line.'

Eileen pressed her palms on the table and pushed herself up. 'You go on and I'll follow. I just want to get a drink of water.'

Bill was halfway up the stairs when he stopped, his brow furrowed. There was something not quite right, but he couldn't put his finger on it. Then it struck him . . . in all the years they'd been married, he'd never known Eileen drink water before going to bed.

His hand pressing on the banister rail, Bill took the stairs two at a time. The living room was in darkness, but from the light in the kitchen he could see Eileen bending over the sink, her face in her hands. He rushed to her, thinking she was sick, then he saw her shoulders shaking and knew she was crying.

'Chick,' Bill took her shoulders and turned her around, 'what's wrong?'

'Oh, Bill,' Eileen sobbed. 'I didn't even 'ave time to say goodbye to all me friends and neighbours.'

Bill held her close and stroked her back. 'You can go up any time and see your friends. It isn't as though we've moved to the other end of the world.'

'But I didn't even have a chance to say goodbye to me little house.'

Eileen swallowed at the lump in her throat. 'And I can't go back there any time, can I?'

Bill wiped her tears away with a finger. He'd expected Eileen to be upset, but he just hoped that when she got used to the new house she'd settle down.

Chapter Six

'Sshush!' Martha Bradshaw put a finger to her lips to quieten the children. 'I think this is Mummy and Daddy.' With her good foot, Martha spun her rocking chair round till it was facing the door. Her neatly combed white hair framed a kind face, with blue eyes that showed her eagerness for news. 'Well,' she asked as Mary came into the room, 'how did it go?'

'Eileen looks as though she doesn't know what day it is.' Mary smiled at her mother as she slipped her arms out of her coat. 'She said for the first time in her life she's lost for words.'

'And that's saying something,' Harry piped in. 'Eileen's not usually short a few hundred words.'

'I've been dying to know how you were all getting on.' Since she'd had a stroke during an air raid in the May blitz, Martha had learned to live within her capabilities. Slowly, and in great pain, she had persevered until she had mastered the crutches given to her by the hospital. Now she could at least get around the downstairs rooms under her own steam. And she never complained because she had so much to be thankful for. A loving daughter, the best son-in-law anyone could ask for, two lovely grandchildren and a nice comfortable home. It was only at times like this that she cursed her affliction. It would have meant so much to her to have been able to help Eileen. To repay, in a small way, some of the happiness the big woman had brought into their lives. 'It'll be nice having them for neighbours.'

'Can we go and see Auntie Eileen, Mummy?' Tony pulled on Mary's skirt. 'You promised.'

'I didn't promise you could see her today. Tomorrow, perhaps, if Auntie Eileen isn't too tired. We could take Grandma with us, in the wheelchair.'

Tony, so serious for his age, went to stand in front of Martha.

'You'll like that, won't you, Grandma?'

Emma, not to be outdone, stood next to her brother. 'If Daddy gets the wheelchair down the steps, Grandma, I'll push you.'

Tony swung his hip and pushed his sister. 'I'm stronger than you, 'cos I'm a boy.'

Harry intervened before there was a crying match. 'You can take turns. One push the wheelchair down, and the other push it back. Okay?'

'I'll make us some tea.' Mary looked from Harry to Martha. 'Will beans on toast do? I'm too tired to cook anything.' As she turned, Mary's eye caught sight of a man passing the window. 'Oh, there's Arthur on his way home. Why don't you give him a lift, Harry? He has to get two buses to the Dingle, and he must be worn out.'

Harry's mind ticked over quickly. Unless he was very much mistaken, Arthur would be calling at Vera's before he went home, and he wouldn't welcome being offered a lift to the Dingle, which was the other side of the city. 'I haven't got much petrol left, and I'm right down on coupons.' Harry stared hard at Mary, willing her to understand. 'Don't forget I've done a lot of running around today, and I've barely enough juice to get me to work on Monday.'

Mary was filled with curiosity. What was going on? She knew Harry could have taken Arthur home, he wasn't that short of petrol. And it wouldn't be because he couldn't be bothered because Harry wasn't like that. He, Arthur and Bill were the best of mates. They all worked in the English Electric on the East Lancs Road, and in work and out, they got on like a house on fire.

'I'll get the tea on.' Mary made her way to the kitchen. She'd get it out of Harry when they were alone.

When Vera opened the door and saw Arthur on the step, her face lit up for a second before her eyes started to twitch nervously.

'It's all right, Vera, there's no one around,' Arthur said. 'Not a soul in sight.'

Vera glanced quickly up and down the street before standing aside and inviting Arthur in. 'It's only Elsie Smith I'm worried about,' she told him as she closed the door. 'I've told you about her . . . the neighbourhood scandalmonger. She's got eyes on her like a hawk and she doesn't miss a trick.'

'There's no harm in a friend coming to visit you. Surely she can't make anything out of that.'

'You don't know Elsie Smith! She spends her whole life pulling people to pieces, and what she doesn't know, she makes up. If she's seen you coming in here, it'll be all round the street in the morning. She likes nothing better than a bit of juicy gossip.'

'Are you going to keep me in the hall?' Arthur asked. 'Or shall I knock on the Smiths' and tell her my intentions are strictly honourable?'

'Don't be daft, and come on in.' Vera opened the living room door. 'She wouldn't believe you, anyway.'

'Uncle Arthur!' Carol threw down the coloured bricks she'd been playing with and flew to wrap her arms around his legs. 'I've been on a ship.'

'So I've heard.' Arthur smiled down into the happy face. 'Auntie Eileen told me all about it.' His eyes moved to the small kitchen. 'Are the boys out?'

Vera nodded. 'Peter's gone to the flicks, and Colin's got a date with a girl from his works.' She moved Carol's toys from the couch and motioned to Arthur to sit down. 'She must be someone special because he took an hour to get ready. He pressed his own trousers and you could cut your throat on the crease in them. His hair is thick with brilliantine and the shine on his shoes is nobody's business.'

'Love's young dream, eh?' There was a hint of sadness in Arthur's smile. 'I wish I had my time over again, don't you, Vera?'

Vera averted her eyes as a deep sigh left her lips. 'If I had a pound for every wish I've made over the last few years, Arthur, I'd be a very rich woman.' She shivered and wrapped her arms around her waist. 'Have you time for a cuppa, or are you in a hurry?'

'I haven't got the energy to hurry.' Arthur lifted Carol on to his knee. 'We've all worked harder today than we do in work. But it was worth it to see Eileen's face.'

'What about the boys?' Vera asked. 'Don't you have to get home to them?'

'I told them I'd be late, and one of their mates is going to stay with them until I get back.'

'Right, I'll put the kettle on and make you a sandwich.'

Vera came down after putting Carol to bed. 'The sea air must have tired her out, she was asleep before her head hit the pillow.'

Arthur watched as Vera sat in a chair on the opposite side of the room. Clasping and unclasping her hands, she was clearly nervous and ill at ease. 'Would you rather I left?' Arthur asked quietly. 'You look worried to death.'

Vera dropped her head to stare at her hands. 'No, I don't want you to leave. It's not very often I get the chance to talk to another adult because I've never really made friends with the neighbours.' She looked at him through lowered lids. 'It's just that I worry about what people think.'

'To hell with what they think!' Arthur sounded angry. 'We're two grown-up people who like each other! If anyone is bad minded enough to read anything into that, then I feel sorry for them. It's you and I who count, and you know I'd never do anything to hurt you, or your reputation, don't you, Vera?'

'I know that,' Vera nodded. 'And it's been marvellous to have you to talk to over the last year, because you understand. Mary and Eileen are the best friends anyone could have, but they've got good husbands and a happy, normal life. They couldn't be expected to know how it feels to be on your own, with no man behind you.'

Arthur leaned forward, his hands clasped between his knees. 'No one to hold you when you're feeling blue, and no one to dry your eyes when the tears come.' A lock of his hair had fallen to cover his eyes and he brushed it away in a gesture of frustration. 'Our lives are a right mess, aren't they? But why us, Vera? What have we ever done to deserve this hell?'

'I stopped asking myself that question years ago.' Vera fixed her gaze on the flickering coals in the large, old-fashioned grate. 'It was when I realised that life without Danny had to be better than the one I had with him.' She tore her eyes away from the fire to gaze around the small room. It was spotlessly clean, but the furniture was shabby, the pattern on the lino had almost disappeared and the curtains were so faded it was impossible to see the flowers that had made them so colourful when they were new. 'I haven't got much to show for nineteen years of married life, not in material things, anyway. And it's a struggle from week to week to make the money spin out. But in spite of that I've got a lot to be thankful for. I've got Carol and the two boys. They're good children and I love them dearly.'

Vera had never spoken at such length before and Arthur sat with his chin cupped in his hands, his eyes noting the changing expressions on her face. He didn't interrupt, afraid that if he did Vera would clam up.

'I don't miss Danny at all.' It was as though Vera were talking to herself, speaking her thoughts aloud. 'It's a much happier house without him and his violent temper. Me and the kids lived in fear of him, never knowing when he was going to lash out with his fists or his feet. The boys hated him, even though he was never really cruel to them. It was me and Carol he always picked on. Carol because he was ashamed of her, and me because I was the handiest. He used me as a punch bag, did Danny.'

'I know,' Arthur spoke softly. 'Remember, I saw a bit of brave Danny's handiwork.'

Vera's head jerked sideways and she looked at Arthur as though surprised at seeing him there. Flustered, her fingers pecked at her lips. 'I'm sorry, I shouldn't burden you with my troubles when you've got enough of your own.'

'A trouble shared is a trouble halved, Vera. God knows I've been glad of you to talk to, to get things off my chest.'

'How are things at home?'

'Sylvia's not well at all. I've asked her to go to the doctor's but she doesn't take any notice of me.' Arthur shrugged his shoulders. 'In fact, if looks could kill I'd have been dead long ago.'

'What a fool of a woman.' Vera sounded angry. 'Doesn't she know how lucky she is?'

'I've gone past caring, Vera. I've nothing but contempt for her and the life she leads.' Arthur sat back and rested his head on the back of the couch. 'It's the boys I'm sorry for. They're growing up now, and when they see their mother going out every night dressed like a tart, how must they feel? And the kids they play with must say something because you know how cruel children can be.' Arthur made a fist of his hand and banged it on the arm of the couch. 'I can't count the number of times I've told myself I should get the boys out of there. I've gone as far as packing a case, but in the end I've chickened out. Sylvia is their mother, after all, and perhaps a bad mother is better than no mother at all. Who am I to decide?'

Vera's heart was full of sympathy for this fine man who, against her better judgement, she'd grown very fond of. She wished she could help him, but who was she to advise when she'd made such a mess of her own life?

'Arthur, it's nine o'clock. I'm not trying to get rid of you, but it takes you nearly an hour to get home and it's late for the boys to be up.'

Arthur breathed in deeply and stretched his arms over his head. 'I don't feel like moving now. You know I like being here with you, don't you, Vera?'

Vera lowered her head and her voice was a mere whisper, 'And I like you being here.'

Arthur stood up quickly. 'I'd better go before I say too much. But thanks for listening to me, Vera. You've no idea how good it is to have someone to talk to.'

'Of course I do! Haven't I just bared my soul to you?' Vera pushed back a wayward strand of hair. 'I've told you more than I've ever told anyone.'

'Another instalment next week,' Arthur laughed. 'Who needs to go to the pictures?'

Vera opened the living room door and stood aside to let Arthur pass. 'I might see you at Eileen's next weekend?'

'Let's not leave it a week before we see each other. I'll call in on me way home from work one night with some sweets for Carol.' Arthur opened the front door, then whispered, 'Would you like to make sure the coast is clear before I go out? Elsie Smith might be lurking in the shadows.'

Vera didn't often laugh out loud, but when she did it was a joy to the ear. Loud and clear it rang out before caution brought her hand up to smother it. 'Blow Elsie Smith! If she's watching through her curtains, like she usually is, it'll give her something to think about.'

Arthur stepped into the street and looked up at Vera who was standing on the top step, her folded arms hugging her slim waist. 'I'm very fond of you, you know that, don't you, Vera? And there's nothing I'd like better than to give Elsie Smith something to gossip about. But I value your friendship too much to risk losing it. So you need never be afraid of me, love.'

'I would never be afraid of you,' Vera said softly. 'I just wish things were different.'

'Who knows what the future holds?' Arthur leaned forward and pecked her on the cheek. 'Goodnight, Vera.'

Vera waited till he was passing the Smiths' house, then called, 'Goodnight, Arthur.' She closed the door behind her and leaned against it, her hand on the cheek Arthur had kissed. 'Why, God,' she whispered. 'Why do you punish me so?'

Elsie Smith let the curtain fall back into place. 'That man's been at

Vera Jackson's again. There's something going on there, I'm telling you.'

Fred Smith sighed wearily. 'Is it any of our business?'

Elsie Smith's thin lips formed a straight line. 'It's not decent having a man in the house when the boys are out. There's something fishy there, mark my words.'

Fred put his *Echo* down and faced his wife. 'Vera Jackson's husband walked out on her, so she's a free agent. If she had ten men in the house, or even a red light put up outside, it's got nothing to do with you, me, or anyone else. She's a good woman and a good mother.'

Elsie folded her thin arms across her flat chest, her nostrils flared and her beady eyes mere slits. 'Well, we'll just wait an' see, shall we? But I bet a pound to a penny there's something going on between Vera and that bloke.'

'Why don't you be honest and say you hope there's something going on?' Fred asked softly. 'Brighten up your life if you had something to gossip about, wouldn't it? With your mind, Elsie Smith, I don't know how you sleep.'

Chapter Seven

'I've never been to an auction before.' Mary gripped Eileen's arm. 'You won't ask me to bid for anything, will you?'

'Oh, don't worry about that, kid!' Eileen said confidently, her wide hips swaying and brushing Mary and Maggie who were walking either side of her. She winked broadly at her mother. 'Me and me mam are old hands at this game, aren't we, Mam?'

'Oh, yes, we're experts.' Maggie smiled at Mary. 'Take no notice of her, lass, we're as green as cabbages.'

'This is it.' They stopped outside Hartley's auction rooms in Moss Street and Eileen grunted when she saw the number of people inside. 'Strewth! We'll be lucky to get in, never mind buy anythin'.' She shook Mary's arm free and straightened her shoulders ready to battle her way through the throng. Her foot was inside the doorway when she turned her head. 'Don't bat an eyelid, kid. If yer blow yer nose or move yer 'ead, yer'll find yer've bought yerself a three piece suite.'

'Ay, Mam, take a gander at those two fireside chairs.' Eileen pointed to two sturdy-looking chairs covered in a beige moquette. 'They'd be just the job for your room.'

'The dealers will probably bid for those,' Maggie said. 'They buy anything saleable.'

'Dealers?' Mary asked. 'What dealers?'

'See that woman in the blue coat, the one who looks as though she's 'asn't got two ha'pennies to rub together? Well she's a dealer . . . got a secondhand shop down Smithdown Road.' Eileen lowered her voice. 'Don't look now, but there's a feller standin' right behind us, the scruffy lookin' one in the long overcoat, he's got a shop in County Road.'

Mary stole a quick glance at the thin, seedy-looking man standing directly behind Eileen. 'It doesn't seem fair that dealers can come in here and buy. Doesn't give anyone else a chance.'

Eileen saw the crowd parting to make way for an officious looking man. 'Here's the auctioneer. Now the fun starts.'

In spite of being afraid to move or turn her head, Mary was fascinated as the sale progressed. With the lift of a finger a painting was bought for thirty shillings, a three piece for ten pounds, a piano for a fiver. The auctioneer moved things along so quickly, Mary couldn't keep up with him. Then the two fireside chairs came up . . . lot 24.

'Who'll start the bidding at three pounds for the pair?' The auctioneer scanned the crowd. 'Am I bid three pounds?'

The dealer in the blue coat lifted her hand. 'Three pounds.'

'Three pounds five shillin's,' Eileen shouted, red in the face.

'Three pounds ten.' The scruffy dealer behind entered the fray.

'Three pounds twelve and six.' As Eileen spoke she stepped back a pace, jerked her elbow with a force that winded the dealer when it came into contact with his ribs. 'Oh, I'm so sorry,' Eileen fussed, standing in front of the man and brushing an imaginary speck off his coat as he fought to catch his breath. 'I do hope I didn't hurt you.'

While Eileen was being profuse in her apologies, the chairs were knocked down to her for three pounds twelve and six.

'What happened?' Mary asked.

'I lost me balance for a second.' Eileen bit hard on the inside of her mouth to keep a smile at bay. 'Must be all this standin' that did it.' She opened her purse and took out a five-pound note. 'Do us a favour, kid, and pay for the chairs, will yer? Give it to the man sittin' at the table just outside the door. He'll give yer a receipt.' She grabbed Mary's arm. 'Don't forget me change.'

Eileen felt a tug on her coat and for the first time saw the little woman standing beside her. She was an elderly woman with white hair, a heavily lined face and pale eyes that told of a life of hardship. 'It's about time someone 'ad a go at 'im.' When she smiled, Eileen saw she didn't have a tooth in her head. 'Blinkin' nuisance those dealers, they don't give anyone else a chance.'

'Here every week, is 'e?'

'Him an' the other one.' The woman nodded across to the dealer in the blue coat. 'Got the money, 'aven't they, so they get all the best stuff.'

A bedroom suite came under the hammer then, and this was what Eileen was waiting for. She held out a hand to silence the woman and joined in the bidding. In less than a minute she was smiling happily, the owner of a wardrobe, dressing table and chest of drawers . . . all for seven pounds fifteen shillings.

Eileen turned her gaze back to the woman. 'What are you after?'

'A bedding bale.' A thin finger pointed to a sideboard with several bundles on top. 'We got bombed out in the war, yer see, and lost everythin' we 'ad. It's taken us years to get a home around us again, but we're short on beddin'.'

Mary came back then and handed Eileen the receipt and change. 'Have you bought anything?'

Eileen pointed to the bedroom suite. 'It's old fashioned, but it's solid mahogany and me mam said it will polish up a treat.'

'Are we going now, then?' Mary's face dropped. 'I'm enjoying meself, I think it's very interesting.'

'Me mam's got 'er eye on that little table over there. It'd look nice in front of the bay window with a plant on. Depends 'ow much it goes for, 'cos by the time I've paid for the furniture, I'll only 'ave a few bob left.'

The table started at five shillings, the scruffy dealer bid an extra half crown, but when Eileen glared at him as she upped it another half crown, he dropped out, thinking she'd probably break his ribs next time. Maggie was delighted. That table wouldn't half set her room off. 'Are we going now?' she asked. 'Me legs are getting tired.'

'Hang on a sec.' Eileen twisted round to face the dealer. His face paled and he stepped back a pace. He didn't trust this big woman one little bit. Eileen put on her best smile. 'I wonder if yer'd do me a favour?'

Suspicion showed in the man's eyes. 'What d'yer want?'

Eileen quickly explained about the old lady being bombed out and what she was after. 'I'm sure you're not interested in beddin', so I wondered if yer'd look after the old lady for me, see she gets what she came for?' Eileen crossed her fingers and asked God to forgive her for telling lies. 'I'll be back soon, I'm only goin' outside for a breath of fresh air, but in case I'm not back in time, can I rely on you to see she gets what she wants?'

The man rubbed the back of his hand across his nose. The woman's barmy, he thought, nutty as a fruit cake. But she was also very big, with muscles on her like Popeye, and he had no intention of crossing her. 'Yeah, OK.'

'Oh, you are kind.' Eileen pulled him towards the woman who was listening with her mouth open in amazement. 'This very nice gentleman is going to help you. He'll make sure yer get what you've come for. And he's goin' to tell his lady friend in the blue coat, aren't you, love?'

The glint in Eileen's eyes warned the man not to argue. 'Yeah, I'll give Hilda the wire.'

'Oh, good!' Eileen beamed. 'We're only goin' outside for a bit, so we'll see yez later.'

'What was all that about?' Mary followed in Eileen's wake as she pushed her way through the crowd. 'I thought we were going home?'

'So we are, kid! I'll explain when we're outside.'

But the smile left Eileen's face when she went to pay for the table and bedroom suite. The man took her money without looking up. 'D'yer want it delivered?'

'Of course I want it delivered! D'yer think I'm goin' to carry the blinkin' things on me back!'

'Ten bob delivery charge.' The man held his hand out. 'We deliver in your area on a Thursday.'

'What! Flippin' daylight robbery!' Eileen could see there was no use arguing, so she turned to Mary. 'Well, money bags, I 'ope yer've got ten bob to lend me.'

'I'll pay for me table when we get home,' Maggie said quietly. 'I've got a few pounds put by.'

'Yer burial money is it, Mam?' Eileen patted Maggie's arm. 'Don't act the goat, missus. Yer know I'm only kiddin'.'

Eileen took one of Maggie's arms, Mary the other, and three happy and well-satisfied women marched out of the shop. And they laughed all the way home on the bus when Eileen told them about the bedding bale. Between guffaws that had all the passengers on the bus looking at them, Eileen said, 'The funniest thing of all is, I told that bloke I was only goin' outside for a breath of fresh air an' I'd be back. He'll probably still be there when the shop closes.'

'It looks a treat, Ma.' Bill's gaze swept Maggie's room. The sideboard, a present from Rene and Alan, had been delivered that day, along with the furniture from Hartley's. 'And when it's decorated, you won't know yourself.'

Young Billy was peering over his dad's shoulder. 'Yeah, it looks great, Nan. Proper posh.'

'When it's all finished, I'll invite you in for tea,' Maggie said with pride. 'In fact, we'll have a party.'

'An' 'ave the neighbours talkin'.' Eileen pushed between her husband and son, sending them flying. 'There'll be no rowdy parties in this 'ouse, missus. It'll be afternoon tea by invitation only.'

Maggie moved the aspidistra plant an inch, then stood back to admire the new table. 'Sets the room off, doesn't it?'

'Yes,' Bill agreed, 'just the finishing touch it needed. Apart from a few odds and sods, the whole house is furnished now.'

'Except for the decoratin',' Eileen reminded him. 'This wallpaper is so dark it gives me the willies.' She linked her arm through Bill's and fluttered her eyelashes at him. 'When are yer goin' to make a start?'

'We've arranged to start scraping at the week-end. If we get all the dirty work done first, it'll be half the battle.' Bill smacked his forehead with an open hand. 'Oh, I forgot to tell you, Arthur didn't turn in to work today. He rang to say his wife was ill.'

'What's wrong with 'er?'

'I don't know. It was his foreman who told Harry.' The three of them worked on different sections in the English Electric, but they met up at lunch time in the canteen. Harry had a good job as a manager, Bill was a joiner and Arthur an electrician.

'I 'ope it's nothin' serious,' Eileen said. 'Arthur told me on Saturday that she looked ill, but she wouldn't go to the doctor's.'

'He'll probably be back at work tomorrow. If not, he's bound to let us know what's going on.'

Eileen pinched at the fat on her elbows. 'I feel sorry for 'im. He's got no friends up there, so he's no one to mind the boys. If 'e didn't live so far away, I'd call an' see if there was anything I could do. But it's bloody miles away.'

'Don't even think about it, chick!' Bill wagged a finger under Eileen's nose. 'You're in no condition to be helping anybody.'

'Bill, I only meant that if they lived nearer, I could 'elp with the boys. See them off to school, like, and let them come 'ere until Arthur got 'ome from work. It's not as if they're babies and need washing an' dressin', for heaven's sake. David's eleven, and Gordon's nine.'

61

'Me dad's right, Mam,' Billy said. 'You've got to look after yerself.'

'Oh, don't you start!' Eileen jerked her head in disgust, but secretly she was pleased. He was a good boy, was Billy, very caring for a boy his age. 'Anyway, what are we gettin' so het up about? Sylvia's probably got a cold an' will be up an' about in a day or two.'

'In the meantime, you stay out of it, right?' Bill's face was stern. 'No taking it upon yourself to go up there, jumping on and off buses.' Eileen took one look at Bill's set face and nodded.

'Our Billy's 'ad 'is dinner.' Eileen placed the plate in front of Bill. 'I think 'e must 'ave a date, 'cos he threw 'is dinner down and dashed upstairs to get ready.'

Bill eyed the plate heaped with mashed potatoes, cabbage and bacon ribs. 'That looks good, chick! Now a bit of beetroot, or some pickled cabbage would go down a treat with that lot.'

'Who was yer servant before I came along, Bill Gillmoss? Anyone would think yer were born with a silver spoon in yer mouth, instead of a flippin' dummy.' Eileen came back with a glass bowl full of deep red beetroot. 'As it so 'appens, me mam did this today.' She watched Bill dip his fork in the bowl, a look of anticipation on his face. 'D'yer remember when I was expectin' our Billy, an' I 'ad a cravin' for a coconut? And with Edna it was crab? Well, this time it's beetroot an' that's why me mam made that. So don't yer scoff the lot.'

Bill looked up, a smile on his face. 'What a time I had getting that crab. I think I tried every fish shop from here to town before I finally got one.'

Eileen asked the question that had been on her lips since Bill entered the house. 'Did Arthur turn in?'

Bill shook his head. 'Didn't ring up, either.'

'Oh, dear.' Eileen rested her elbows on the table. 'I wonder what's up?'

Bill had a piece of bacon rib in his hands and was chewing on the meat. He didn't answer till the bone was clean and he placed it at the side of his plate. 'Harry said if there's no word tomorrow, he'll run me up there tomorrow night.'

'I've got a feelin' in me bones that there's somethin' drastically wrong,' Eileen said. 'I don't 'alf feel sorry for Arthur. He's such a nice feller, he deserves a better life than he's got. An' the kids, too, poor buggers.'

Bill put his knife and fork down and reached across to pat her arm. 'We don't know how lucky we are, do we, chick? Always enough coal on the fire, food in the larder, good kids and a happy marriage. Who could ask for more in life?'

Eileen grinned. 'Yeah. We could conquer the world, you an' me, Bill Gillmoss.'

Eileen suddenly sat back in the chair, her two hands covering the lump in her tummy. 'This little feller is certainly lettin' me know he's 'ere. Been at it all day, he 'as.'

'Why do you keep calling it a "he"? There's a fifty-fifty chance on it being a girl.'

'Uh, uh,' Eileen smiled knowingly. 'It's a boy all right. A footballer, too! Been kickin' like mad all day.'

'I'll put his name down to play for Liverpool the day he's born then.' Bill smiled back. 'They could do with a good half-back.'

Maggie was sitting comfortably in her new chair listening to the wireless. She hadn't bothered to close the curtains because the street lamp outside the house gave her all the light she needed in the room. It was from this light she saw Arthur pass the window. 'Arthur's here,' she called, as she made her way down the hall. 'I'll open the door.'

Arthur's face was white and drawn as he stood in the middle of the room, his hands nervously running round the rim of his trilby hat. 'I've come from the hospital, that's why it's a bit late.'

'Is Sylvia in hospital, then?' Eileen took Arthur's hat and put it on the sideboard. 'Take yer coat off and sit down.'

'They took her in the Southern this morning.' Arthur sat down heavily, his breath coming in quick gasps. 'Visiting is half seven to eight, and I got the bus right down here.'

'Who's lookin' after the boys?'

'One of the neighbours.' Arthur saw the look of surprise on Eileen's face and nodded. 'I find it hard to believe meself. For two years all they've ever done is pass the time of day. But when the ambulance arrived this morning, two of them knocked on the door and asked if they could do anything to help. I was glad of it too, I can tell you.'

'And Sylvia,' Bill asked, 'what's wrong with her?'

'They don't know yet.' Arthur said, his gaze resting on Edna who was all ears. He shrugged his shoulders. 'They'll know more in a day or two.'

'Have yer 'ad anythin' to eat?' Eileen asked briskly.

'All I've done all day is drink cups of tea. I don't feel hungry, I've gone past it.'

'Rubbish! Yer've got to eat or yer'll be ill yerself.' Eileen dug her elbow in Bill's ribs. 'Give Edna two bob an' she can go for some fish an' chips.'

'Ah, ray, Mam!' Edna complained, frightened of missing something.

'Now then, young lady, you just do as you're told.' Bill passed the coin over. 'The shop's only at the top of the road.'

Maggie had been standing inside the door, now she bustled towards the kitchen. 'I'll put the kettle on and butter some bread.'

Eileen waited for the slam of the front door, then leaned forward. 'Do they know what's wrong with Sylvia?'

Arthur rubbed a hand across his forehead. 'I asked the Sister tonight but she wouldn't commit herself. Said they'd be keeping an eye on her for a few days before doing any tests. But when the doctor said he was sending her to hospital, I asked him what he thought was wrong with her. He didn't want to say anything at first, but I kept on at him that much he finally said he thought it was T B.'

'Oh, dear God, no!' Eileen's face drained of colour. 'People die of T B, don't they?' Too late Eileen realised what she'd said and clamped a hand over her mouth. 'I'm sorry, Arthur, I shouldn't 'ave said that. I don't know what I'm talkin' about, anyway, so take no notice.'

'You've only said what I'm thinking,' Arthur said. 'And the best of it is, the doctor blamed me.' There was bitterness in his voice. 'Threw the book at me for not making Sylvia get some attention before now.'

'But didn't yer tell 'im?' Eileen asked angrily.

'I did in the end. Told him the lot.' Arthur lifted his hand and snapped his fingers. 'And he changed, just like that. Couldn't have been nicer or more understanding. Said it explained Sylvia's terrible colour. Too much drinking over too long a period had probably damaged her liver.'

'Poor woman,' Bill said softly. 'Poor silly woman.'

'Poor woman?' Arthur's nostrils were white with anger. 'Bill, I could kill her with me bare hands! If she had no thought for herself, at least she should have had some thought for her two sons. They're at home now, Bill, crying their eyes out because their mother's sick. She wasn't a good wife, and certainly not a good mother, but she's the only one they've got! That's the only reason I've stayed with her.'

'Doctors don't know everythin', yer know, Arthur.' Tears were stinging the backs of Eileen's eyes. She didn't like Sylvia, but she certainly wouldn't wish this on her. 'She's in the right place in the hospital, they'll sort 'er out.'

'I think the doctor was right,' Arthur said. 'If you'd seen the change in her over the last six months, you'd know what I'm talking about. She lost so much weight she was only skin and bone. And her cough got so bad over the last few weeks she could hardly breathe.' Arthur was silent for a moment, then said, 'If only she'd done as I asked all those months ago, it mightn't have gone this far. But no, she had to go her own way. Out every night dressed like a floosie, coming home all hours the worse for drink. Bleary-eyed every morning, sending the boys off to school any old way. And never without a cigarette dangling out of the corner of her mouth. But for all that, she's the mother of my two sons and they love her.'

'What will you do now, Arthur?' Bill was so affected he had to struggle to get the words out. 'Will you have to stay off work?'

'Mrs Wright next door has offered to see to the boys for me, at least until we know what's happening. They're old enough to see to their own breakfast and get themselves off to school, so it's only for a few hours at night, until I get home.' There was a trace of sadness in Arthur's voice. 'From what I gathered this morning, listening to Mrs Wright and Mrs Summers, they've felt sorry for me since I came back from the army. Oh, they didn't say it in so many words, but it was Sylvia's way of life they objected to and that's why they kept their distance.'

They probably had plenty of reasons for not liking Sylvia, Eileen thought. She was so hard-faced and brazen, she wouldn't worry what the neighbours thought of her. Knowing Arthur was a prisoner of war, and seeing her out with every Tom, Dick and Harry, it was only natural that decent people would distance themselves from her.

Edna arrived back with the fish and chips and put a stop to any intimate conversation. It was when Arthur was leaving, Eileen asked him to let her know if it would be all right for her and Mary to go in and visit his wife. He threw her a look of gratitude and promised to see Bill in work and let him know how the land lay.

Chapter Eight

'Are you going to the shops?' Mary asked. 'I'll walk up with you if you like, give you a hand.'

'No, I got all me shoppin' in yesterday.' Eileen stood in the middle of Martha's room, dressed in her swagger coat that was fast becoming too small. 'I'm goin' up to Bray Street to see all me friends. I didn't get a chance when we moved and they'll think I'm terrible doin' a flit without saying goodbye after being neighbours for all those years.'

'D'you want me to come with you?' Mary asked. 'You really shouldn't be going that far on your own.'

'Our Edna's comin' with me. She'll be 'ere soon. I sent her upstairs to get a proper wash. She said she'd 'ad one, but it must 'ave been a cat's lick an' a promise 'cos she 'ad a flippin' big tidemark.'

'Sit down while you're waiting,' Martha said, pointing to the couch. 'Take the weight off your feet.'

'Mrs B, if I sat down there, yer'd need a crane to get me up. I'll just park meself on yer bed, if yer don't mind.' Eileen lowered herself slowly. 'It's like a mad house down there, I was glad to get out. Bill's started on the hall with our Billy 'elping 'im, Harry's doin' the livin' room an' our Rene's in the front parlour. Honest, I'll be glad when it's all finished.'

'It won't take long. I've trimmed half the rolls of paper and I'll do the rest when I've got the dinner prepared.' Mary sat down beside Eileen and put an arm across her shoulder. 'Come on, cheer up! Just think how nice it'll be when it's all finished.'

'It's not only that that's makin' me feel miserable,' Eileen admitted, heaving a huge sigh. 'I can't get Arthur an' Sylvia off me mind.'

'It's not good news, is it, lass?' Martha said. 'It must be serious if they've transferred her to Fazakerley Hospital.'

'I keep thinkin' about the boys, poor beggars. They're too young to know what T B is. They know their mam's sick, but that's about all.'

'Look, Eileen, in your condition you shouldn't be getting yourself all upset.' Mary's pretty face clouded with concern for her friend. 'All the worrying in the world won't change things, so try and put it out of your mind.'

'I can't 'elp it, kid, yer know what I'm like. Arthur's 'ad such a lousy time, an' now this on top of everythin' else.'

There was a tap on the window and Eileen held her hands out to Mary to help her up. 'That'll be our Edna. I'd better go an' see if the tide's gone out.'

As soon as they turned into Bray Street, Edna skipped ahead. 'I'm goin' to see Janet.'

'Hey, buggerlugs,' Eileen shouted after her. 'Don't you go doin' a disappearin' act! I'll meet yer in the corner shop about three.' Eileen walked slowly up the street and with each step her heart became heavier. Further up she could see some of her old neighbours standing at their doors chatting, while the laughter of children at play filled the air. God, what a difference, Eileen thought. we may be living in a posh house in a swanky neighbourhood, but give me this any time.

Edna had spread the news and people appeared as if by magic. In no time Eileen found herself surrounded, everyone smiling and asking how she was and how she liked the new house. Putting a brave face on, Eileen gave a glowing report on her new home, stopping only briefly to cross her fingers and ask God to forgive her once again for telling lies. They're not really lies, she reminded Him. It is a nice house, it's just that I wish it wasn't me living in it.

Cissie Maddox pushed her way through the crowd that had gathered. 'Well, at last yer've remembered yer old friends. We were beginnin' to think we weren't good enough for yer now.'

'As if I could forget you, Cissie Maddox.' Eileen eyed Cissie up and down before casting her eyes down to her own swollen body. 'I'm bigger than yer now, Cissie, so watch yerself.'

Cissie stepped forward and to everyone's amazement gave Eileen a big hug. 'I 'aven't 'alf missed yer, Eileen Gillmoss. It's been like a graveyard without that fog-horn voice of yours bawlin' loud enough to wake the dead.'

'Got no one to fight with, eh, Cissie?' Eileen was overwhelmed by the reception and tears were not far away.

'It has been quiet without you, Eileen,' Ada Wilson said. 'Tommy was only saying that this morning.'

'Come an' 'ave a cuppa.' Cissie linked arms with Eileen. 'You can tell me all yer news.' As they neared her house she glanced sideways. 'Good, but yer not half a size! Yer seem to 'ave sprouted in the last few weeks.' Eileen waved goodbye to the other neighbours, saying she'd see them again soon, then turned to Cissie with a grin on her face. 'Yer not kiddin'! Look at me coat, fits where it touches! When I bought it, it was a loose swagger . . . now it's edge-to-edge.'

Eileen left Cissie's half an hour later feeling more cheerful than she'd done for months. She crossed the road to have a word with Tommy Wilson so she wouldn't have to pass her old house, thinking it was no good upsetting herself. It was over and done with now and she'd just have to make the best of it.

Eileen leaned on the counter of the corner shop and gave Milly Knight a beaming smile. 'Like old times, eh, Milly? Am I still good for a bit of stuff on tick?'

'Oh, it's lovely to see you.' Milly's smile lit up her face. 'D'you know, I haven't had a good laugh since you moved.'

'Well, I 'aven't done much laughin' meself, Milly. Between you and me and the gate post, me new neighbours are a miserable lot. Yer seldom see them, and when yer do they just nod their 'eads. I was beginnin' to think they were all deaf an' dumb until I 'eard them at the shops.' Eileen straightened up. 'D'yer want a little impersonation?'

'Oh, yes, please.' Milly's eyes gleamed in anticipation. 'Make it a good one so I can remember it, 'cos from the looks of you, I won't be seeing you round here until after the happy event.'

'Yer'll 'ave to use yer imagination for this one.' Eileen waved her arm around the shop. 'Pretend this is a butcher's shop and you're the butcher. I'm one of me neighbours, a Mrs Elmsley. She's only 'alf my size an' she speaks very posh.' Eileen coughed and walked to look in the window. 'I'll have ha lamb chop, Mr Jones. No, not that one, it's far too fatty. My husband his very fussy, you know. Now let me see,' Eileen tapped a finger on her teeth. 'Could Hi see the third

69

one along hon the front of the tray? Yes, that's the one.' Eileen's eyes moved from the window to where Milly was standing and pretended to inspect the imaginary chop. 'Mmmm, I don't know. Could you cut that piece of fat off? That's fine, now would you weigh hit for me?'

Eileen lowered her voice, 'I'll do your bit.' In a deep growl she asked, 'D'yer only want the one chop, Mrs Elmsley?'

'Yes, thank you, Mr Jones. I'm having some nice boiled ham for my tea with bread hand Anchor butter.'

Eileen grabbed a piece of paper off the counter and folded it before handing it to Milly. 'That'll be sixpence, Mrs Elmsley. I 'ope yer 'usband ch . . . enjoys it.'

Eileen looked towards the door. 'This is me an' Bob Jones watching Mrs Fussy bloody Elmsley walk through the door. As soon as she's out of sight we burst out laughin' and Bob says he almost said what he was thinking, that he hoped Mr Elmsley choked on the fiddlin' bloody chop.'

'Oh, Eileen, you're priceless.' Milly wiped her eyes. 'It'll never be the same again around here without you. Still, you've moved to a nice place and I hope you'll be very happy there.'

Eileen leaned her elbows on the counter. 'Milly, I 'aven't said it to anyone else, but I'd give every penny I 'ad right now to be back in me own little 'house.'

Milly saw the sadness in Eileen's eyes but decided that sympathy now wouldn't help. So she kept her tone light. 'Oh, aye, and how much have you got right now?'

This brought a smile to Eileen's face. 'A tanner! We bought wallpaper for the whole 'ouse an' it's left us boracic lint . . . skint.'

'I can let you have some things to tide you over.'

'Nah! I've got all me shoppin' in, an' if we run short we'll 'ave to live on fresh-air butties.'

Bill opened the door to Eileen. 'You look tired, chick.'

'I'm absolutely whacked! I 'ad to tell our Edna to go on, I couldn't keep up with 'er.' Eileen puffed her way down the hall. 'How's it goin'?'

Bill pulled on the back of her coat as he pushed open the parlour door. 'Have a look.'

Eileen's jaw dropped. 'I don't believe it! Oh, it's lovely!'

Maggie was sitting in an arm chair, her arms folded, a smug smile of satisfaction on her face. 'Well, what d'you think of it?'

The wallpaper, beige with sprigs of pink flowers, made the room look bright, warm and comfortable. 'Oh, Mam, it looks beautiful! Yer wouldn't think it was the same room.'

'Our Rene's worked like a Trojan, honestly she deserves a medal. Young Billy did the pasting and she had the strips up in no time. When Edna came home and said you were on your way, she was determined to get the last two strips up, and she moved like those blue flies you're always talking about.'

Eileen was still taking it all in when Bill took her arm. 'Come on, there's more to see.'

When Eileen saw the living room it was too much for her and she pulled out a chair to sit down. They'd chosen a pink paper for this room, patterned in diamonds in a darker shade. 'I never thought yer'd get this far,' she said quietly. 'I expected to come 'ome to a right mess.'

'I'm glad Harry gave me a hand with the ceilings last night,' Bill said. 'Having them done was half the battle.'

'Where is Harry? And our Rene, where's she got to?'

'She went upstairs to give Harry a hand. He's started on our bedroom, but I think I'll call a halt. We've done enough for one day.' Bill cupped Eileen's face in his hands. 'I'd have been lost without Harry and your Rene, they've been great. And our Billy's been a real cracker.'

'Where is Billy?'

Bill grinned. 'Getting ready to go out. If I tell you something, will you promise not to say anything to him?'

'Yeah, go 'ed.'

'I overheard him talking to Harry. He's got a date tonight with Mavis Radford.'

'Mavis Radford from Bray Street?' Eileen didn't know whether to laugh or cry. Her lovely son with a girl . . . she didn't think she liked the idea of another woman in his life.

Bill nodded. 'He met her at the Holy Name dance and made a date to take her to the pictures tonight.' Bill saw the look in Eileen's eyes and wagged a finger under her nose. 'Remember, you promised. He doesn't know I overheard him telling Harry.'

Eileen rested her chin on her hands when Bill ran upstairs to tell the workers to knock off. It had been a long day and the extra weight she was carrying around with her had drained her energy.

71

★ ★ ★

When Arthur called with his two sons, Eileen was sitting on a straight chair with her bare feet resting on two cushions. 'Yer'll 'ave to excuse me, Arthur, but I couldn't move if I tried.' She smiled at the two boys. 'Come an' give Auntie Eileen a hug.'

If anybody else had asked for a hug, the two boys would have said they were too old for soppy things like that. But they were drawn to this big, cuddly woman, and they didn't hesitate to fling their arms around her.

'Been to see yer mam, 'ave yez?'

'Er, no.' Arthur's eyes sent a warning. 'They don't allow children in the ward Sylvia's in.'

'Oh, did yez 'ave to wait outside?'

Again Arthur answered for the boys. 'I'd been told they couldn't go in, so I left them with Vera for a few hours.' Looking decidedly uncomfortable, Arthur went on quickly, 'I would have brought them here, but I knew you'd be up to your necks.' He turned to Bill. 'I'm sorry I couldn't give you a hand, like I promised, but under the circumstances I know you'll understand.'

'That's the least of your worries,' Bill said. 'You've more than enough on your plate.'

Arthur gazed around the room. 'This looks very nice.'

'Yer should see me mam's room,' Eileen said. 'She's sittin' there lookin' like Lady Muck.'

'Come on, I'll show you.' Bill led Arthur and his sons out, saying, 'I can't take any credit for this, Rene did it with the help of our Billy.' While they were out of the room, Eileen tried to pull her dress down to make herself more respectable, but as soon as she let go of the material it wrinkled up again over her knees. 'Blast it,' she muttered, 'I'm like a flippin' elephant!'

A few moments later Arthur returned. 'They must have worked hard to have done all this.' There was a faint smile on his drawn face. 'You're a real slave driver, Eileen Gillmoss.'

'Oh, I've been out,' Eileen tried again to cover her knees but the dress wasn't having any. In the end she gave it up as a bad job. 'I'm not soft, yer know, Arthur, I don't stay around when there's work to be done. I've been visitin' me old neighbours.' Her eyes kept straying towards the door. 'Where's David and Gordon?'

'Maggie's showing them some photographs. She must be a mind reader, your mother, 'cos I wanted a word with you on your own.'

Arthur sat down and stared at his clasped hands before meeting Eileen's eyes. 'Sylvia is very sick. The boys don't know and I'm not going to tell them, yet, anyway. I've got to take them to Walton Hospital one day next week, the three of us have to be tested to make sure we haven't contracted the disease.'

Eileen gasped, 'Oh, no!'

'It's all right, Eileen, there's not much chance of any of us having it. The boys didn't see enough of Sylvia, and she wasn't affectionate with them when she did see them. So they should be clear. And as for me,' Arthur said bitterly, 'I haven't slept with her, or had any physical contact with her for two years. Except for two nights, when I first came back from the army, I've slept in the boys' room.'

'Thank God for that!'

'I suppose I should say the same thing, but all I feel is sadness. It could have been so different if only she'd given it a chance. But as it is, it's David and Gordon who'll suffer the most and I can't find it in my heart to forgive her for that.'

Chapter Nine

Joan stood on tip-toe as she leaned towards the mirror over the fireplace. With one hand on top of the tiled grate to steady herself, and her Tangee lipstick in the other, she peered at her reflection. This was the first tube of lipstick she'd ever had in her hand and she didn't know where to start. To make matters worse, her mother and sister were watching. She brought the lipstick towards her mouth and puckered her lips. No, that wasn't how the girls in work did it, they stretched their lips.

Behind her, Edna mimicked every action, winking at her mother as she did so. Although she was two years younger than Joan, there wasn't much difference between them in height. In fact, they could be taken for twins. Through the mirror, Joan caught sight of her sister's antics and spun round, her face red with embarrassment and anger. 'If you don't move, I'll clock yer one.'

Edna stuck her tongue out. 'You an' whose army?'

'Mam, will yer tell this one off?' Joan gave her sister one more dirty look before turning to Eileen who was sitting on one of the dining chairs, her elbows resting on the table, watching the performance. 'She's nothing but a blinking . . .' Joan's words trailed off when she saw the look on her mother's face. 'What's up?'

Eileen's jaw dropped with horror as she gazed at the vivid orange slash that covered her daughter's mouth. 'In the name of God, are yer lips under that lot?'

'I might have known you'd say somethin' like that,' Joan said angrily. 'I never do anythin' right, do I? Not like this one 'ere,' Joan glared at Edna, 'she's mammy's girl, can't do no wrong.'

Edna put her two thumbs to her temples, wiggled her fingers and stuck out her tongue. 'Cry baby, cry baby . . .'

'Hey, knock that off,' Eileen warned. 'Get out of 'ere before I get me hands on yer an' give yer a thick ear.'

When Edna had left, Eileen turned sympathetic eyes on Joan. 'Take a good look in the mirror, sunshine, an' yer'll see what I'm on about. Yer must 'ave half the tube of lipstick on, an' it's all over the place, no shape to yer lips at all. If yer Dad comes down an' sees yer like that there'll be ructions. Tell yer what, why don't yer 'ave a swill, then nip up to Auntie Mary's an' ask 'er to show yer how to make yer face up properly?'

'Where's our Joan off to?' Bill asked. 'She's just flown out of the door as though the devil was on her tail.'

Eileen rolled her eyes. 'I don't think I'm our Joan's favourite person at the moment.' Eileen went on to tell him what had happened.

'She's too young to be wearing lipstick,' Bill said. 'She's only fourteen, for heaven's sake.'

'Yeah, but I remember when I was that age, I kept wishin' I was older so I could do the things the girls in work did. Joan's just the same, wishin' 'er life away. When she gets older she'll be wishin' she could lose a few years.'

Eileen leaned back, causing the chair to creak in protest. She ran a hand across her forehead before resting it on her swollen tummy. 'I'll be glad when the next month's over.'

'Not long to wait now, chick, only two more weeks.'

'Can't come soon enough for me.' Every part of Eileen's body felt drained and weary. She hadn't had a proper night's sleep for weeks because she couldn't get comfortable in bed. And every night, lying awake listening to Bill's even breathing, seemed like an eternity. 'I'll be glad when it's all over.'

Bill stood behind her, his arms wrapped around her neck. 'Shall I bring some pillows down and you can try and get comfortable on the couch?'

Eileen shook her head. 'No, yer never know who'll come.'

'Eileen, you can't spend all the time sitting on a hard chair. I'll get a couple of pillows, you can sit in my chair and I'll ask Ma if we can borrow one of hers so you can put your feet up.' Bill made for the door. 'And Ma said you haven't had your bottle of Stout today, so I'll get you settled then nip up to the Walnut and get a couple of bottles.'

On his way to the pub, Bill called in to the Sedgemoors'. Eileen was really down in the dumps and needed someone to have a good natter to, someone to cheer her up and get a smile on her face.

★ ★ ★

When Joan came back, Mary was with her. 'Well, the state of you and the price of fish!' Mary laughed when she saw Eileen, a pile of pillows at her back, stretched between two chairs with a glass of Stout in her hand. 'There's nothing like comfort.'

'You're tellin' me!' Eileen tried to sit forward but the effort was too much. 'I just wish I 'ad it!'

'Look at me face, Mam.' Joan leaned towards her mother. 'Auntie Mary did it up for me. Cream, powder, rouge, the lot.'

Eileen gazed at the thin face and saw, for the first time, the attractive woman her daughter was going to be. 'Now that's more like it. Yer look a real treat, sunshine.'

'Can I go over to Hanford Avenue to show Marjorie?' Joan was so excited she hopped from one foot to the other. 'I won't stay long, I promise. I'll be back before it gets dark.'

'Who's Marjorie?' Mary asked when Joan had gone.

'Someone she works with. They travel to work together.' Eileen winced when she tried to move to a more comfortable position. 'Yer know, kid, I wouldn't go through this again for a big clock.'

Mary pulled a chair forward and sat near her friend. When she smiled, her set of perfect white teeth gleamed. 'We all say that.'

'Yeah, well I mean it. Bill was right when 'e said we were too old for this lark.'

'When you've got the baby in your arms, you'll forget all about the trouble and discomfort.' Mary tossed her head and her long hair fanned out before resting on her shoulders. 'Me and Harry have been talking about sending Emma to learn how to play the piano. There's a woman in Wembley Gardens who gives lessons.'

'But yer 'aven't got a piano!' A smile seldom seen these days lit up Eileen's face. 'I was goin' to say we 'ad one but the leg fell off, but it's a stale joke, isn't it, kid?'

'Not up to your usual standard, Eileen Gillmoss, but under the circumstances it'll do,' Mary told her. 'Anyway, I told Harry we could get a piano cheap at Hartley's.'

'Aye, it'd be nice for a party. Yer can't beat an old joanna for a proper knees-up. Me mam used to 'ave one, before me Dad died, and we used to 'ave some parties at 'er 'ouse, believe me.'

'Who played the piano, your dad?'

'No, me mam! She never 'ad lessons like, but she only 'ad to hear

77

a tune once and she could belt it out on that old joanna of theirs like no one's business.'

'Well, fancy that! I'd never have thought.'

'Oh, there's lots yer don't know about me mam. She was a nice-lookin' woman, always dressed up to the nines, an' the life an' soul of any party.' Eileen pulled a face. 'Then me dad died, she gave the joanna away when she came to live with us, an' she's never played since.'

Bill came back to see his wife more lively and talkative than she'd been for weeks, and he was glad he'd asked Mary to come and sit with her for a while. It had done her more good than all the Stout in the world.

'Where is your mam?' Mary asked as she set the chair back by the table.

'Need yer ask? Gone to the first 'ouse at the Rio, to see James Cagney an' Pat O'Brien in somethin' or other. When she comes in I'll get the whole story, actions an' everythin'. An' if it's a sad story, we'll both end up cryin' our eyes out.' Eileen handed Bill the empty glass. 'I'd 'ave another one, but it might make me laddo, here,' she patted her tummy, 'drunk.'

'Still kicking like mad, is he?' Mary jerked her head back and tutted. 'Look, she's got me calling it "he", now! We'll all get our eye wiped if it's a girl.'

'Now as yer mention it, I 'aven't felt it for a few hours. Must be feelin' sorry for me, givin' me a rest.'

'He probably got bored stiff listening to you two and he's gone to sleep,' Bill laughed. 'Wait till we get into bed and then he'll start.'

'Mam, I 'aven't felt the baby kickin' for days now, should it be like that?' Eileen was sitting on her usual hard chair peeling potatoes into the colander on her knee. The potato knife clutched in her hand, she looked across the room to where Maggie was on her knees wiping the tiled fireplace with a damp cloth. 'I should feel somethin', shouldn't I?'

Maggie fell back on to her heels and turned her head. 'Can't you feel anything at all?'

'Not a thing. The last time I felt it movin' was the day yer went to the Rio, an' that's four days ago. I 'aven't mentioned it before 'cos I thought it might be on account of me gettin' near me time.'

Maggie put her hands on the raised tiles and pushed herself up.

With the corner of her pinny she wiped the sweat from her forehead. 'I'm not very well up on these things, lass, so I can't tell you. Perhaps you'd better go an' see Dr Greenfield.'

'No, I won't bother 'im. I'm due to go to the hospital clinic tomorrow, so I'll wait till then. It's probably nothin' to worry over, so don't say anythin' to Bill. I don't want 'im fussin' round me.'

But Maggie did worry, and on her way to the shops she called at Mary's and asked if she could have a word with her mother. 'What d'you think, Martha?'

'I don't know any more than you, Maggie, but to be on the safe side I'd advise her to see the doctor.'

Mary was hovering by the door, an anxious look on her face. 'Perhaps Eileen's right, and a baby does stop kicking when it's getting ready to be born.'

Maggie was fidgeting nervously. 'She's told me not to tell Bill, but I'm going to have to whether she likes it or not. As soon as I can get him on me own, I'm telling him.'

'I'll slip up later and tell her I'll go to the clinic with her,' Mary said. 'Doris next door will mind the children for a couple of hours. We'll get a taxi to the hospital.'

Eileen lay on the couch in the clinic, her heart pounding as the doctor moved the stethoscope across her stomach and bent to listen for the sound of the baby's heartbeat. He didn't speak and she could read nothing from his expression. Why didn't he say something?

The doctor straightened up and let the stethoscope fall to hang on his chest. 'Well, Mrs Gillmoss, I think we'd better have you in.'

Eileen tried to turn on her side but found she couldn't move. She'd only been able to get on the couch with the help of two nurses. 'Is there somethin' wrong with the baby, doctor?'

The doctor was middle-aged with dark hair falling on to his forehead, and the brown eyes that looked down on Eileen were sympathetic. 'I can't say, I'm afraid. I want to do some tests and that's why I want you in immediately.'

Worry made Eileen speak sharply. 'Look, will somebody 'elp me off this ruddy couch? I want to know what's goin' on.'

The nurse who'd been standing near the door came forward and with the help of the doctor raised Eileen's back and swung her body round so her legs were hanging over the side. 'Is that better?'

'Never mind about me, what about me baby?'

'I'll tell you that when you've had a proper examination in the morning. I want you to go home now, pack a few things and come straight back.' The doctor bent to look more closely at Eileen's face. 'Hey, they're not tears, are they? Come, come now, there's no point in crying until you've got something to cry about. Dry your eyes and the nurse will help you on with your clothes.'

Mary was waiting by the front door when Harry came in and she quickly explained. 'Eileen wouldn't go back to the hospital till Bill came in from work. Said she wanted him with her.'

Harry gave her a peck on the cheek before turning on his heels. 'I'll run them down.'

'There's no point in you waiting, Harry,' Bill said as they helped Eileen from the car outside the main doors of the hospital. 'I'll stay with her till she's settled in a ward.'

Harry looked at Eileen's downcast face and wished there was something he could say to cheer her up. But what was there to say?

Harry drove through the hospital gates, saw Eileen's face in his mind's eye and instead of turning left, turned the steering wheel to the right and towards Dr Greenfield's surgery.

Through eyes blurred with tears, Eileen saw John Greenfield walking down the ward towards her, and she held out her hands to him. 'Oh, thank God you've come.'

John held her hands in his, and smiled. 'It's a coincidence, really,' he lied. 'I had to visit a patient on the men's ward, and while I was here I thought I'd call and see a friend who was in the Army Medical Corps with me. He's a doctor on the maternity wards now. I happened to mention you'd be coming in any day now, and told him he'd better look after you. Imagine my surprise when he said you'd come in last night.'

'Did 'e tell yer anythin'?' Eileen squeezed his hands so hard, John winced with pain. 'I mean about the baby?'

'Now, you know what we doctors are like, Eileen. Until we're sure, we never commit ourselves. They'll be giving you a thorough examination later today, and then they'll know more.'

Eileen released his hands to wipe away a tear. 'I'm very stupid about things like this, Doctor. Does 'e think there's somethin' wrong with the baby?'

Oh, Lord, John groaned inwardly. How was he to answer that?

He was praying that everything would be all right, but it would be wrong to raise her hopes. He let out a long, deep sigh. 'Eileen, you wouldn't want me to lie to you and I'm not going to. Dr Groves isn't certain of anything, and neither am I. If we were, I'd tell you, honest.' John looked at his watch and grimaced. 'I'll have to be on my way. The surgery will be overflowing with patients.'

'Will yer come in again an' see me?' Eileen sniffed. 'I 'ate hospitals, they're all disinfectant and bed pans.'

John smiled. 'I'll slip in as soon as I get a chance. Keep your chin up and stop crying or you'll make yourself ill.'

Eileen saw a nurse walking towards them and muttered, 'If she's got a bed pan in 'er 'and, hit 'er over the 'ead with it for me, will yer?'

The Matron was waiting for Bill when he came through the doors leading to the corridor outside the wards. 'Mr Gillmoss, Doctor Groves would like a word with you. He's in my office.' Her starched uniform crackled as she led the way. 'In here, please.'

Dr Groves looked up from the notes he was reading and pointed to a chair on the opposite side of the desk. 'Sit down, please, Mr Gillmoss.'

Bill, his face haggard, watched the doctor shuffle the papers into a neat pile and place them in the wire tray on top of the desk.

'I've got some sad news for you, Mr Gillmoss.' Dr Groves removed his glasses and pinched at the bridge of his nose. This was one part of his job that he hated. 'I'm sorry to have to tell you that the baby your wife is carrying will be stillborn.'

Bill slumped in his chair and covered his face with his hands. He couldn't speak for a while, and when he did, it was in a whisper. 'Have you told my wife?'

'Not yet. I thought it best to see you first and ask whether you would prefer me to tell her, or whether you would rather do it yourself. I am prepared to break it to her, but perhaps she would take it better from you.'

'She's going to take it bad no matter who tells her.' Bill closed his eyes as despair and anger built up within him. 'How can it be? She's been so well for the whole time, did everything she was supposed to do. Drank orange juice, took her Glucodin religiously every day and had a bottle of Stout every night.'

'It's one of those unsolved mysteries, Mr Gillmoss. It happens, and nobody knows why. It certainly hasn't been caused by anything your wife did.'

'Then why?' Bill's clenched fist came down heavily on the desk, causing the wire tray to jump several inches in the air. 'Why did it have to happen to her? She was so looking forward to this baby,' his voice broke, 'she wanted it so much.'

The office door opened and Matron came in with a cup of tea, her eyes showing the sympathy she felt. 'Drink this, Mr Gillmoss, you'll feel much better.'

'I can't face her,' Bill said, his head moving from side to side. 'I know I sound a coward, but I couldn't do it.'

'Then I'll tell her.' The doctor pushed his chair back. 'Wait here till I come back.'

Bill's hand holding the cup and saucer was shaking so badly the tea splashed on to his hands. It was the pain of the hot liquid burning his skin that cleared his head. He put the cup down and stood up. 'No, it's only right I should be the one. I couldn't live with meself if I let her down now.'

'Matron will go with you and draw the screens so you'll have a bit of privacy,' the doctor said. 'If Mrs Gillmoss gets upset or hysterical, ask Matron for something to calm her down.'

'Before I go, will you tell me what's going to happen? My wife is bound to ask, and I want to know meself.'

'We will induce labour either tomorrow or the next day. It depends upon how your wife is. It will be like a normal birth, except, except . . .'

'Except that the baby will be dead,' Bill finished the sentence, his voice bitter.

'There's no easier way of saying it, Mr Gillmoss, I just wish to God that there was. But if it helps, John Greenfield will be here with her.' When he saw the surprise on Bill's face, Dr Groves told how he knew Eileen's doctor and about his visit early that morning. 'He rang to ask about the results of our examination, and said to make sure I told your wife he'd be here with her the whole time.'

Matron walked down the ward ahead of Bill and when Eileen saw her hand reach out to draw the screens, she took one look at Bill's drawn face and burst out crying.

Chapter Ten

'I want to go 'ome, Bill.'

'You can't, chick!' Bill looked shocked. 'It's only been two days and the doctor said you'd be in at least ten days.'

'I don't care what the doctor said, I want to go 'ome.' Eileen was a shadow of her former self. The once rosy cheeks had lost their glow, her eyes were dull and her thin hair was lank and lifeless. 'How d'yer think I feel seein' all the happy mothers with their new babies? Honestly, Bill, if I stay 'ere much longer I'll lose me sanity.'

Bill gazed up and down the ward. He'd been so concerned about Eileen he'd never really looked around before, but now he took in the cots at the end of each bed, some with proud fathers cooing down at their new babies. He leaned forward to take Eileen's hand. 'I know it must be upsetting for you, love, but they won't let you out yet.'

'They wouldn't be able to stop me if you signed me out.'

'I couldn't do that! You know what happens if anyone signs themselves out against their wishes, they wash their hands of you. And what would happen if you got sick? I'd be the one to get the blame.'

'You just said it must be upsettin' for me, but 'ow the hell do you know what it's like, eh, Bill Gillmoss?' Eileen asked angrily, snatching her hand away. 'I'm not sayin' they're not good to me, 'cos they are, the nurses and the other women in the ward. They're only bein' kind and friendly when they bring their babies to me, but they don't understand 'ow much it hurts.' The fire suddenly went out of Eileen's voice and she whimpered, 'I'm not made of stone, yer know, Bill.'

Bill screwed his eyes up. 'I'm sorry, chick, I had no idea.'

'Sign me out, please?' Eileen implored. 'I promise I'll go straight to bed at 'ome, an' I'll be all right.'

The pleading in Eileen's voice was like a knife turning in Bill's heart. But the responsibility was too much for his shoulders alone. He'd never forgive himself if anything went wrong. 'Look, love, I don't like seeing you so unhappy, and I'd do anything for you, you know that. But for my own peace of mind I'd like to have a word with Dr Greenfield first, see what he says. I'll try and get hold of him tonight and ask Mary if she'll slip in tomorrow and let you know.' He saw the disappointment on Eileen's face and knew he couldn't leave her in this state without a ray of hope. 'Whichever way it goes, chick, I promise you'll be home in a few days, even if I have to carry you out. But let me speak to Dr Greenfield first, eh?' Trying to coax a smile, his hand made a cross over his heart. 'Scout's honour, two days at the most.'

The last patient had left and John Greenfield was clearing his desk before going through to his living quarters for his evening meal. It had been a long, trying day, and he was looking forward to putting his feet up for half an hour before making an evening call on a patient he was concerned about. He heard a knock on the front door and his housekeeper's voice saying that surgery was over and would the caller come back tomorrow.

John sighed, pushing his fine, wayward hair off his forehead. He had to go through the hall to get to the dining room and was just in time to see Bill Gillmoss before the housekeeper shut the front door on him.

'Mr Gillmoss.'

Bill was closing the gate behind him when he heard John's voice. He turned and walked back up the path. 'I'm sorry to bother you, Doctor. I left the hospital ten minutes before the end of visiting time hoping to catch you before surgery closed, but I'll call back tomorrow on me way to the hospital.'

'No, come in now. I can spare five minutes.'

The two men faced each other across the desk as Bill explained why he'd come. 'She's heartbroken, Doctor, honestly. In all our married lives I've never known her so depressed. It's doing her more harm than good being in there.'

'They should have left her in the small room where she was the first day, then she wouldn't have had to see the babies in the ward. But, unfortunately, they needed it for an urgent case.' John tapped the desk with his pen, his face thoughtful. 'Eileen would be better off at home with her family around her. I could get a district nurse to call in every day to keep an eye on her, and I could give her tablets to stop her breasts from filling up.' He threw his pen down. 'No, I can see no reason why she can't be discharged.'

'Then she can come home?' Bill's whole body slumped with relief. 'Thank God for that.'

'It's up to the doctor on the maternity ward, and it's too late to ring tonight. I'll give him a call first thing in the morning and have a word with him. You're not on the phone, are you?'

Bill shook his head. 'We're not, but the Sedgemoors are.' He gave the number and stood up. 'Thank you, Dr Greenfield, for everything. It's no wonder Eileen says you're the best doctor in the world. You've certainly taken a load off my shoulders tonight.'

'Well, Mrs Gillmoss, you're leaving us today.' The Matron's stern face relaxed into a smile. 'Now isn't that good news?'

Eileen's face dropped on to her chest as a lone tear trickled down her cheek. She wiped it away and met the Matron's gaze. 'It's not that yez haven't been good to me, 'cos yez 'ave. But I want to be with me family, I miss them so much.'

'I understand. I'll get you a list of do's and don'ts, and you must promise to abide by them. An ambulance will be taking you home, but I can't tell you exactly what time that will be. So while you're waiting, sit on the side of the bed and clear your locker out.' Matron walked away a few steps, then turned. 'You've got a very handsome husband, Mrs Gillmoss. Very distinguished looking.'

'Keep yer eyes off 'im, Matron, he's all mine.' For the first time since she'd come in hospital, Eileen didn't have to force a smile. 'Yer don't think I'm daft enough to marry an ugly beggar, do yer?'

Sitting on the side of the bed, her belongings in a small case by her feet, Eileen talked to the group of women who'd gathered around to say goodbye. But her eyes kept going to the clock on the wall at the end of the ward. Come on, ambulance, her thoughts ran, don't you know I'm dying to see me mam and the kids?

When a nurse finally came with a wheelchair, Eileen couldn't get into it quickly enough. She was afraid the doctor might change his mind and keep her in. With her case on her knees, she said to the nurse, 'Home, James, an' don't spare the 'orses.' She waved to the women as she was wheeled out of the ward. 'Look after yerselves! Ta-ra, now!'

★ ★ ★

Maggie had been pacing up and down by the window for over an hour, and when she saw the ambulance turn the corner she cried, 'It's here.' She hurried to the door, followed closely by Mary, Vera and Carol. Nervously picking at her pinny, she watched the men open the back doors of the ambulance and climb inside. She gripped Mary's arm when she saw her daughter being carried out on a stretcher and Eileen heard her cry of distress.

'Don't worry, Mam, it's not as bad as it looks.'

Mary dashed upstairs to pull the bedclothes back and was standing by the bed smiling when Eileen was transferred from the stretcher. 'Welcome home, Eileen Gillmoss.'

'Hi-ya, kid.'

Eileen thanked the ambulance men, then let out a sigh when they left the room. 'Thank God for that! I've never been so glad to be 'ome in all me life.'

Maggie came bustling in and bent to kiss her daughter. She was shocked by Eileen's appearance but hid it as she straightened the counterpane. We'll soon have her back to her old self now she's home, she consoled herself.

Carol was hanging on to Vera's coat, a puzzled look on her face. Why was Auntie Eileen in bed in the middle of the day?

There was an awkward silence until Vera walked towards the bed. She struggled to find the right words, but someone had to mention the baby no matter how painful. They couldn't carry on as though nothing had happened. 'I'm so sorry, Eileen.'

Those few words were all that were needed to start the four women crying. Maggie went to Eileen and held her close, rocking her like a baby. 'There, there, lass, you cry as much as you want.'

'Why me, Mam? What did I do wrong?'

'You did nothing wrong, lass.' Maggie's tears ran unchecked on to Eileen's head. 'These things happen and nobody knows why.'

Mary and Vera were crying unashamedly. Both would have given anything to be able to help Eileen, the one person they had both turned to when they were in need of a friend. But there was nothing they could do to take the hurt away, only grieve with her.

'It was a little girl, Mam.'

Carol's lips started to tremble. She didn't understand why everyone was upset, except that it had something to do with Auntie Eileen and a little girl. She squeezed between Eileen and Maggie.

'I'm your little girl, Auntie Eileen.'

Through her tears, Eileen saw Carol's face pushed under her mother's arm and her sobbing eased. She ran a hand across her nose, then sniffing loudly she reached out to stroke the fair hair. 'Of course yer my little girl, sweetheart. An' the best little girl in the whole world.'

Using the corner of her pinny to wipe her face, Maggie stepped back to let Carol near the bed. They say these children bring their own love, she thought, well Carol certainly did. She was a Godsend right now.

When Carol sat on the bed and tried to cuddle Eileen, the big woman quickly put her arms out to protect her breasts. 'Not too close, sunshine. Auntie Eileen's got a pain.'

Eileen pulled a face at Vera. 'Me breasts are full of milk an' they're awful sore.' She turned to Maggie. 'We'll 'ave to find an old sheet to tear into strips, an' yer can bind them up for us.'

'I've got an old sheet,' Mary said. 'And I'll do it for you.'

'Thanks, kid, but we've got plenty of old sheets, 'aven't we, Mam? In fact they're all flippin' old.' Eileen tried to stifle a yawn, but it wasn't lost on Maggie.

'I think it's time for you to have a rest.' Maggie reached across and took one of the pillows from Bill's side of the bed. 'Lift your head and I'll make you comfortable.'

'Come on, Vera, we'll go and let Eileen have a bit of peace and quiet, she looks all in.'

It took some persuading to get Carol off the bed. Only a promise that she could come again tomorrow did the trick.

Mary looked back from the doorway. 'Can Harry come and see you tonight, or would you rather he left it a few days?'

'Now, kid, 'ave yer ever known me refuse to 'ave a man in me bedroom? Tell 'im I'm lookin' forward to seein' 'im.'

Bill gazed around the table as the children ate the hot-pot Maggie had made for their dinner. Usually meal times were noisy affairs, with jokes, laughter and arguments. But tonight, after seeing their mother looking so pale and tired, they were quiet.

'How long will me mam be in bed, Dad?' Billy asked, putting down his knife and fork. 'She doesn't look very well, does she?'

'No, son, she doesn't.' Bill pushed a potato around his plate. His normal hearty appetite had deserted him and if it wasn't for upsetting Maggie, the whole lot would have gone in the bin. 'You know how much she was looking forward to having this baby, all the plans she'd made. I know we were all looking forward to it, and we all feel sad, but it's much, much worse for your mam.'

There was a lump in Billy's throat which wouldn't go no matter how hard he tried to swallow. Embarrassed, he picked up his plate and made for the privacy of the kitchen. 'I can't eat any more, Nan, I'm sorry.'

'That's all right, son,' Maggie called after him. 'None of us are very hungry tonight.'

Edna pushed her plate away and dropped her head on the table, her thin shoulders shaking with sobs. 'Me mam said I would 'ave had a little baby sister.'

Bill ran a hand over her head, his voice soft. 'I know, love, but your crying isn't going to help your mam. We've all got to pull together now to help her get better.' He turned to Joan, whose hands were lying in her lap, her eyes fixed on her plate. 'D'you hear me, Joan?'

Joan nodded, not trusting herself to speak. She hadn't wanted a baby in the house, but she would rather have had a hundred babies than see her mam looking so unhappy.

'So we've all got to get stuck in and give Nan a hand with the housework for the next few weeks. This house is far too big for her to keep clean, as well as see to your mam and do the washing and cooking.'

'I can stay off school an' help me nan,' Edna said. 'If yer give me a note for the teacher, I won't get shouted at.'

Bill thought about it, then said, 'I don't like you staying off school, but I don't think it would do any harm just this once. You could help in the house and be company for your mam. That's what she needs, someone to take her mind off things.'

'Can I go up an' tell her?' Edna was off her chair and out of the room before Bill had time to stop her. They could hear her taking the stairs two at a time and Maggie shook her head. 'She's a live wire, that one. Just like her mother was.'

'I'm glad they've all gone.' Eileen lay back on the pillows, her face showing her tiredness. 'I knew Mary an' Harry were comin', but I didn't expect our Rene an' Alan. How did they know I was 'home?'

'Rene's been ringing Mary every day,' Bill said, sitting down on the side of the bed. He took Eileen's hand in his and rubbed his thumb gently over the skin. 'It's good to have you home, chick. I haven't half missed you.'

Eileen's eyes were fastened on the wall behind the door. 'Where's the cot?'

'Gone. Everything's gone, love.' Since he'd got in from work Bill had been dreading this moment. But what had been done was for the best. 'I asked your Rene to come down and clear everything out.' He saw the pain on Eileen's face and said quickly, 'It had to be done, chick! It would have broken your heart if you'd had to do it.'

'Where've they gone?' Eileen could see in her mind all the small matinee coats, the nightdresses and tiny pillowcases Maggie had embroidered, and the cot and pram sets. She remembered how she'd folded them all neatly away, ready for when the baby came. Tears smarted her eyes. 'Who did they go to?'

'A young couple in Walton. They'd only just got a house and were struggling to save the money to furnish it when the girl found out she was in the family way. Just the sort of couple you would have given them to yourself.'

'Yer've never said anythin', Bill.' Eileen's voice was low. 'But were yer very disappointed?'

'More than disappointed, love, I was heartbroken. But Dr Greenfield had a good talk to me after the baby was born, and although I didn't appreciate what he said then, I've had time to think it over and he was right.'

'What did he say to yer?'

'Not tonight, Eileen, I'll tell you some other time. You've had enough for one day.'

Eileen struggled to a sitting position. 'Tell me now.'

Bill sighed and ran his fingers through his mop of white hair. 'I know you'll be upset, but he said we were lucky.' When the bed creaked with Eileen's movement, Bill lifted his hand. 'You wanted to know, so hear me out. There's lots of children dying every day, and as the doctor said, it would have been much worse if we had known the baby and grown to love her.' With a catch in his voice, Bill went on, 'We're luckier than some 'cos we've got three children, and we've got each other.'

Eileen was silent as she watched Bill's face working to keep the tears at bay. And without warning her mind went back in time to when Bill was taken prisoner in the war and she didn't know whether he was alive or dead.

Eileen held out her open arms. 'Hold me, Bill.'

After a week of only being allowed to walk round the bedroom or go to the toilet, the nurse pronounced Eileen well enough to go downstairs on the understanding she didn't overdo things. But there was no need for the nurse's warning because Mary and Vera were there every day to give Maggie a hand, and they wouldn't even let Eileen wash a cup. 'This is the life.' Eileen was sitting on the couch munching a Fry's Chocolate Cream bar, watching Mary doing some ironing. 'Nice work, if yer can get it, eh, kid?'

Mary spat on her finger and tested the iron. 'Ow, that's hot!' She smiled at Eileen. 'Serve me right if I burnt meself. Harry's always telling me off about it.'

'You and Vera 'ave been smashin'. An' our Rene, of course. I don't know 'ow me mam would 'ave managed without yez.' Eileen licked some melted chocolate off her fingers. 'But another week should see me back on me feet.'

'You'll do as you're told and take it easy for at least a month.' Mary folded the sheet she'd finished ironing. 'Me and Vera don't mind, we enjoy having a natter.' She didn't say that there was an understanding between her and Vera, and Rene, that Eileen shouldn't be left on her own too much. She never talked about the baby, but the pain and heartbreak could be seen on her face when she thought no one was looking.

Eileen wiped her sticky fingers on the silver paper before throwing it in the fire. 'I'll make it up to yez, kid. When I'm feelin' better I'll mug yez to a meal in Sampson and Barlows.' She gazed at Mary's bent head for a while, then asked. 'What's wrong with Arthur Kennedy these days? Nobody 'as mentioned 'im, an' he 'asn't been to see me. That's not like Arthur.'

Mary put the iron down while she turned a pillowslip. 'Oh, he hasn't forgotten you, he asks about you all the time. But with you being so low, healthwise, Bill thought it better if he didn't come.'

'That's daft, that is, an' mean,' Eileen said. 'Anybody would think Arthur 'ad the plague.'

'Bill was only being careful, and we all agreed with him, even Arthur.' Mary folded the pillowslip and placed it on top of the pile on the sideboard. 'In your condition it was better to be safe than sorry.'

'How did 'im an' the kids get on when they went for a test?'

'Fine. They got the all clear.' Mary could see the line Eileen's thoughts were taking and said, 'That had nothing to do with Bill asking him not to come. It's just Arthur going to the hospital to see Sylvia, Bill was frightened he might have picked up a germ on his clothes.'

'Load of rubbish,' Eileen said. But she wasn't displeased. How could she be, when Bill only had her interests at heart? 'How is Sylvia?'

'Arthur doesn't go in every night now. He said it was a waste of time because Sylvia wouldn't talk to him. He can sit by the bed for an hour and she won't open her mouth. Arthur said it's as though she's blaming him for everything.'

'Does he still take the boys to Vera's?'

Mary's eyes went to the door of the kitchen where Maggie and Vera were preparing the dinner. Her voice low, Mary said, 'I think so, but Vera doesn't say much.'

'I'll 'ave to get meself better soon, won't I, kid? Get up-to-date with all the news.' Eileen was looking more like her old self. She was eating everything put before her and was feeling stronger every day. But inside, the pain and heartache were as strong as ever. She managed to hide it during the day, and only Bill knew how she was suffering. Because it was in his arms she cried herself to sleep every night.

Mary noticed Eileen shiver, and quickly put the iron down. 'Are you cold, Eileen? Shall I put some more coal on?'

'No, I'm all right, kid. Just someone walkin' over me grave.' It was still an effort to smile, but when Eileen saw the concern on her friend's face she managed to raise one. 'I was just thinkin', yer not very good at repeatin' gossip, are yer, kid? I bet yer don't know 'ow many blankets next door 'ave got on their bed, or who the milkman's 'aving it off with.'

'Oh, go way with you,' Mary laughed. 'You should have Elsie Smith for a neighbour. You'd be in your element then.' Mary cocked an ear. 'There's a knock on the door. I'll go.'

Eileen could hear raised voices but couldn't make out what they were saying. She was watching the door when Mary came back with her arm around Edna's shoulders. Eileen cried out when she saw the bandage wrapped around her daughter's head. 'Oh, my God, what's happened?'

91

Edna ran to sit next to her mother on the couch while Mary explained. 'One of the teachers brought her home. Apparently she fell in the playground and cut her head open.'

'Is it bad?' Eileen held Edna away from her to look closely at the bandaged head. 'Have yer 'ad it seen to?'

Maggie and Vera came hurrying from the kitchen. 'Oh, lord, what is it now?'

Maggie's hand went to her mouth. 'If it's not one thing, it's another.'

'All right, Mam, don't be gettin' yer knickers in a twist.' Eileen put her fingers under Edna's chin and raised her face. 'Tell us what happened, sunshine.'

Edna, her face ashen, said, 'We were playin' football in the playground an' me an' Marie Ashton ran to kick the ball and we banged into each other. I went flyin' and landed on me head.' Edna was reduced to tears and Eileen couldn't get another coherent word out of her.

'Whoever brought her home said she's been to the hospital and has had four stitches in the wound,' Mary said. 'I think it must have been one of the teachers.'

'It was our headmistress, Miss Bond,' Edna sobbed. 'She took me to the 'ospital in her car. An' she said I was to stay off school till the stitches are out.'

'Is it sore, sunshine?' Eileen put her arm around the thin shoulders and could feel her daughter shaking. 'I think yer'd better take some aspirin and go to bed for a couple of hours. You go on up an' I'll get yer a hot drink an' two tablets. When yer dad comes in, he'll know what to do.'

'You stay where you are, I'll see to her.' Vera took Edna's hand. 'I'll settle her down if you'll make a cup of tea, Mary. Weak with plenty of sugar in.'

Bill took his shoes off and let them fall to the floor. 'There's not much I can do, chick. She says it's sore, but I'm not touching the bandage 'cos I'll never get it back on properly.' He stood up and struggled with the stud at the back of his collar. When it slipped from his fingers and fell to the floor, he cursed, 'The blasted thing's rolled under the tallboy and I'm not moving that tonight.'

Eileen was leaning back against the headboard, a worried look on her face. 'Shall I call the doctor out tomorrow?'

'That won't be necessary, unless she's in a lot of pain.' Bill slipped between the sheets. 'And you know what a good actress our Edna is, so only believe half of what she says. She'll do a Bette Davis on you and have everyone running round after her.' He stretched his arms over his head and yawned. 'Ask Mary if she'll be a pal and ring the school tomorrow to find out when the stitches are due to be taken out. I'll have to take a couple of hours off work to take her to the hospital.'

Eileen watched Bill snuggle down in the bed, the clothes pulled up to his chin. 'I've been lying here thinkin',' she said. 'All the runnin' round, movin' to this 'ouse an' havin' to decorate an' buy new furniture, an' all for nothin'. We could 'ave stayed in our old house.'

Bill pushed himself up and held her close. 'It wasn't for nothing, love. We've got a nice house here. You haven't had time to appreciate it, but when you're feeling better you'll see the difference. Ma's got her own room and we've got a bathroom and washhouse. We couldn't ask for anything more.'

Eileen bit on the inside of her lip. 'Don't start shoutin' at me, Bill, but I feel it in me bones that this isn't goin' to be a lucky 'ouse for us.'

'Ye gods and little fishes!' Bill was exasperated. 'You can't blame the house for what happened to you, or 'cos our Edna fell and cut her head. That's just being superstitious. There's no such thing as an unlucky house and you know it.'

Eileen shrugged off his arm. 'Okay, Bill Gillmoss, 'ave it your own way. But don't say I never warned yer.'

Chapter Eleven

'It was a crackin' game yesterday, wasn't it, Dad?' Billy leaned forward to look past Edna who was sitting next to him at the table. 'That goal of Bob Paisley's was brilliant.'

'Yes, it was a masterpiece,' Bill answered with a smile. 'All the lads played well, Liddell, Stubbins, Balmer, every one of them.'

'Yeah.' Billy munched happily on a roast potato. At twenty, he was a replica of how his Dad had looked at his age. And like his Dad he was a fanatical supporter of Liverpool Football Club. 'We play Arsenal away next week, don't we?'

'In the name of God, can't you two talk about anythin' but football?' Eileen asked, a smile creasing her face. Sunday was the one day of the week she looked forward to, when the extension leaf on the table was pulled out and the family sat down to eat together. Her eyes were bright as they looked around the table. Next to her sat Joan, eighteen now, then her mother, Maggie. Opposite, sat Bill, Edna and young Billy. 'I bet if I put a Liverpool shirt down to yez for yer dinner, yer'd eat the blasted thing!'

'I would if it had salt and pepper on.' Billy grinned cheekily. 'And a drop of the old tomato ketchup.'

'Oh, ha-ha, very funny.' Eileen saw Joan pick up her plate and scrape her chair back. 'You've been quick. What's the hurry?'

'I'm meeting Joyce Harrison, we're going for a walk.'

Joan had grown into a very attractive girl. Her figure was slim and curved in the right places, her long legs shapely in the high-heeled shoes she wore. Her fine, mousy-coloured hair was long and straight, and today it was combed to fall across one side of her face in the style of Veronica Lake, one of her favourite film stars.

'Are yer sure it's Joyce yer meetin', and not some feller?' Eileen asked, jokingly. 'Yer've gone to a lot of trouble with yer appearance just to go out with a girl. There's enough make-up on yer face to sink a flippin' ship.'

'I've told you, I'm going out with Joyce.' There was no answering smile on Joan's pink flushed face. She might have inherited the colour of Eileen's hair and her hazel eyes, but she certainly hadn't inherited her sense of humour. It had rubbed off on Billy and Edna, but somewhere along the line it had passed Joan by. 'Anyway, what difference would it make if I was meeting a boy? I'm eighteen years of age, not a kid.'

Bill could see Eileen's hackles rising and stepped in to prevent a row developing. 'You may be eighteen, young lady, but that doesn't give you the right to be cheeky to your mother. We'll have a little respect, if you don't mind.'

Joan bounced out to the kitchen and they heard her plate being banged on the draining board in temper. Then she reappeared and marched through the room without a glance at anyone. They heard her footsteps running up the stairs and Eileen clicked her tongue. 'She's a bad-tempered little faggot, that one. And selfish into the bargain. Never thinks about anyone but herself. She won't even wash a cup in case she breaks one of 'er flippin' nails.'

'All right, chick, don't get yourself all het up. I know you were only joking about who she was meeting, but Joan obviously didn't. Just forget it.'

'She wouldn't know a joke if it jumped up an' hit 'er in the face,' Eileen grumbled. 'The only time yer get a smile out of 'er is when she's gettin' her own way.'

'Don't be worryin' about her, Mam,' Billy said. 'She's full of herself now, but she'll grow out of it.'

'Our Billy's right, Mam.' A mischievous grin lit up Edna's face. 'Did yer notice she's Veronica Lake today? I wonder who she'll be tomorrow . . . Joan Crawford or Alice Faye?'

Maggie chortled. 'Your mam will never be dead while you're around, lass.'

Bill was trying hard to keep his face straight. 'You shouldn't be making fun of your sister.'

'Oh, come on, Dad, we're only acting daft,' Billy said. 'Mind you, our Joan is a pain in the neck sometimes.' He started to collect the dirty plates. 'Me and Edna will wash the dishes.' He gave his sister a playful dig. 'Won't we, kiddo?'

'No, I'll do the dishes,' Eileen said. 'You two go about yer business.'

'Are you going up to Bray Street, Billy?' Even as she asked, Edna knew it was a daft question. Billy had been courting Mavis Radford from their old street for three years now, and he spent all his free time up there. Except, of course, for the Saturday afternoons Liverpool were playing at home. 'If you are, I may as well wait an' come with you, 'cos I'm goin' to Janet's.'

Edna went upstairs for her coat and when she came down she pulled a face. 'Our Joan's got a right gob on her. Didn't look at me or say a word.' Edna, at sixteen, was as tall as her sister and very like her in looks. But her body hadn't filled out yet, and every time she had a bath she inspected herself for signs that her bust was growing. The girls she worked with behind the counter of George Henry Lee's told her to be patient, that some girls blossomed later than others, but every time she looked down at her flat chest, she doubted they were right.

'What's she doin' up there?' Eileen asked.

Edna nearly blurted out that her sister was doing what she spent most of her life doing, standing in front of the mirror titivating herself up. But it was no good starting her mam off again. 'She's just pottering around.'

Billy came in then and Eileen eyed him with pride. He looked so handsome in his best suit, his black hair sleeked back with brilliantine. 'Can I bring Mavis back for tea, Mam?'

'Of course yer can. She'll 'ave to take pot luck though 'cos I haven't made a jelly or anythin' fancy.'

'She won't worry about that.' Billy jerked his head at Edna. 'Come on, Sis, shake a leg.'

'I might stay at Janet's for me tea,' Edna said as she followed her brother. 'But I won't be late. I'll be home before it gets dark.'

'Okay, sunshine. Ta-ra!'

It was half an hour later when Joan came down, her hair and make-up perfect, her perfume pervading the air. 'I'm having my tea at Joyce's, Dad. Can I take a key with me, just in case I'm late getting home?'

'We won't be going to bed till after eleven,' Bill said. 'You should be in by then.'

'Oh, I probably will be! But we sit and listen to records in their parlour and the time flies over.'

Listen to records me eye, Eileen thought. She's tellin' lies, but Bill can't see it. 'What sort of records d'yer listen to?' Eileen spoke to Joan's back.

'Er, em, Frankie Laine and, er, Pat Boone.'

'Oh, I like Frankie Laine.' Eileen's voice warned that while Joan might be able to pull the wool over her father's eyes, she certainly wasn't fooling her. 'I'll 'ave to borrow them sometime.'

Bill, oblivious to the undercurrent, handed Joan a key. 'Don't be too late now, d'you hear?'

'Okay, Dad,' Joan answered meekly. 'I won't be late.' She reached the door, then without looking back, said, 'See you later, Mam.'

Eileen saw Billy grimace and bend down to rub his ankle. She saw him mouth the words, 'That hurt!' and Mavis, bending her head until it was on a level with his, mouthed back, 'Well, tell them, then.'

'Oh, aye!' Eileen grinned. 'Tell us what? Come on, Billy, spit it out.'

Flushing a bright red, Billy gave one last rub to the ankle Mavis had kicked under the table, then grinned back at his Mother. 'Me and Mavis are getting engaged at Christmas.'

'Well, 'ow about that!' Eileen pushed her chair back and sprang to her feet. Grabbing Mavis in a bear-like hug, she kissed her cheek. 'I'm over the moon, love. Welcome to the family.'

Bill, pride showing on his face, shook hands with Billy. 'Congratulations, son! I'm very happy for you.'

Maggie pushed Bill aside and threw her arms round her grandson's neck. 'Oh, I am happy, Billy. You couldn't have picked a better lass.'

When the excitement had died down, Bill sank into his favourite chair and lit a cigarette. 'So, you're getting engaged at Christmas, eh? And when d'you think you'll be getting married?'

'Why, Dad?' Billy's face was flushed with happiness as he sat with Mavis's hand gripped tightly in his. 'Are you anxious to get rid of me?'

'Of course he's not!' Eileen answered for Bill. 'He just can't wait to be a father-in-law, can yer, Bill?'

'I dread you leaving home, son, if you must know.' There was a glint in Bill's eyes. 'Just think, I'll be the only man in the house, then! I won't stand a dog's chance if the women all gang up on me.'

'Ah, God 'elp 'im! Eileen dabbed her eyes and pretended to sob. 'Let's all say "aaah" for our Dad. All together now, aaaah!'

Mavis squeezed Billy's hand, her shoulders heaving with a fit of the giggles. She couldn't wait to get married and be one of this family. They were always so happy and Eileen was guaranteed to have you laughing before you had time to sit down. Mavis was an only child and she loved her parents dearly, but it was so quiet in their house compared to the Gillmosses'.

When Edna came in and was told the news, she shrieked with delight. 'I'm goin' to be a bridesmaid, goody goody!'

'Hey, give us a chance, we're not even engaged yet!' Billy looked sideways at Mavis and winked. 'Would you want this ugly duckling to be one of your bridesmaids? She'd probably spoil the weddin' photographs.'

Edna spread her elbows on the table. 'When are yer buying the ring, our Billy?' Then without waiting for a reply, she asked, 'Are you gettin' a solitaire, Mavis? When I get engaged, I'm getting a solitaire.'

'Oh, my God!' Eileen put a hand over her heart in mock horror. 'Don't tell me you've got a secret feller hidden somewhere! I couldn't stand two shocks in one day.'

'Don't be daft, Mam. You're not gettin' rid of me that easy.' Edna patted her mother's arm. 'I know when I'm well off.'

'Well,' Billy smiled at Mavis with that special look in his eyes of someone in love. 'Put our Edna out of her misery. Are you getting a solitaire?'

'I don't mind.' Mavis blushed. 'We'll go together and choose it.'

Billy's chest swelled with pride. He was a man now, with responsibilities. 'We'll have to pull our horns in and start savin' like mad, otherwise it'll be a tanner ring from Woolworths.'

Rubbing her hands together gleefully, her face creased in a smile of pure bliss, Eileen warned Bill, 'And you, Bill Gillmoss, 'ad better start workin' all the hours God sends, if yer get the chance, to save up for the weddin'. 'Cos when my only son walks down the aisle, I want to be dolled up to the nines.'

'Mam, me and Mavis wouldn't care if you turned up at the church with curlers in yer hair and an apron on, as long as you turned up.'

'What! An' give these toffee-nosed snobs round 'ere somethin' to talk about?' Eileen shook her head before adopting a haughty pose. 'As Eliza Doolittle would say, my dear son, "not bloody likely"!'

Eileen lay on her back staring up at the ceiling. The illuminated

99

clock told her it was turned twelve and she still hadn't heard Joan come in. All the others were in bed and, like Bill, were probably well away by now. She could hear her husband's rhythmic breathing and wished she'd been able to drop off as quickly as he had, then she wouldn't be lying here on pins wondering where Joan had got to.

Through the silence, Eileen heard the soft click of the key in the lock and she glanced sideways at the fingers on the clock. Twenty past twelve. This was no time for a young girl to be coming home.

Eileen turned on her side and pulled the clothes over her shoulder. Wait till the morning, she'd give the little madam the length of her tongue. Her ear cocked, Eileen listened for the soft pad of footsteps on the stairs, but there was no sound. For ten minutes she waited, her anger rising. 'There'll be no gettin' her up in the morning,' she muttered under her breath.

Slowly, so as not to disturb Bill, Eileen slid out of bed and groped for her dressing gown. She closed the bedroom door quietly behind her and holding on to the banister rail lowered herself gently down each of the stairs. If she woke Bill, he'd come down and there'd be hell to pay. When she reached the bottom stair, a puzzled look crossed her face. There was no sound and no light coming from under the living room door. She leaned back against the wall, telling herself it must have been a noise from outside she'd heard and had mistaken it for a key in the door. She was probably wrong about Joan not being in, too. Here she was calling the poor girl for everything when she was probably tucked up in bed and fast asleep. Eileen was about to pull herself up the first stair when she heard a sound, almost like a whisper. No, she shook her head, it's my imagination playing tricks on me again. If I keep this up they'll be carting me off to the looney bin. Then the sound came again, and this time, Eileen knew it wasn't her imagination.

As she opened the living room door with one hand, Eileen felt for the light switch with the other. And when the room flooded with light, she saw the couple on the couch disentangling themselves from each other's arms, surprise and embarrassment written on their faces.

Eileen took in Joan's ruffled hair, the smudged lipstick and the dress riding high on her hips. She opened her mouth to give vent to her anger, but just in time remembered the sleeping household and closed the door softly. Then she stood with her hands on her wide hips. 'What the hell d'yer think you two are up to?'

'Nothing, Mam! Honest, we . . .'

'You keep quiet, young lady, or I won't be able to keep me hands off yer.' Eileen turned her wrath on the young man who was blinking fifteen to the dozen, his face a bright crimson. 'Who the 'ell are you?'

The youth swallowed hard before stammering, 'Me name's Philip Ryan.'

'Oh, it is, is it? Well, Philip Ryan, what 'ave yer got to say for yerself, eh?' When Philip didn't answer, Eileen asked, 'D'yer make a habit of sneakin' into girls' 'ouses when their parents are in bed?'

'It's all my fault, Mam,' said a tearful Joan. 'I asked Philip in.'

'I'll deal with you in the mornin', my girl,' Eileen warned. 'Right now you can get up those stairs.'

Joan looked from Philip to her mother. 'But, Mam . . .'

'Do as yer told. I'll see yer friend out.'

'No, Mam!' Joan had never felt so humiliated in her life. All the girls were after Philip Ryan but he'd chosen her. Now her mother was making a fool of both of them and he'd never look at her again. 'Please, Mam!'

'If yer've any brains in that thick head of yours, yer'll do as yer told an' get up them stairs. An' if yer wake yer dad, then heaven help yer.' Eileen opened the door just wide enough for Joan to slip through, then closed it again. She looked Philip up and down until he squirmed with embarrassment. 'Well, young feller me lad, what 'ave yer got to say for yerself?'

'Joan invited me in and said you wouldn't mind.' Philip's eyes were on his shoes. 'I'm sorry.'

He's telling the truth, Eileen told herself. The poor bugger's probably terrified. Still, I'm not having those sort of goings on in my house. 'No matter what Joan said, yer own common sense should 'ave told yer it's not proper to go into a girl's house without 'er parents knowin', an' sittin' in the dark snoggin'. Yer not that daft that yer don't know what I'm gettin' at, are yer?'

When Philip shook his head, Eileen asked, 'Where d'yer live?'

Terrified the big woman was asking for his address so she could go and see his parents, Philip croaked, 'Childwall.'

'Then yer'd better be off an' see if yer can get a bus.' With a finger to her mouth for him to be quiet, Eileen opened the door. They made not a sound as they crept down the hall, and as Philip stepped down on to the pathway, he'd never been so glad to be out of a house in his life. But Eileen wasn't finished with him yet and he nearly jumped out of his skin when she grabbed his arm in a vice-like grip.

'Yer know that song about the daring young man on the flying trapeze? The one who floats through the air with the greatest of ease? Well,' Eileen hissed, 'if yer ever again pull a trick like yer pulled tonight, yer won't need to get a bus 'ome, 'cos I'll kick yer backside so hard yer'll be flyin' through the air like that feller on the trapeze. Except it won't be with the greatest of ease.' She gave Philip a push. 'Now, scarper before I test me kickin' power.'

As she watched Philip run down the road as though his feet had taken wings, Eileen didn't know whether to feel sorry for him or angry. It was more Joan's fault than his, but what might they have got up to if she hadn't come down when she did?

As she climbed the stairs, Eileen sighed. Didn't her daughter realise that no bloke would respect her if she played so easy to get? It wouldn't have been so bad if Joan had been going out with Philip and the family knew him, but a complete stranger? She needed a good talking to, that young lady, and she'd get it in the morning.

Bill turned on his side and asked, sleepily, 'What's wrong, chick?'

'I've only been to spend a penny. Go back to sleep.'

It was always a rush in the mornings, getting Bill and Billy out to work, then starting breakfast for the two girls. Edna usually left the house before Joan, and Eileen was biding her time until she was alone with her wayward daughter, who'd avoided her eyes and had barely answered when spoken to. But Joan had other ideas. She had no intention of staying around for the ticking off she knew was coming, so when Edna left for work, Joan followed close on her heels, saying, 'I'll walk up the road with you.'

'The cute little faggot.' Eileen spoke to the empty room as she cleared the breakfast dishes. 'But if she thinks she's gettin' away with it, she's got another think comin'. Just wait till tonight, she'll get a piece of me mind.'

But as the day wore on and Eileen had time to think it all through, she wondered if it wouldn't be wiser to let the whole matter rest. If Bill heard them arguing and found out what it was about, he'd go mad. He'd be angry with Joan, but he'd be upset too, 'cos he thought the world of his children. They could do no wrong in his eyes.

In the end, Eileen couldn't make up her mind what to do and sought her mother's advice. After telling Maggie in detail about the events of the night before, Eileen asked, 'What shall I do, Mam? Have a good talk to 'er, or leave it an' see 'ow she behaves in the future?'

'She deserves a good telling off,' Maggie said. 'Fancy bringing a boy in when we were all in bed! And the lies she told, too, saying she was going to her friend's. I'm surprised at our Joan.'

'I'm not,' Eileen said with a sigh. 'She's different to the other two. They're like an open book, tell me everythin'. But not Joan, she's as deep as the ocean. I've noticed her changin' over the years, an' she's a right little snob now. Seems to look down 'er nose at us, as though we're not good enough for 'er. And haven't yer noticed, Mam, that she never brings any friends 'ome with 'er? Our Edna goes back to Bray Street every week to see her old friends, but Joan's never been back once.' Eileen banged the table with her clenched fist. 'It's this bloody 'ouse that's done it! She thinks we've gone up in the world now an' we're too good for our old neighbours. I feel like knockin' some sense into 'er.'

Maggie was thoughtful for a while, then said, 'I'd leave it be, lass. See how she behaves in future. She probably got the fright of her life last night and it might have taught her a lesson.'

Eileen managed a smile. 'I've got me doubts about our Joan 'aving learned a lesson, but Philip Ryan certainly did. I bet he wouldn't touch 'er with a barge pole now.' The smile turned into a laugh. 'I can see the funny side of it now, Mam. Yer should 'ave seen 'im runnin' down the road as though a ghost was after 'im. I wouldn't be surprised if he 'adn't wet 'is kecks with fright.'

With an imagination as good as her daughter's, Maggie could visualise the scene and she chuckled, 'He'll give Joan a wide berth in future, that's for sure. So let's hope they've both learned a lesson and forget it, eh? No good upsetting Bill and causing a bad atmosphere in the house. You'll just have to keep your eye on her, that's all.'

'I'll be watchin' her like a bloody hawk, don't worry. If she steps out of line again, I'll definitely tell Bill an' he can sort 'er out.'

Chapter Twelve

'I'll never be ready in time.' Eileen plumped up the cushion on Bill's chair and glanced around the room. 'Everything's done, but look at the state of me, I look like the wreck of the bloody Hesperus.'

'Don't panic, chick!' Bill was gazing into the mirror, wrestling with the knot in his tie. 'You've got half an hour before they come.'

It was Boxing Day, and young Billy and Mavis were having a party to celebrate their engagement. Because the Radfords' house was too small for the number of people invited, Eileen had happily volunteered to have it in their house. 'We should 'ave put the Christmas tree in me mam's room,' she fretted. 'We'll need all the space we can get.'

The tie now to his liking, Bill turned to his wife. 'Go upstairs and get yourself ready. I'll carry the tree through.'

'Do as you're told, lass.' Maggie's voice came from the kitchen where she and Mary were arranging sandwiches and sausage rolls on plates. 'You're fussing that much, you've got everyone a bundle of nerves.'

'Well, look who's talkin'!' Eileen waddled to the kitchen door. 'And who is it, pray, that's been rushin' round like a blue-arsed fly all day?'

'Not me.' Maggie gave Mary a sly dig. 'I've been as cool as a cucumber.'

'Eileen, for heaven's sake will you move yourself?' Mary covered a plate of salmon sandwiches with a damp tea towel to stop them from going dry and curling up. 'It's a big occasion for Billy and he'll want his mother looking nice.'

Eileen stood to attention and gave a smart salute. 'Aye, aye, sir.'

When she came down later, she gave a twirl to show off the dress Bill had bought her for Christmas. 'Well, 'ow do I look?'

'You look champion, chick.' Bill squinted through the haze of cigarette smoke. 'It looks a treat on you.'

Mary, her head to one side, nodded in agreement. The dress really suited Eileen. It was a loose-fitting crepe dress, deep blue with three-quarter sleeves and a cowl collar. 'It looks lovely on you, Eileen.'

'Me hair spoils it.' Eileen pulled a face at herself in the mirror. 'Old tatty 'ead.'

'Heat the curling tongs on the gas stove and I'll put a few curls in the front,' Mary said. 'It'll only take a few minutes.'

Mary was just putting the finishing touches to Eileen's hair when Harry's car pulled up outside bringing Billy, Mavis and Mr and Mrs Radford. After that, Eileen was in a whirl as the other guests arrived. 'Blimey,' she whispered to Mary, 'where we goin' to put them all?'

Billy had invited four of his mates from work, and Eileen had asked Milly and Jack Knight, Cissie Maddox and her husband George, and Doris and Jim from next door. With her sister, Rene, and her husband, Alan, Vera, Arthur Kennedy, Mary, Harry, and Harry's parents, Lizzie and George, there were twenty-seven people squashed into the living room and kitchen.

'Spread out, will yez, folks? The eats and drinks are in me mam's room,' Eileen shouted, pushing her way through the mass of bodies, her face glowing with happiness. After all, it wasn't every day your only son got engaged. She felt on top of the world in her new dress, and Mary had done her hair a treat. 'Help yerselves an' get stuck in.'

It was later, when all the food had been eaten, the dishes put away, and everyone had a drink in their hand, that Bill made his planned speech and Billy placed the solitaire engagement ring on Mavis's finger. 'A toast to the happy couple.' Bill raised his glass, his face flushed after a few drinks. 'May they have all the luck in the world.' He saw the tears rolling down Eileen's face and added, 'If they're as happy as Eileen and I have been, they won't go far wrong.'

'Go on, yer soppy beggar,' Eileen gulped before wrapping her arms around her son's neck, her tears falling on his shoulder. 'Yer a good lad an' yer've got yerself a smashin' girl.'

'Let's have some music.' Harry looked through the records and put one of Jim Reeves' on the turntable. 'Take your partners, but you'll have to dance on the spot 'cos there's no room to move.'

Eileen noticed Billy's friends looking ill at ease. 'Why don't you young ones go in me mam's room? You don't want to be with all us oldies.'

Billy, his arm around Mavis, took his friends out, followed by Joan. But Edna hung back. 'I'd rather stay here.'

'Go on,' Eileen urged. 'Yer might get a click.'

'Come on, George.' Cissie Maddox pulled her husband up. 'It's years since we 'ad a dance together.'

'Vera?' Arthur held his hand out. 'Shall we?'

Jack Knight winked at his wife. 'How about it, Milly?'

Soon the room, and the kitchen, were packed with bodies swaying to the strains of a waltz, then a quick step. 'I think we should 'ave booked Buckingham Palace,' Eileen whispered in Bill's ear as he held her close. 'There's no room to breathe.'

'It's a good excuse to hold you tight.' Bill nuzzled her neck. 'I feel all romantic.'

'That's the drink talkin',' Eileen laughed. 'It's amazin' what a few pints will do.'

The drinks flowed freely and the noise grew louder. Harry put on a Mrs Mills record of party songs and Eileen gave Cissie the nod. 'Come on, girl, let's give 'em a treat.'

With their arms across each other's shoulders they stood in the middle of the room and belted out the old tunes for all they were worth. The sight of two eighteen-stone women who were more than a little merry, with their mouths doing contortions as they sang, had everybody in stitches as they clapped and cheered them on. They made so much noise, Billy and his friends came through to see what was going on and it wasn't long before their voices joined in.

Everyone was too occupied to notice the sullen look on Joan's face. Why did her mother have to make a spectacle of herself? It was bad enough her being so big and fat without making a show of herself. It made her feel ashamed of saying she was her mother.

One of Billy's friends, Benny, was standing next to Joan and he turned to her with a huge grin on his face. 'They're dead funny, aren't they?'

'D'you think so?' Joan's lips curled. 'I'm going back in the front room, are you coming?'

Benny hesitated, looking to his friends. 'D'you think we should?'

'Yes, come on.' Joan took his elbow. 'The others will follow.'

From the other side of the room, Edna was watching. She saw the look of bewilderment on Benny's face as her sister pulled at his arm and knew he must be wondering what was going on. This was the first time he'd met the girl and he'd only exchanged half a dozen words with her.

She's a fly one, our Joan, Edna thought. But if she messes around with Benny, Billy will have her guts for garters.

Lizzie Sedgemoor and Milly Knight had joined Eileen and Cissie in the middle of the room to add their voices to 'My Old Man' and 'Maybe It's Because I'm a Londoner'. Then they started on all the old Irish songs, raising the roof with their enthusiasm.

Edna laughed and clapped with the others, but her eyes were on the door all the time. Half an hour later, Joan and Benny still hadn't put in an appearance and Edna was worried. She'd kill their Joan if she did anything to upset her mother or Billy. Edna knew what her sister was like when there were boys around. She'd gone to one or two dances with Joan but was so disgusted with the way she flirted with every boy she danced with, Edna refused to go out with her again.

Bill was laughing at Eileen's antics as he went round topping up glasses. She was now doing her impersonation of Mae West and the audience were doubled up as she hitched up her enormous bust before standing with one hand on her hip and the other patting her hair. 'It's not the men in my life,' Eileen's hips swayed and her eyes narrowed, 'but the life in my men.'

'Aren't you having a drink, love?' Bill stood in front of Edna with a bottle of sherry in his hand. 'How about a sherry with lemonade in?'

'No, thanks, Dad,' Edna said. 'I'm just going up to the bathroom.' She elbowed her way through the crowd but in the hall she stopped at the bottom of the stairs and made sure no one was looking before stepping back to the half-open door of the front room. Not a sound. Oh, dear, Edna sighed, what do I do now? I can't barge in or our Joan will give me the height of abuse and make a fool of me.

Edna made her way slowly upstairs. She sat on the lavatory seat and told herself she didn't care what their Joan did. If she wanted to flirt with boys, that was her business. But tonight of all nights, and with a friend of Billy's, surely she should have more sense.

Edna made her way downstairs and on the pretence of looking in the mirror of the hallstand, she cocked her ears. Still no sound. Not even the sound of anyone talking. And if they weren't talking, what were they doing?

'What yer doing out here, Sis?' Billy had been on his way to the bathroom when he spotted Edna. He gave her an affectionate hug. 'Why aren't you in there enjoying yerself?'

Billy had had a lot to drink but something clicked in his fuddled mind when he looked at Edna. He remembered someone asking where Benny had got to and now he put two and two together. His eyes went from Edna to the half-open door and without further ado, he pushed the door fully open. 'What the hell d'yer think you two are doing?'

Edna caught a glimpse of Joan and Benny standing in the middle of the room with their arms around each other and their lips locked. She just heard Benny's gasp of surprise before fleeing back to the party to witness Cissie Maddox doing her impression of Norman Evans' 'Over The Garden Wall' sketch.

'Well, I'll not forget our Billy's engagement in a hurry.' Eileen flopped down after waving goodbye to most of the guests. 'It's been one 'ell of a night, eh? What d'yer say, folks?'

'One of the best parties I've ever been to.' Harry's words were slurred, his smile that of a man who has had more than enough to drink. 'We should do it more often.'

'You, Harry Sedgemoor, are drunk.' Mary tried to look severe but there was laughter in her voice. 'You made a show of yourself doing that tango with Cissie.'

Arthur and Vera had stayed behind, with Mary and Harry, to give Eileen a hand to clear away the mess. But first, Eileen had insisted, a cup of tea and a sit down were called for.

'I don't think I've ever laughed so much in all me life,' Arthur said. 'You and Cissie make a very good double act.'

'Don't put ideas into her head.' Bill handed Arthur a cigarette. 'She's bad enough as it is.'

'Hey! "She" is the cat's mother, Bill Gillmoss! I'll 'ave me full title if yer don't mind.'

'Young Billy enjoyed himself,' Vera said. 'You certainly did him proud, both of you. And he's got a nice girl in Mavis.'

'Yeah, I'm made up for both of them,' Eileen said, kicking off her shoes and sighing with relief. 'Our Billy's a good kid an' he deserves the best.'

Mary took Harry's cup. 'Come on, let's get cracking and clear this lot up. The men move the furniture back and the women will wash up.'

'Bloody slave driver,' Eileen grunted, rubbing her swollen feet. 'Me plates of meat are killin' me.'

'You stay put, and me and Mary will wash up.' Vera rolled her sleeves up. 'Half an hour and we'll have the place back to near normal.'

'Except for me mam's room.' Eileen heaved herself off the chair. 'That looks as though a bomb's hit it. She's gone to bed with glasses and half-eaten sandwiches all over the floor, God love 'er.'

'I didn't see much of our Joan.' Bill's brows drew together. 'In fact I don't remember seeing her at all until she came over to say she was going to bed.' He shook his head. 'I must have had too much to drink because I counted four of our Billy's friends when they came, but I only saw three leaving.'

Eileen laughed. 'There were four, but Benny left early 'cos he had promised to go on to another party. Billy said he didn't say goodbye because there were so many people here he was shy. And as for our Joan, she went to bed early 'cos it's work temorrer.' Eileen bent and grabbed hold of the front of Bill's shirt. 'Now, Bill Gillmoss, if that answers all yer questions, get off yer backside an' get stuck in.'

There were no buses running and very few cars on the road as Arthur and Vera walked along Rice Lane. Now and again a group of revellers would pass, on their way home from parties, but otherwise the streets were deserted. Harry had offered to drive them to Vera's, pick up his two boys and take them to the Dingle, but Arthur said it would be better if they walked. Harry was more than a little drunk and it wasn't worth taking a chance.

It was a clear night but bitterly cold, and they walked briskly to keep warm. 'You can't walk all the way home,' Vera said. 'By the time you got there it would be time to go to work. You'd better stay at ours and get a couple of hours' sleep on the couch. The boys can stay till you pick them up after work.'

'What about Elsie Smith?' Arthur chuckled. 'Aren't you afraid she'll label you a scarlet woman?'

'You're not walking all that way home at this time of night, Elsie Smith or no Elsie Smith. Let her think what she likes.'

But when they reached Vera's front door, Arthur held her arm as she reached to put the key in the lock. 'I'll leave the boys here because it would be a shame to wake them, but I think it would be better if I didn't stay. I don't want you getting a bad name.'

Vera pulled her arm free and opened the door. 'Arthur Kennedy, you are not walking all the way to the Dingle and that's that!'

The fire had died out and there was a chill in the room. 'I'll put the electric fire on to warm the place up. I don't know about you, but I'm chilled to the marrow.'

Arthur stood just inside the door, making no effort to move. 'Vera, what about the children? My two will still be in bed when I leave for work, but Colin and Peter will be up. Aren't you worried what they think?'

'What is there to think?' Vera asked. 'Colin and Peter know you well enough by now, they're certainly not going to read anything into you sleeping on our couch.' She slipped out of her coat and threw it over a chair. 'I'll make us a hot drink and then I'm off to bed.'

Sitting close to the warmth of the electric fire, her hands around a mug of steaming cocoa, Vera asked, 'Have you been to the hospital since I saw you last?'

Arthur nodded. 'Several times. But Sylvia still refuses to see me. The Sister said Sylvia gets so agitated when they mention my name, it's best if we leave things as they are.' He sipped his cocoa. 'When I went on Christmas Eve with some presents from the boys, I was leaving them in the Matron's office when Sister Duffy came in. She said Sylvia was in a deep sleep, so if I wanted I could see her without her knowing.'

'And?' Vera coaxed, seeing the distress on Arthur's face. 'You'll feel better if you talk about it.'

'I talk to Sister Duffy when she's on duty, she's very understanding. She told me the doctors don't know how Sylvia has hung on for the last two years.' Arthur met Vera's eyes. 'And I don't know meself, after seeing her. She looked so old, like a wizened old woman, it knocked me for six. I wouldn't have recognised her, would have walked past the bed if Sister hadn't been with me.'

'I'm sorry, Arthur.'

'If God has any mercy, he'll take her.' Arthur's voice cracked. 'I can understand why she refuses to see me. Sylvia was always proud of her looks, she wouldn't want me to see her the way she is now.'

Vera could hear the distress in Arthur's voice and she stood up.

Holding out her hand for his mug, she said, 'I'll get a pillow and something to throw over you, and you can put your head down for a few hours.'

When she came downstairs, Arthur was still sitting where she'd left him. 'Come on, take your coat off.' Vera put the pillow and blanket on the couch and turned round to find Arthur standing close behind her. There was a look of such despair in his eyes, she held her arms open and he walked into them. 'What would I have done without you these last three years?' he asked. 'You've been a tower of strength, my anchor.'

Vera stroked his head. 'It cuts both ways, Arthur. You've helped me as much as I've helped you.'

When Arthur put his arms around her waist and held her tight, Vera didn't resist. This was what he needed, physical and moral support. But wasn't it what she needed, too?

'I've stuck to the promise I made all those years ago, that I would never do anything to hurt you,' Arthur whispered into her hair. 'But holding you close like this, it's hard to keep that promise.'

'Arthur, there's been times over the years when I've cursed you for making that promise, and for being the decent, honest man you are. If you had made any advance towards me, I wouldn't have turned you away.'

'Oh, Vera.' Arthur's cry was like that of a hurt animal. 'Don't say that or I'll lose what little self control I've got. I've wanted you so much, for so long, there's times I thought I'd go mad with the need for you.' He held Vera from him. 'I think you should go to bed now, Vera, before I go too far. I'm only human and I can stand only so much.'

'I'm not made of wood myself, Arthur.' Vera gave a nervous laugh. 'But seeing as it's Christmas and friends usually kiss each other at Christmas, there's no harm in a little kiss.'

Arthur looked down at Vera's upturned face and cupped it with his hands. His lips touched hers, like a feather at first, then they came back, hard and demanding. Vera could feel the hunger in Arthur's kiss and her body responded. Somewhere in her mind a warning sounded but it was quickly dispelled. For three years they'd kept each other at arm's length, played everything by the book. Surely now they were entitled to a little happiness? Just one hour, no one could begrudge them that.

Chapter Thirteen

'D'you know what I fancy, Mary?' Harry folded the *Echo* and placed it down the side of his chair. 'A bag of chips, with plenty of salt and vinegar on.'

'What?' Mary's finely arched eyebrows rose in surprise. 'After that big dinner you had? Well, you greedy guts!'

'That was four hours ago, pet.' Harry grinned. 'Anyway, it's not so much that I'm hungry, but it's ages since we had chips from the chippy and ate them out of the paper. And you know they don't taste the same once you put them on a plate.'

Mary lowered her knitting to rest on her knee. She was knitting a pullover for Tony and was in the middle of a row of a complicated pattern. 'It's half past ten.'

'What difference does that make? The children are fast asleep, your mam is sitting up in bed reading, and we'd only be a quarter of an hour.'

Mary gazed into Harry's deep brown eyes and couldn't refuse. 'Just let me finish this row. You go and tell me mam and bring me coat off the hallstand.'

They walked up the road, their joined hands swinging between them. They were passing the entry at the top of the road when Harry happened to glance sideways into the dark passage. The street lamp at the corner cast enough light into the alley for him to make out the figures of a young couple locked together in a passionate embrace. He could only see the back of the boy and the long hair of the girl who was pressed up against the wall.

They were past the entry in a few strides so it was impossible to be sure, but there was something familiar about the girl's hair that reminded Harry of Joan. He didn't say anything to Mary as they turned the corner . . . after all, he could be wrong.

There were only a couple of people in the chip shop and Mary and

Harry were quickly served. Outside, they stood while they tore a hole in the newspaper wrapping to get to the bag of chips, giggling like school children given a special treat. 'Mmm, don't they smell delicious?' Harry opened his mouth wide and drew in the night air to cool the red hot chip burning the inside of his mouth. 'Lovely, tell your ma.'

'I feel like a big soft kid.' Mary's laugh tinkled in the quiet road. 'It's years since we did this.'

When they were passing the entry again, Harry slowed his pace to look more closely at the young couple. They were still locked in an embrace, but this time Harry could see the boy's hand inside the girl's coat, moving and exploring. He still couldn't see the girl's face but there was no mistaking that hair style. It was Joan all right.

Harry waited until they were in the house before asking casually, 'Did you notice the courting couple in the entry?'

'No, why?'

'The girl was Joan.'

'Joan! In the entry with a boy! Eileen would kill her!' Mary had slipped her coat off and stood with it over her arm. 'Are you sure it was her?'

'Yes, darling, I am sure it was Joan. And they weren't just kissing, either. The bloke was all over her. If any of the neighbours see her, she'll be getting herself a bad name.'

Mary's face clouded. 'Eileen would go mad if she knew.'

'Don't tell her, for heaven's sake.' Harry leaned forward. 'It's none of our business.'

'I've no intention of telling her. She's upset enough as it is, and I'm sure Joan's got something to do with it.' Mary laid her coat over the arm of the couch and sat down. 'Eileen was telling me the other day that she heard Joan and Billy having a terrible row the day after his engagement party, but when she asked what it was about, neither of them would tell her. But whatever it was, Billy hasn't spoken to Joan since. He won't even look at her, never mind speak to her, and Eileen said the atmosphere in the house is terrible when they're both in.'

'Well, perhaps I'm just being bad minded,' Harry said. 'For all we know, she might be courting the bloke. I'm sure she wouldn't go down a dark entry with any Tom, Dick or Harry.'

'No, I'm sure she's not like that.' Mary picked up her coat. 'Stick the kettle on, love, will you? The chips have given me a thirst.'

114

★   ★   ★

Bill gave Eileen a peck on the cheek as he struggled out of his coat. 'The hospital rang the Admin up today, with a message to ask Arthur to go there right away. Sylvia must have taken a turn for the worse.'

'Oh, my God.' Eileen wiped her hands on her pinny. 'Mind you, from what Arthur's told me, it would be a blessing if God took 'er.'

Bill walked to the kitchen to wash his hands. 'Harry's going up to the Dingle after tea and I said I'd go with him. See if Arthur needs any help, like.'

'I'll go with yez. The boys might need a woman to comfort them.' Eileen moved quickly for a woman of her size. She set Bill's dinner on the table, asked Maggie to see to the girls when they came in, and hurried upstairs to get changed.

'Am I all right to go like this?' Bill asked when Eileen came down. 'I don't need to put me suit on, do I?'

Eileen looked him over. Bill was very particular over his appearance. Shaved every morning before he went to work, he always had to wear a clean shirt. 'You look fine, love.' She chucked him under the chin. 'Yer vain enough as it is, but I'll still tell yer, you are the handsomest man in Liverpool.'

'Don't be so mean with your compliments, chick.' Bill grinned. 'You mean I'm the handsomest man in the world.'

Maggie had come in and she stood listening. 'I think you both mean the most handsome man, don't you, not the handsomest? Your grammar is terrible.'

'Oh, 'ere she is,' Eileen groaned. 'The walkin' encyclopaedia. Don't yer ever wonder, Mam, 'ow anyone as clever as you could 'ave a bird brain like me for a daughter?'

'Come on, love,' Bill urged. 'We don't want to keep Harry waiting.'

Eileen picked up her bag and stuck it under her arm. As she followed Bill out, she whispered in Maggie's ear, I've always told yer the 'ospital gave yer the wrong baby. I'd sue them, if I were you.'

Arthur opened the door, his face white and drawn. He seemed to have aged ten years overnight. 'It's nice of you to come,' he said as he closed the door behind them. 'I appreciate it.' He put a finger to his lips and nodded towards the living room. 'The boys are in a

115

terrible state. I've just had to tell them that Sylvia died this afternoon.'

'Oh, my God, the poor things. Shall I go in to them?' Eileen asked, her heart bursting with pity.

Arthur nodded. 'If you would, while I have a word with Harry and Bill. I don't want to say too much in front of the lads because they're upset enough.' He waited till Eileen closed the room door. 'Will you tell them in work, Harry? I'll have to take a week off to see to everything, and I'm keeping the boys off school.' He sighed as he ran a hand through his hair. 'There's such a lot to do, me head's splitting. Tomorrow I've got to go back to the hospital for the death certificate, then to Brougham Terrace. When that's done, I've got to see to the funeral arrangements.'

'Are you all right for money?' Harry asked. 'Because I can always . . .'

Arthur shook his head. 'Thanks, but I'm all right. I knew this was going to happen sooner or later, and I've been putting some money by each week.' He leaned back against the wall, his head lowered. 'It's the boys I'm worried about. When Sylvia went into hospital, I honestly thought she was going to get better and I kept telling them she'd be coming home soon. And it wasn't a lie, because the doctor on her ward told me she had a fifty-fifty chance. But in me own heart I've known for a long time that she wasn't going to get better, and I'm asking meself now if I shouldn't have told them the truth. Prepared them, so it wouldn't have come as such a shock.'

'Don't be blaming yourself,' Bill said. 'You only did what you thought was best for them.'

'You did the right thing, Arthur,' Harry said. 'They're bound to be upset, it's only natural. But they're young and they've got their whole lives ahead of them. It may take a while, but they'll get over it.'

Arthur led the way down the hall. He threw the door open and stopped on the threshold, tears forming in his eyes at the sight that met him.

Eileen was sitting in the middle of the couch with an arm around each of his sons. She was rocking gently, kissing one bowed head, then the other. She looked up at the three men crowded in the doorway. 'Gordon and David are comin' 'ome to our house an' they're goin' to stay for a few days, aren't you, boys?'

Two tear-stained faced looked up into Eileen's face and they nodded.

'We can, can't we, Dad?' There was pleading in David's eyes. He didn't want to move from this big woman who gave out so much love and sympathy. It was what he and his brother needed right now.

'Are you sure, Eileen?' Arthur could feel the relief course through his body.

'I wouldn't ask if I wasn't sure.' Eileen winked over the heads of the boys. 'I've told them you've got a lot of runnin' round to do, so they're goin' to keep me company.'

'Can I go and get me pyjamas, Dad?' Gordon slid to the end of the couch, eager to be away in case his Dad changed his mind.

'I'll pack some things for you.' There was gratitude in the faint smile Arthur gave Eileen before making for the stairs.

'Arthur!' There was surprise written on Vera's face. 'I didn't expect to see you.' She looked at his face more closely. 'What's wrong?'

'Can I come in?'

Vera held the door wide. 'Of course, need you ask?'

'Are you alone?'

'Yes, I've just put Carol to bed and Colin and Peter are out dancing somewhere.'

There was a frown on Vera's face. 'What's all the mystery about?'

Arthur dropped into a chair, his whole body weary. 'Sylvia died this afternoon.'

Vera gripped the edge of the table for support. She closed her eyes. 'What can I say, Arthur? Sorry seems so inadequate.'

'I've been expecting it for years but it's still come as a shock.' He was silent for a while, then said softly, 'I thank God once again for Eileen. I was at me wits' end trying to comfort the boys, and then Eileen turns up and takes charge of them. They're in her house now and she said they can stay there until after the funeral. She's fussing over them, giving them the kisses and hugs that they need . . . something a man isn't as capable of as a woman.'

Arthur looked up at Vera and their eyes locked. This was the first time they'd been alone since the night of Billy's engagement party, and the memory of that night filled Vera with a guilt that lay heavy on her heart.

'Vera.' Arthur knew what she was thinking. It was as though, at that moment, he could read her mind. 'Don't reproach yourself, please. If you want to blame anyone for what happened that night, then blame me.' He stood up and put his hands on her shoulders.

'I'm not sorry it happened and I don't feel any guilt. Sylvia hadn't been a wife to me for over five years . . . ten if we count the war years when I was away. She didn't want me for a husband, didn't want me in her bed. So why should I feel guilty about the one and only night I held a woman in my arms? Especially as I love that woman and I hope she loves me.'

Vera laid her head on Arthur's chest as tears rolled down her cheeks. 'I don't regret what happened that night, Arthur, it's just that I feel it was wrong, when Sylvia was so ill.'

Arthur held her close. 'Don't cry, love, please? We're not bad, you and me. Just two ordinary human beings who needed to be loved.'

Vera sniffed. 'I haven't got a hankie.'

'Here, use mine.' Arthur dropped a light kiss on her forehead. 'I'll have to go now, 'cos I've got a busy day tomorrow.'

'If there's anything I can do, you will let me know, won't you? If you need someone to help on the day of the funeral, you've only got to say the word.'

As Arthur was walking away, Vera called him back. Her eyes on the pavement, she said softly, 'I'll slip up to church tomorrow and light a candle for Sylvia and you and the boys.'

'All hands are swappin' beds tonight,' Eileen said as she took David's and Gordon's coats. 'Joan and Edna, you're goin' in Billy's bed, and Billy can sleep in your room with the boys.'

'Ah, ray, I don't have to sleep in the same bed as this one, do I?' Edna's smile was wide as she winked at the two boys. She felt so sorry for them, they looked so lost and defenceless. 'She snores something terrible, you know, and talks in her sleep.'

'I'm not moving out of my room,' Joan said, her flared nostrils white with temper. 'Why can't they have Billy's bed and he can sleep on the couch?'

'Because I said so, that's why.' Eileen glared at her daughter. How could she be so unfeeling?

'Well, I refuse to move.' Joan tossed her hair back over her shoulder, a sullen look on her face.

Bill had entered the room in time to catch Joan's statement and his face flooded with colour. 'Did I hear you say you refuse? Well, let me tell you this, young lady, while you're living in this house, you'll do as your mam tells you.'

Joan's chair crashed back and she flounced out of the room. Eileen looked at Bill and shrugged her shoulders, then put her arms around David and Gordon. 'Take no notice of her, she's a bad-tempered little madam. I'll make yez a nice drink and then Edna will take you up and show yez where yer sleepin'. An' she'll find an empty drawer for yez to put yer clothes in.'

'Where's Billy?' Gordon asked shyly. 'Will we see him tonight?'

'He's gone up to see his girlfriend,' Edna told him. 'But he promised to be back early so you can all go to bed together.'

'That Joan's a hard-faced little faggot,' Eileen said when all the family were in bed and she was alone with Bill. 'She thinks of no one but 'erself. Not one word did she speak to those poor boys.'

'She certainly needs taking in hand,' Bill answered. 'She's getting far too big for her boots.'

Eileen was standing in front of the mirror putting a few dinkie curlers in the front of her hair. She lowered the comb, her face thoughtful. 'Bill, I've been thinkin'. Arthur's got no family, and neither had Sylvia, apart from a sister in America that Arthur hasn't heard of for years. There'll be no one to go to the funeral, only us and the Sedgemoors.'

'What have you got in your mind, chick?'

'It's the two boys I'm thinkin' of.' Eileen tapped the comb against her teeth. 'I don't want them to think their mother had no friends, that no one mourned her death.'

'So?'

'Couldn't we make it a good turn out, for the sake of the kids? Ask all the people that know Arthur to rally round? Doris and Jim next door, they like Arthur. And there's Lizzie and George, Harry's parents, I know they'd come if they were asked.'

'Eileen, the funeral will be in the Dingle. How are they all going to get there? It would mean Arthur ordering enough cars for them all and he might not be able to afford it.'

'I've thought it all out.' Eileen sat down and took Bill's hands in hers. 'That's if you'll go along with it.'

'Do I have any choice?' Bill grinned as he squeezed her hand. 'Go on, spit it out.'

'Harry and Jim 'ave got cars, so they could take us. Arthur would only need to order one funeral car for him and the boys. And they could all come back here for a bite to eat.'

119

'You have got it all worked out, haven't you, chick?'

'I couldn't bear it if there were only a couple of people at the funeral, the church would be empty. It would be so sad for Arthur and the boys.'

'I agree with you and as far as I'm concerned, you can do what you think best. But you'd better have a word with Arthur first, see what his plans are.'

When Arthur came the following day, he looked completely worn out. He'd never sat down, he told Eileen, but now, thank God, everything had been seen to, all the arrangements made. He'd been to the Co-op undertakers and said they had taken everything in hand. The funeral was in three days' time.

'Have yer thought about who's goin' to the funeral?' Eileen asked.

'Not much to think about is there? There's only me and the boys.' The sadness and bitterness in Arthur's voice brought a lump to Eileen's throat. She was glad she'd sent David and Gordon on a message to Woolworths in Walton Vale. She wouldn't have wanted them to see their dad so downcast. He was all they had left. 'D'yer mean yer not goin' to ask me an' Bill to come? Or Mary and Harry?'

Arthur lifted his head. 'Will you come? I didn't like to ask but I'd appreciate it if you would.'

'Of course we will.' Eileen tilted her head to one side. 'Shall I tell yer what I'd really like to do, that's if yer've no objections, like?' While Eileen was telling him of her plans, Arthur's eyes lost some of their sadness. While he'd been rushing around all day, dreadful visions had been flashing through his mind. a huge church, the coffin in front of the altar, and all the pews empty except for himself and his two sons. He was worried about the effect it would have on David and Gordon.

'Well,' Eileen asked, 'will that be all right with you?'

Arthur opened his mouth but no words would come. He couldn't express his feelings for this mountain of a woman who had a heart to match her size. Many times over the last five years he'd needed her kindness and her thoughtfulness, and she'd never let him down. But what she was offering now was more than a gesture of kindness, it was a lifeline for him and the sons he adored.

'I don't know what to say.' Arthur coughed to clear his throat. 'I should say "no", it's too much to ask of you. But right now, Eileen,

I need help more than I've ever needed it.' Arthur pressed two fingers to his eyelids to relieve the pressure. 'I'd be more than grateful to take you up on your offer, and you have my heartfelt thanks.'

'Oh, it's not only me,' Eileen said, her hand waving away his thanks. 'Yer've got some good friends, yer know, Arthur, and they've all offered to 'elp. After all, what are friends for if they're not there when yer need them?' Eileen put her hands on the chair and pushed herself up. 'I'll put the kettle on for a cuppa. David and Gordon should be back soon and they'll be made up to see you.' She stopped by the kitchen door and turned her head. 'When Bill and Harry get in from work, we'll get our heads together and sort things out.'

Arthur took the cup Eileen held out to him. 'I'll give you the money for the food, but won't it be a lot of work for you to make a spread for so many?'

'Nah! There'll only be a dozen and that'll be child's play.' Eileen took a sip of tea, watching Arthur over the rim of her cup. 'Anyway, I'm not doin' the eats. Me mam and Vera are doin' them.' She saw the change of expression on Arthur's face at the mention of Vera.

'Have you seen Vera, then?'

'Yeah, she called this mornin'. She won't come to the funeral because of Carol, but she'll be 'ere to give me mam a hand.'

They were silent as they drank their tea, each wrapped up in their own thoughts and neither knowing that they were both thinking of the same person. And both with hope in their hearts.

Chapter Fourteen

'Can I take your key, Dad, in case I'm late tonight?' Joan was standing in front of her father, dressed up to the nines, with her hair and make-up perfect. 'I'm going to the Grafton and it means getting two buses.'

Eileen was sitting at the dining table, the *Echo* spread out in front of her. Joan never asked her for a favour. She always went to Bill because she knew he was a soft touch, believed everything she told him. But Eileen was wise to her daughter. She'd found her out in so many lies, she now took everything she told her with a pinch of salt.

'What time's the dance over?' Bill asked.

'It'll be late tonight because Ivy Benson and her band are on. About twelve o'clock, I imagine.' Joan saw the look of doubt cross Bill's face and hurried on to say, 'Oh, but I won't stay till the end. I might even be home before you go to bed.'

'Aye, an' pigs might fly,' Eileen muttered, rustling the paper.

Joan turned around and glared. 'I think you forget I'm turned eighteen now, I'm not a kid.'

'Eighteen or not, I don't like the idea of you walking all that way home if you miss the last bus,' Bill said. 'It's not safe for a girl to be walking the streets that time of night.'

Joan's attitude changed and she said meekly, 'I promise I won't miss the last bus, honest, Dad.'

'Make sure you don't.' Bill slipped the front door key off his keyring and handed it to her. 'You be in here by twelve o'clock at the latest.'

Having got her own way, Joan smiled. 'Thanks, Dad.'

'She's got you for a right sucker,' Eileen said when they heard the front door bang. 'You always give in to her.'

'She's too old now to tell her to be in by ten o'clock. You're too hard on her, chick. I remember going to the Grafton with you when we were her age, and your mother never used to worry about what time we got in.'

'Because me mam knew who I was with, that's why she didn't worry.' Eileen glowered. 'We never know who our Joan's with 'cos she never brings any of her friends home. Don't you think it's funny that the only friend of hers we've seen is the one from Hanford Avenue? And that's only every Preston Guild.'

Edna was sitting quietly in a chair by the window, a romantic novel open on her knee. She'd been reading when Joan came into the room, and kept her finger on the line she was up to as she watched her sister through lowered lids. If me mam and dad knew what our Joan got up to, they'd have a duck egg, she thought. She never brought a girl friend home because she hadn't got one. She was only interested in men, and according to what she told Edna each night, in the privacy of their bedroom, it was a different bloke every night. And they were always handsome, like Clarke Gable or Errol Flynn, had plenty of money and were smashing dancers. But if these blokes were all as good as Joan said, how come they were replaced the following night by another film star look-alike? Edna went back to the heroine in her book. If her sister landed herself in hot water it would be her own stupid fault 'cos she was asking for it.

'Bill, wake up.' Eileen shook Bill's shoulder. 'It's one o'clock and our Joan's not in yet.'

Bill turned on his side, squinting in the glare of the light. 'What's that, chick?' He rubbed the sleep from his eyes. 'Did you say our Joan's not in yet?'

'No, and it's one o'clock.'

Bill shot up. 'Are you sure?'

Eileen clicked her teeth. 'Of course I'm sure! I 'ad a feelin' she knew she was goin' to be late, so I stayed awake, listenin' for 'er. But I expected her before now an' I'm worried.'

Bill slid his legs over the side of the bed and reached for his trousers which were folded over the back of a chair. 'She probably missed the last bus and has had to walk.'

'I wouldn't mind if I knew that's what's 'appened, but I've been lyin' here thinkin' all sorts of things.'

'I'll get dressed and go and look for her.' Bill struggled into the legs of his trousers. 'She'll get a good telling off for this.'

Eileen made a pot of tea when Bill went out and as she sat at the table her inside was churning over. It was dangerous for a young girl to be out at this time, you never knew who was hanging around. And when Bill came in, shaking his head, her nerves were at breaking point.

'I walked as far as the station, but there's not a soul to be seen,' Bill said. 'It was no use walking any further because I don't know which direction she'll be coming from.'

'Here, get this hot tea down yer.' When Eileen saw Bill's worried face, her anxiety was mixed with anger. If that little so-and-so was out there gallivanting while they were worried sick, she wouldn't half give her what for. 'You go to bed an' I'll wait up for 'er.'

'I couldn't sleep, not knowing where she is,' Bill said. 'I'll stay up with you.'

'It's daft both of us sittin' 'ere an' you need yer sleep more than I do.' When Bill went to object, Eileen said, 'She's probably strollin' 'ome with some of 'er friends, without a care in the world. She won't know we're sittin' here on pins.'

'Well, give me a call if she's not in soon,' Bill said, shaking his head as he walked through the door thinking of what he'd say to his daughter the next morning.

But when Bill came down at half past six, followed closely by Billy, Eileen shrugged her shoulders. 'She's not come 'ome.'

'And you've been up all night?' Bill pulled his braces over his shoulders and fastened them to the buttons on his trousers. 'Where the hell can she have got to?'

'Don't ask me,' Eileen said, putting their breakfast plates on the table. 'I've been sittin' 'ere worried to death.'

'What's up?' Billy yawned, stretching his arms over his head.

When Eileen explained, Billy raised his eyes to the ceiling. 'I wouldn't worry about our Joan, she's quite capable of taking care of herself.'

'I keep tellin' meself not to worry, that if there was anythin' wrong we'd 'ave heard by now. They say bad news travels fast.'

'I'll have something to say to her when . . .' Bill broke off when there was a knock on the front door. 'This'll be her now.'

'It won't, yer know,' Eileen said, hurrying along the hall. 'Don't forget, yer gave 'er yer key.'

It was Mary standing in the pathway. 'I've just had a phone call from your Joan. She said she missed the last bus so she stayed at her friend's house.'

'I'll break 'er bloody neck for 'er!' Eileen roared. 'D'yer know, kid, I've been up all night, and Bill was up half the night, worried sick?'

'I told her she was very naughty and that you'd be worried,' Mary said, 'but she said she'd explain tonight, and then put the phone down.'

'I'll phone 'er, when I get me hands on her.' Eileen's face was red with anger. 'The little flamer!'

'I'll see you later,' Mary said, hurrying away. 'I've got me mam's breakfast on.'

When she got home, Mary said, 'Eileen's in a hell of a temper. She's been up all night.'

Harry broke off a piece of toast and popped it in his mouth. 'You can't blame her being in a temper. Can you imagine what we'd be like if Emma was Joan's age and she stayed out all night?' He reached for another slice of toast. 'I know you'll say I'm bad minded, but I'd like to bet it wasn't a girl she spent the night with.'

'Oh, you can't say that, Harry!' Mary said. 'The girl's probably telling the truth.'

'And I'm a monkey's uncle,' was Harry's answer.

Joan was first home from work and Eileen was waiting for her, hands on hips. 'Well, what 'ave yer got to say for yerself?'

Joan raised her brows, a look of disdain on her face. If only her mother could see herself. Big, fat, untidy and loud mouthed. I bet she never had many boys running after her when she was young. 'I told Mary to tell you I missed the bus and slept at my friend's house. There's no law against that, is there?'

'Don't you be so hoity-toity with me, you little madam, or yer'll feel the back of me hand.' Eileen gritted her teeth. 'Now, I want to know where you were all night. What's the name of yer friend an' where does she live?'

'Her name's Doreen and she lives in, er, Everton.'

'Whereabouts in Everton?' Eileen asked, trying hard to keep a rein on her temper. 'What's the name of the road?'

Caught unawares by the question, Joan floundered for a second. Then she brazened it out. 'I didn't take any notice of the name of the road but it's up near Liverpool's football ground.'

'Yer can tell that to the marines,' Eileen growled. 'I don't believe a word yer've said. It's a terrible thing to say about me own daughter but you are a liar, Joan, and yer don't fool me for one minute. But I'm not sayin' any more, I'll let yer dad sort yer out.'

There was an uneasy tension round the table as they ate their meal, and as soon as they were finished, Billy and Edna made for their bedrooms out of the way. Joan stood up to follow, but Bill motioned for her to stay. He moved from the table to his chair and took out his packet of cigarettes, all the time his eyes on his daughter's face.

He waited till his cigarette was lit, inhaled deeply, then said, 'Well, I think you've got some explaining to do, so let's have it.'

Joan put on her timid, little girl look and said she'd left the Grafton early enough to get the bus but it drove away just as she got to the bus stop. 'I was frightened to walk home on my own, Dad, so Doreen said I could sleep at their house. I couldn't let you know because we're not on the phone and it was too late to ring Auntie Mary's.'

Eileen shook her head slowly in disbelief. What a bloody good actress her daughter was! So different in her attitude now she was talking to her father. Eileen could see by Bill's face that he was being talked around and she pushed her chair back in disgust. He's falling for it again, she thought as she ran the water on the dirty dishes. She can twist him around her little finger and he can't see it. 'He's making a rod for his own back and mine,' Eileen muttered as she banged a plate down on the draining board in temper. 'He'll come to his senses when it's too late.'

'Well, I never expected to see you tonight.' Eileen's face showed her surprise when Bill ushered Vera into the room. 'Where's Carol?'

'Colin's having a night in, so he's minding her.' Vera's eyes were shining. 'I've got some news for you.'

'I 'ope it's good news 'cos I've 'ad me belly full of bad news. I need somethin' to cheer me up.'

'Where is everybody?' Vera asked. 'Are they all out?'

'Billy's gone to see Mavis, an' the two girls are upstairs. Edna's washin' 'er hair, and Joan's got a fit of the sulks because we wouldn't let 'er go out. She's probably sittin' on 'er bed callin' me an' Bill fit to burn.' Eileen clicked her tongue. 'The little faggot stayed out all night and 'ad us worried to death. And for once, Bill put 'is foot down an' made her stay in tonight as a punishment.'

Very couldn't wait any longer to tell her news. 'I heard today that me divorce is coming through.'

'Oh, smashing'!' A smile lit up Eileen's face. 'So yer'll soon be a free agent, eh?'

'Yes.' Vera rubbed her hands together, 'I didn't expect it so soon, but from what the letter said, because I filed for it on the grounds of desertion, and it's four years since Danny walked out, there's no opposition and it will go through quickly.'

Bill came in from the kitchen with a cup of tea in each hand. 'I'm sorry we've nothing stronger to celebrate with, Vera.' He smiled as he handed her a cup. 'It is good news, isn't it?'

My goodness, Eileen thought, he hasn't half changed. At one time the very thought of anyone getting divorced would have horrified him. You made your vows at the altar to love, honour and obey, and in Bill's eyes those vows were not to be broken. Mind you, he wasn't the only one who had changed since the war. I mean, who'd have ever thought the day would come when women would be seen smoking in the street, or going into a pub without being accompanied by a man?

'D'yer think yer'll ever get married again, Vera?' Eileen's face was a picture of innocence. 'Do yer good to 'ave a man about the 'ouse again.'

Blushing, Vera pushed her hair behind her ears. 'Now who would have me, at my age?'

'Ay, don't be runnin' yerself down.' Eileen leaned forward. 'Yer a nice-lookin' woman an' any man with half a brain would grab yer, aren't I right, Bill?'

Bill knew Eileen was probing and his eyes flashed a warning. 'Vera will sort her own life out, given time.' He smiled at Vera. 'Eileen is right about one thing, though, you are an attractive woman, Vera, and you'd make some man a very good wife.'

'If yer did get married again, it would 'ave to be in a register office,' Eileen said, ignoring the look on Bill's face which was telling her to drop the subject. 'They wouldn't marry you in a church.'

'Eileen, if the time ever came when I did marry again, that would be the least of me worries.' Vera wasn't to be drawn. 'But you know what they say about "chance being a fine thing".'

Upstairs, Edna sat on the side of her bed watching Joan file her long nails before covering them with a bright red nail varnish. 'Where did you get to last night?'

Joan completed the painting of one nail before looking up. 'I told you, I went to the Grafton and missed the last bus home.' Her face was thoughtful as she studied Edna's face. 'If I tell you, will you promise not to tell me Mam?'

'I've never clatted on you before, have I?' Edna stood up and turned the bed clothes back. 'But if yer don't want to tell me, then don't bother.'

But Joan wanted to tell her. She'd had such a marvellous time the night before, she was dying to tell someone. 'If you repeat this to anyone, I'll never speak to you again.' She screwed the top back on the nail varnish bottle and put it on the chest of drawers. The sullen look disappeared from her face as she began to speak. 'I did go to the Grafton, and I met this American. He asked me for a dance, then stayed with me when it was over.' Her eyes were bright with excitement. 'He was lovely, Edna, very good looking and very polite.'

'What was his name?' Edna had climbed into bed and was leaning back against the headboard.

'August, but they call him Augie.'

'August!' Edna tittered. 'What sort of a name is that when it's out?'

'If you're going to make fun, I'm not telling you any more.'

Edna held her hand up. 'Sorry! I promise I won't laugh.'

'Anyway, he was with a friend who's going out with a girl from Woolton, and they joined us. The boys are stationed at Burtonwood, and Valerie, that's Augie's friend's girl, often goes up to the base 'cos they've got a bar there and there a games room. Anyway, she was going back with them last night, and they asked me to go too.'

Edna's mouth gaped. 'You went to Burtonwood?'

'The boys were in a Jeep, and they said they'd get me back home for twelve o'clock. But I was enjoying meself so much, I didn't realise the time until it was one o'clock. I couldn't come home then because me mam knows there's no buses running that late.'

Edna was all ears. 'Where did you stay, then?'

'At the camp.' Joan heard Edna's sharp intake of breath and hurried on. 'I slept with Valerie, so you can take that look off your face. And Augie ran me to work this morning in the Jeep.'

'You're asking for trouble, our Joan. If me mam and dad knew that, they'd kill you.' Edna wrapped her arms around her drawn-up knees. 'I've heard the women in work talking about the girls who go to Burtonwood and they say they're no good. And they say that most of the Yanks have got wives or girlfriends back in America.'

'Augie's not like that,' Joan protested. 'He hasn't got a girl back home, and he didn't try to get fresh, he only kissed me. I was supposed to meet him tonight, but they wouldn't let me out.'

Edna was sorry now Joan had told her. She didn't want to share that sort of secret, not when she thought their parents had a right to know. 'Don't tell me any more, Joan, 'cos if yer get caught and me mam finds out I knew what you were up to, I'd get into trouble, too.'

Edna's words had no effect on Joan. As usual, the only person she was interested in was herself. 'He probably won't want to see me again after letting him down tonight,' she moaned. 'But I've got the phone number of Burtonwood so I'm going to ring him tomorrow.'

Edna snuggled down between the sheets. 'Bring him home and let me mam and dad meet him. If he's as nice as you say, they won't mind you going out with him and then you wouldn't have to sneak behind their backs.'

'I'm not bringing him here!' Joan flashed. 'If he met me mam, I'd never see him again!'

Edna shot up. 'What's wrong with me mam? She's easy to get on with and everyone likes her.'

'But she's so fat and common! She doesn't . . .'

Edna was out of bed like a flash and she slapped her sister so hard across the face Joan's head snapped back. 'Don't you ever say anything like that about our mam. I've a good mind to go down now and tell her what you've been up to.'

'You promised!' Joan held on to Edna's arm and coaxed, 'Don't tell her, please?'

Edna shrugged her arm away as though she found her sister's touch distasteful. 'From now on keep your lies to yourself. I don't want to know what you do, where you go or who you go with. In fact, you can do me a favour and don't even talk to me. Me mam is the best mother in the world, and let me tell you something else, I'm ashamed to say you're me sister.'

Chapter Fifteen

'Yer know, you an' our Billy are like a couple of daft kids on a Saturday.' Eileen was relaxed on the couch as she smiled up at her husband. She tried in vain to cross her legs but gave up in disgust. She should really try and lose some weight, but it would mean going without chips and roast potatoes, a sacrifice too great for someone who loved their food. 'Yez go out of 'ere with yer red and white scarves on, grinnin' like a pair of Cheshire cats. It's a wonder yer don't buy yerselves one of them big rattle things.'

Bill was combing his hair in front of the mirror over the fireplace and his eyes met Eileen's through the glass. 'You must be a mind reader, chick, I was going to ask you to buy me one for Christmas.' Bill grinned as he plucked the stray hairs from the comb and threw them in the fire. 'I don't know why you don't come to the match with us one Saturday. You wouldn't half enjoy it, the atmosphere is marvellous when the Kop start singing. They make up their own words to the songs and they're dead funny.'

'Oh, aye!' Eileen pinched at the fat on her elbows. 'An' 'ow would I get through the turnstile . . . jump it?'

They heard footsteps running down the stairs and both pairs of eyes turned to the door. 'There's no hurry, son, we've plenty of time.' Bill smiled. 'I was just telling your mam she should come with us one day. She'd enjoy it, wouldn't she?'

'I'll say!' Billy chuckled as a thought struck him. 'She'd probably march down the pitch and thump the referee if she didn't agree with him.'

'I think two fanatics in the family is enough,' Eileen said as she looked from father to son with love shining in her eyes. 'My two handsome men.'

'What are you going to do with yourself, chick?' Bill asked as he slipped his coat on. 'Are you going to the shops with ma?'

'Me mam's gone to Mary's to sit with Mrs B for a few hours. Since they got that television she's never away from there. She can't understand 'ow yer can sit in yer own room and watch pictures comin' out of a little box. Mind you, I can't understand it meself, but I wouldn't tell 'er that.'

'I'll get you a television one of these days,' Bill promised. 'It'll keep you company.'

'I can do without one, thank you. We'll need all the money we can get for when me laddo here gets married.'

'I come out of me time in three months,' Billy said proudly. 'I won't know meself, getting a man's wage.'

'We'd better get a move on,' Billy said. 'We'll see you later, chick.'

Eileen went to the door to see them off and when she came back to the living room a wave of loneliness swept over her. God, but it was miserable when they were all out. She sat down at the table thinking that if she was still in her old house she wouldn't have to wonder what to do with herself. All she'd have to do was open her door and there were bound to be neighbours in the street to talk to. Or she could go up to the corner shop and spend an hour chatting to Milly.

Eileen pushed the chair back and stood up. 'I'm not stayin' here on me tod,' she told the empty room, 'or I'll go crazy. I may as well join me mam in front of Mary's television.'

There was a murder mystery on the television and Eileen wouldn't budge until she knew who the murderer was. She kept looking at the clock, telling herself it was time to get the tea started, but her backside stayed glued to the chair until the play was over. 'I'd 'ave sworn it was the feller with the moustache who did the killin'. Yer could have knocked me over with a feather when it turned out to be the girl that did it.'

'It just goes to show,' Maggie said, 'you can't trust anyone.' She took the television very seriously and sometimes Eileen wondered if her mother really knew it was all make-believe.

'It was a good film, was it?' Bill asked as Eileen bustled round setting the table. 'I bet it wasn't as exciting as the match, though.'

'We won again, Mam.' Billy was so happy you'd have thought he'd scored the winning goal. 'And Everton got beat.'

'I just can't understand men.' Eileen stood with the knives and forks in her hand. 'This city 'as got two football teams and yer'd think yer'd be glad when either of them won. But no, the fans are divided into two camps and they're daggers drawn! Harry came back from watchin' Everton with 'is chin touchin' 'is chest because they got beat, an' when he sees you he's goin' to get 'is leg pulled soft. Next week it'll be the other way round an' he'll 'ave the laugh on you. Honest, I wish yer'd grow up.'

Bill had bought the *Echo* on the way home from the match, and he'd been reading while Eileen was talking. 'Hey, Billy, listen to this. It says here that Liverpool might be getting a new manager.'

'Go way!' Billy sat down near his father, his face agog. 'What does it say?'

'They might be signing Don Welsh from Brighton, to take over from George Kay.'

'In the name of God, can yez think of nothin' else but bloody football?' Eileen banged the cutlery on the table. 'Bill Gillmoss, take that coat of yours off the couch and hang it on the hallstand. If the kids left theirs lyin' around, yer'd soon 'ave somethin' to say.'

'All right, chick, keep your hair on.' Bill winked at his son. 'Make a good referee, wouldn't she?'

'Well 'ave less of the "she", if yer don't mind.'

'I think I'll go out and come in again.' Bill was still grinning. After such a good match it would take a lot to dampen his spirits. 'See if I can get you in a better mood.'

'Yer know, I am in a bad mood.' Eileen was surprised herself. 'And I don't know why, unless that murder film's given me the willies.'

'I'll take you out for a drink tonight, cheer you up.' Bill dropped his head in his hands for a second, wondering whether he dare say what he was thinking. His shoulders started to shake with laughter that he couldn't hold back. 'We could take Harry for a pint to drown his sorrows after Everton's defeat.'

'Ooh, yer can be a bad bugger sometimes, Bill Gillmoss,' Eileen said. 'Yer sit there gloatin' when Liverpool win, but yer've got a right gob on yer when they lose.'

'It's only in fun, chick.' Bill stretched his legs. 'And Harry can give as good as he gets.'

Eileen and Bill were calling for the Sedgemoors at half seven and they were getting ready to go out when Vera arrived with Arthur. It was so unusual to see them together, Eileen couldn't hide her surprise. 'Gettin' daring, aren't yez, walkin' out together? What's brought this about, 'as Elsie Smith died, or somethin'?'

A deep laugh rumbled in Arthur's throat. 'Vera's decided that seeing as how she is now a single woman, we don't have to worry about Elsie.'

'Has yer divorce been finalised, then?'

Vera nodded, her happiness showing on her face. 'All over and done with.'

'Yez are a lousy pair, deprivin' Elsie of a juicy bit of gossip.' Eileen laughed. 'I wonder who she'll pick on now?'

'I don't care as long as it's not me.' Vera stole a shy glance at Arthur before saying, 'We thought you might like to come out for a drink to celebrate. Harry's mam's minding Carol for us, so we don't have to hurry back.'

'Well, you're just in time,' Bill said. 'We're going out with Mary and Harry so you can join us and we'll all celebrate.'

They sat in the snug of the local pub and Harry bought the first round. Raising his pint glass, he smiled at Vera. 'All the best, and may you have lots of happiness.'

Eileen lifted her sherry glass and said, ''Ear, 'ear.' She put the small glass down on the table and fixed her eyes on Arthur. 'When are yer goin' to make an honest woman of 'er?'

'Eileen!' Bill was shocked. 'It's none of our business!'

'Oh, God, 'ere he goes.' Eileen was sitting on a round stool which was completely hidden under her huge body, so when she slid round to face her husband she appeared to be moving on air. 'They're two of me best mates, aren't they? And best mates don't 'ave secrets from each other, so there!' She nodded to emphasise her words. 'If yer don't want to listen, Bill Gillmoss, then close yer lug 'oles.'

Bill shook his head. 'I give up. What would you do with her?'

Mary leaned forward, her hair swinging from her shoulders to frame her face. It only needed one glass of sherry for Mary to lose her shyness. 'Do what we all do, Billy, enjoy her.'

Arthur was watching Vera's face as he wondered how to answer Eileen's question. It was six months now since Sylvia died, time enough for him to sort himself out and help the boys come to terms with losing their mother. They were beginning to smile again, mixing in with other boys and starting to enjoy life as young boys should. Arthur felt it was time now to look to his own happiness and he had no doubt that it lay with Vera. He knew their feelings for each other were mutual, but each time he'd talked of marriage, she'd said they should wait until she was a free woman before discussing a future together.

Arthur shook his head to clear his mind when Eileen put a hand on his knee. 'Wakey, wakey, Arthur! We've 'ad two more drinks while yer've been asleep.'

Arthur blushed. 'Sorry about that, I was miles away.'

'Well, the men are goin' to drink in the bar so we girls can 'ave a good natter.' Eileen swivelled again to face Bill. 'I can't enjoy meself with my feller breathin' down me neck.'

Bill picked up his pint to follow Harry and Arthur. 'If she gets too personal, Vera, tell her to mind her own business.' He bent and kissed Eileen on the cheek, much to her embarrassment. 'Behave yourself.'

Eileen watched him walk away. 'He's an old stick in the mud, but I love the bones of him.' She hung on to the table as she lumbered to her feet. 'Shove up an' let me sit next to yer. I can only get one cheek of me backside on this fiddlin' little stool and it's gone all numb.'

'If you're after a confession, then you're out of luck,' Vera said. 'I've nothing to tell you.'

'Stop actin' the goat,' Eileen said, her eyes rolling. 'We all know you an' Arthur 'ave fancied each other for years, an' there's nothin' to stop yez gettin' married now.'

'It's not as easy as that,' Vera said. 'I only wish it was. But I don't know whether Arthur realises what he would be taking on. Carol will be with us for life. She'll never marry and leave home like other girls do, and I want to be sure he understands.'

'Vera!' Mary looked at her friend in disbelief. 'Carol's lovely! Any man would be glad to have her for a daughter.'

'Her own father didn't.' Vera sounded bitter. 'He was ashamed of her.'

'You stupid nellie!' Eileen's voice rose. 'Arthur's not Danny! Has 'e asked yer to marry 'im?'

Vera lowered her eyes. She couldn't count the number of nights she'd lain awake going over all this in her mind. 'He's mentioned it several times, but I keep putting him off. Now the divorce is through, though, I've no excuse for putting it off.'

'I don't believe I'm hearin' this,' Eileen said, her voice angry. 'If you're stupid enough to turn Arthur down, I'll never speak to yer again.' She picked up the three empty glasses and snorted, 'This is more like a ruddy wake than a celebration. I'm goin' for more drinks, and I don't know about you two, but I'm goin' to get blotto.'

Eileen banged the glasses down on the bar counter. 'Get those filled for us, Bill, will yer?' She jerked her head at Arthur. 'Come over 'ere a minute, I want a word with yer.'

They were a noisy, happy group when they left the pub at closing time. The drink had loosened their tongues and filled them with a sense of well-being. The three women walked in front of the men, their arms linked, with Eileen in the middle telling one of her endless supply of funny stories. They were too interested to notice the Jeep parked on the opposite side of the road, or the young girl sitting in the passenger seat.

Joan slid down in the seat and lowered her head to hide her face. 'There's my mum and dad.'

Augie viewed the group with interest. 'Which one's your mom?'

Joan heard Eileen's raucous laugh and groaned. How could she tell him that the loud-mouthed, fat woman was her mother? 'The one on the end with the long auburn hair,' she lied.

'She's a nice-looking woman. Why don't we just go out and say hello?'

'No,' Joan said sharply, 'not tonight.'

'Honey, are you ashamed of me?' Augie drummed his fingers on the steering wheel. 'It sure seems that way.'

'Of course not! It's just that since I stayed out all night that time, me mum and I haven't been on friendly terms. And I didn't tell her the truth,' Joan admitted. 'I told her I'd missed the last bus and stayed with a girl friend.'

'Oh, and you thought I'd let the cat out of the bag? Well, since I know, I wouldn't mention it. So there's no reason why you can't take me to meet your folks, is there, honey? We've been going out together for months now, and I would sure like to meet them.'

'I'll take you home soon, I promise,' Joan said, knowing it would be impossible now after the lie she'd just told.

Vera rubbed the sleep from her eyes and looked at herself in the mirror on the window ledge in the kitchen. There were dark circles under her eyes through lack of sleep, and as she ran the cold water to swill her face she thanked God it was Sunday and the boys and Carol were having a lie in. She'd have time to tidy around and make herself presentable before they came down for breakfast.

By ten o'clock Vera had finished her work. The living room was tidy, the fire had been raked out and reset, and she was washed and dressed. But although she'd kept herself busy, she couldn't keep her thoughts away from Arthur. Last night she'd had a good excuse for saying goodnight to him at the bottom of the street because she had to pick Carol up from the Sedgemoors', and as she'd said, it was late. But he was coming this afternoon at two o'clock and she knew he wouldn't listen to any more excuses. Vera took a deep breath and the pain in her chest was like a knife turning. She didn't want to send Arthur away, didn't want to lose him. She loved him so much she couldn't bear the thought of never seeing him again. But the fear in her heart wouldn't go away.

Vera called Colin and Peter as she climbed the stairs. 'Come on, sleepy heads, time to get up.' She knocked hard on their bedroom door. 'It's nearly dinner time.'

Carol was already out of bed and trying, in her own way, to pull her dress over her head. 'That's a good girl.' Vera pulled the dress down and fastened the three pearl buttons at the back. Carol was twelve now, and although she was a big girl for her age, she had the mentality of a four year old. She was able to do most things for herself but needed watching constantly. Vera never allowed her to play out in case she wandered off and got lost, and she'd never asked the other children in the street to keep an eye on her because she knew from experience that children could be very cruel.

'Come on, down we go.' As Vera walked down the stairs behind her daughter, her thoughts were on Arthur. He was very kind to Carol and very patient, and Carol thought the world of him. But would it work out?

These were the thoughts running through Vera's mind as she stood in the tiny kitchen frying bacon and eggs for breakfast. And when the children were sitting at the table talking she couldn't concentrate on the conversation.

'You're very quiet, Mum,' Colin said. 'Have you got a hangover?'

'I don't drink enough to get a hangover, you know that.' Vera smiled at her elder son. Colin was twenty and, like Peter, favoured Vera in looks. He was courting and spent much of his time at the home of his girlfriend, Glenda. 'I think I'm in for a cold, 'cos my head's splitting.'

Peter rubbed a piece of bread in the bacon dip and his face took on a look of pure bliss when he took a mouthful. 'You can't beat a Sunday breakfast,' he said, with his mouth half full. 'Did you go out with Arthur?'

Vera nodded. 'And the Gillmosses and the Sedgemoors. We had . . .' A knock on the front door took Vera's eyes to the clock on the mantelpiece. Half eleven, and Arthur wasn't due till two. 'I wonder who that can be?'

'Shall I go?' Colin asked.

'No, I'll go.' Vera stood up. 'It's probably a kid to say his ball's gone over the backyard wall.'

When Vera opened the front door and saw who was standing outside, all her strength drained away and she had to hold on to the door to stop herself from sliding to the floor. She opened her mouth but no sound would come.

'Hello, Vera.' Danny Jackson was wearing a smart suit, his hair was slicked back, and he looked as sure of himself as he ever had.

Vera was staring at him as though he was a ghost, and when she didn't answer, Danny said, 'Aren't you going to ask me in?'

'Who is it, Mum?' Colin came to look over his mother's shoulder, and his face darkened. 'What do you want?'

Danny stepped back a pace. He'd expected to see a boy, not the man Colin had grown into. 'I came to see how you all are. There's nothing wrong with a man wanting to see his family, is there?'

Colin moved Vera aside. 'You've left it a bit late, haven't you? Anyway, we don't want to see you, so go back to where you've been for the last four years.'

Temper flared in Danny's eyes but it disappeared quickly and a smile crossed his face. 'I don't mean no harm. Surely I can come into me own house?'

Vera pulled on Colin's arm. 'Let him in before he starts yelling and the neighbours hear.'

Peter, a trickle of fat running down his chin, stared open mouthed. And Carol, though not recognising their visitor, ran to put her arm around Vera's waist. 'Mummy.'

'It's all right, darling, go and finish your breakfast.' Vera stood by the table, her gaze on Danny's face. What was he doing here after all this time? What was he after?

'Is there a cup of tea in the pot?' Danny walked over to his old chair and sat down. 'How are you, Peter?'

Peter gulped, not knowing what to do. He could see his mother was upset and Colin's face was red with anger. Why had they let him in? They should have chased him, sent him packing. Anyway, he thought, I'm not having anything to do with him.

Peter picked up his plate and marched silently out to the kitchen. Seconds later he reappeared, passed his father without a glance and made for the stairs. 'I'm getting dressed, then I'm going out.'

Colin rubbed his thumb across the corner of his mouth. He could see his mother was in a state of shock and didn't want to make things worse for her, but somebody had to ask the question. 'What did you come for, Dad?'

'I told you. I just wanted to see me family.' Danny's hands hung loose between his legs. 'I didn't come to cause trouble.'

'I'll make a fresh pot of tea.' Vera escaped to the kitchen. This wasn't the Danny she remembered. he was slimmer, quieter, better dressed and not so quick with his temper. The old Danny would have lashed out at Colin if he'd dared answer him back. Perhaps he's changed, Vera thought as she filled the kettle.

'You know me mum's not married to you now, don't you?' Colin fixed Danny with an icy stare. 'You're divorced now.'

'I know, son.' Danny spread his hands out. 'Honestly, I just wanted to see you all. I've wanted to for a long time.'

'You've left it too late.' Colin towered over his father. 'Four years too late.'

Vera came through carrying the tea pot, Carol hanging tightly on to her skirt. She saw the anger on Colin's face and felt the tension in the air. The last thing she wanted to see was father and son fighting. 'Aren't you supposed to be going to Glenda's, Colin?'

'There's no hurry.' Colin was remembering the times he'd seen his mother taking a hiding from this man. He'd been too young then to stop him, but things were different now, he was a man. 'I want to know what's brought him here after all this time?'

'I'll deal with this, you go and get ready.' Vera nodded, her eyes sending the message that it would be all right. She wasn't afraid of Danny any more. 'Glenda will be waiting for you.'

Vera sat Carol on the couch with her coloured picture book, then poured Danny a cup of tea. She didn't speak or meet his eyes as she handed him the cup. Then she began clearing the breakfast dishes.

Anything to kill time until both boys were out of the house. It was only when she heard the door bang, and the shadows of her sons passed the window, that Vera sat down. 'Well, Danny, what did you come for?'

'Why will nobody believe me? I've been wanting to come for a long time because, to tell yer the truth, I've missed you . . . all of you.'

'What's the matter, Danny, did your Dutch girlfriend throw you out? Is that it?'

Danny's expression gave no hint that Vera had hit the nail on the head. It would spoil his plan if she knew the truth. 'Leaving you was the most stupid thing I've ever done in me life, and that's bein' honest. I didn't know when I was lucky. I'd 'ave come back ages ago, but I was too proud to admit I was wrong.' Danny clasped his hands together and gazed into Vera's eyes. He had to make her believe him because he had nowhere else to go. That bitch had thrown him out, lock, stock and barrel. 'I want to know if you'll 'ave me back, Vera?'

Vera studied Danny's face. He's either a very good liar, or he really has changed, she told herself. But as Colin had said, he'd left it too late. Too late for her, and the children.

There was a rap on the window and Vera jumped. 'I'll see who it is.'

'I know I'm early, but I couldn't wait any longer.' Arthur stepped into the tiny hall and bent to kiss Vera's cheek. 'I had to see you.'

Vera put her hand on Arthur's arm, intending to tell him who was sitting in the living room, but changed her mind. Let whatever was going to happen, happen. No whispering, no secrets, everything above board.

Arthur stared at the man who was sitting at ease in the chair he usually sat in .'Hello.' He let his hand ruffle Carol's hair as she clung to his coat. 'We haven't met before?'

'Arthur, this is Danny.' Vera's voice was calm. 'Danny, this is a friend of mine, Arthur Kennedy.'

The smile left Arthur's face and he stared with dislike at Danny. 'What are you doing here?'

'What's that got to do with you?' Danny glared back. 'Seein' as this is my house, I should ask you what you're doin' here?'

'No, Danny,' Vera said. 'This is not your house, it's mine. Your name was taken off the rent book when you did a bunk and left your family.'

'Well, I'm here now.' Danny's face was turning purple, his breathing heavy. 'I've come back to you.'

Danny could feel his anger rising and lowered his head to try and control his emotions. He felt like thumping the bastard, whoever he was, but to show his temper now would only jeopardize his chances with Vera.

When he looked up his face showed no trace of the rage burning within. He ignored Arthur and appealed to Vera, his voice soft. 'Couldn't we have a talk in private, like? I'd like to ask yer some personal questions and I don't need a stranger present.'

'Forget it, mate!' Arthur didn't give Vera a chance to answer. 'I'm not going anywhere.'

Danny jumped up, unable to hold his temper in check any longer. 'Don't you poke yer nose in my affairs or I'll flatten it for yer.' He saw the look Arthur gave Vera and his lips curled. 'Oh, I get it!' He sneered, 'He's yer fancy man, is he?'

Vera stepped between the two men. 'You had me fooled for a while there, Danny. I actually felt sorry for you, believing you really missed your family and cared for them. Not that it would have made any difference because I wouldn't have you back for all the money in the world. But I would have felt some sympathy for you. But it was all an act, you haven't changed, not one little bit.'

Danny pushed Vera aside so forcibly she stumbled into the table. His face ugly with venom, he poked his finger into Arthur's chest, roaring like a bull, 'You sling yer hook and leave me an' me wife to sort this out. You've got no business here.'

Arthur pushed Danny's hand away before grabbing him by the lapels of his jacket. 'I'm warning you, don't you dare lay a finger on me. And for your information I am not Vera's fancy man. Oh, I would have been if she'd let me, but your ex-wife,' he stressed the last two words, 'has too much self respect for that. So watch that mouth of yours, unless you want me to close it for you.'

Carol, frightened by the shouting, pulled at Arthur's coat. 'Uncle Arthur, he's bad man.'

Without releasing his grip on Danny, Arthur looked down into wide eyes filled with fear. 'It's all right, sweetheart, you go to mummy. The man is just leaving.'

'Who the 'ell d'yer think you are?' Danny blustered. He hadn't expected this. It had never entered his head that Vera would have a new man in her life.

141

'I'll tell you who I think I am.' Arthur let go of Danny's lapels and pushed him away. 'I'm the man who's going to marry Vera.'

'Oh, aye!' Danny turned to Vera and the venom she saw in his eyes took her breath away. The mask had slipped and she saw him for what he'd always been. A violent, bad-tempered, wicked man. 'Yer don't believe he'll marry yer, do yer? D'yer think he's daft enough to take her on?' Danny nodded to where Carol was cowering behind her mother. 'He's havin' yer on so he can get what he wants. He'll fill his boots, then bugger off and leave yer.'

'That does it, I'm not standing here being insulted by a loud-mouthed slob.' Arthur nodded to Vera to open the door, and he moved so quickly Danny was caught off guard. Before he knew what had hit him, he'd been spun round, grabbed by the scruff of the neck and propelled through the door and into the street.

'A word of warning,' Arthur said from the height of the top step, 'which I would advise you to heed. If I hear you've been within a mile of Vera, I'll have the police on to you. That's after I've given you the biggest hiding you've ever had in your life.' With that Arthur slammed the door so hard it could be heard the length of the street.

Danny raised his foot in anger but checked himself before it came into contact with the door. If he made a scene the neighbours would be out and he wasn't going to fill their mouths, or give them the satisfaction of saying Danny Jackson had come crawling back and been thrown out.

Danny straightened his jacket, adopted a jaunty air and strode down the street. He wasn't finished, not by a long chalk. He'd come back when Vera was on her own. If that bloke hadn't turned up, another half an hour and he'd have had her eating out of his hand. Oh, he'd be back all right, and next time he'd be here to stay.

Elsie Smith let the curtain fall back into place. She'd seen Danny pass earlier and was still at the window when Arthur went by. She hadn't even started the dinner because she was too frightened of missing anything to leave her spec by the window. 'There's been some right goings-on at the Jacksons.' She folded her arms across her flat chest, the lines on her forehead deepening. 'Danny didn't stay long when the queer feller arrived. I told you there was something fishy going on with Vera and that bloke but you wouldn't have it. But he must have his feet under the table 'cos he's just thrown Danny out.'

Her husband, Fred, turned a page of the *News Of The World*. For two hours now he'd had a running commentary on the comings and goings at next door but one. He thought his wife was going to have a fit when she saw Danny passing, she was that excited. And when Arthur arrived she was so beside herself with curiosity her head nearly went through the window pane.

Fred laid the paper down. He didn't know why he bothered buying the *News Of The World* when his wife contained more gossip than the paper. 'I'm surprised Danny had the nerve to show his face in the street after all this time. He certainly won't get a welcome off any of the neighbours.'

Elsie's thin lips formed a straight, tight line. 'I'd love to know what's goin' on between Vera and that other feller. He's there nearly every night.'

'You'll find out soon enough.' Fred crossed his legs and picked up the paper. If anyone could find out, it was his wife, and she wouldn't rest until she did.

Elsie glared at her husband's back as she passed on her way to the kitchen. He never got excited about anything. All he lived for were the boys, his work and reading the blasted papers.

Elsie opened the oven door to get the roasting tin out. Her husband forgotten, her thoughts went again to the Jacksons. She'd have given anything to have been a fly on the wall when Danny and Arthur met. I bet there was a right bust up, she thought. Anyway, she'd get talking to Lizzie Sedgemoor tomorrow and just casually mention she'd seen Danny. Lizzie was friendly with Vera, so she was bound to know what was going on. Elsie bent to light the gas in the oven, a half smile on her face. Yes, that's what she'd do.

Chapter Sixteen

It was Wednesday afternoon and Mary was sitting across the table from Eileen telling of Tony's exploits at school while they waited for Vera. It was Eileen's turn for their usual get-together when they exchanged gossip over tea and cakes.

'He fell and scraped his knee,' Mary said. 'It looked really sore but he said it didn't hurt. In fact he looked quite proud of himself.'

'You don't know how lucky yer are with 'im. Remember what our Billy was like? A real tearaway, he was!' Eileen grinned. 'He broke more windows in our street playing footie than all his mates put together. We had many a good laugh over our Billy's antics though, didn't we?'

Mary flicked her head, sending her blond hair cascading over her shoulders. 'If our Tony grows up to be as nice as him, I'll consider meself lucky.'

'Yeah, he's a cracker.' Eileen's eyes shone with pride. 'Yer don't get many like 'im in a pound.'

When the expected knock came, Mary stood up. 'I'll go.'

'I'm sorry I'm late.' Vera cast a nervous glance at Mary. 'I hope you don't mind, but I met Maggie coming back from the shops and when she said she was calling in to see your mam, I asked her if she'd mind Carol for half-an-hour.'

'Course I don't mind.' Mary closed the front door. 'Me mam's always glad to see Carol.'

'Where've you been?' Eileen asked. 'We'd almost given yer up.'

'I called into Mary's for a few minutes.' Vera slipped her coat off and threw it over the arm of the couch. 'I've got something to tell you and I didn't want Carol to hear, so I've left her with your Mam and Mrs B.'

Eileen leaned her elbows on the table and cupped her face in her hands. 'Is it something excitin'?'

'It depends what you mean by exciting.' Vera pulled a chair out and sat down. 'I got the shock of me life.'

'Well, out with it,' Eileen said, shuffling to the edge of her chair. 'If yer keep me in suspense much longer I'll 'ave to run to the lavvy.'

Taking a deep breath, Vera related the events of Sunday, leaving nothing out. She carried on talking through the gasps of disbelief from her friends, until she reached the part where Arthur had banged the door on Danny.

'Well, I'll be blowed!' Eileen bellowed. 'Yer mean the cheeky sod just knocked on yer door, after all that time, an' expected to be welcomed back with open arms? I'd 'ave broken 'is bloody neck for 'im.'

'That's not all,' Vera told them. 'He came back again on Monday when he knew the boys would be out at work. He probably thought if he got me on me own, he could sweet talk me round.'

Vera gazed from Eileen to Mary, then lowered her head to watch her finger making circles on the table. 'He was as nice as pie at first, you'd have thought butter wouldn't melt in his mouth. But when he realised I meant it when I said I wouldn't have him back, he changed his tune and ranted and raved. He even lifted his hand a few times as though he was going to give me a belt, and I didn't turn a hair. I just stood there, staring him out, letting him see that I'm not the least bit frightened of him any more.'

'Well, I never!' Eileen's layer of chins moved when she shook her head. 'I know Danny's a hard clock, but I didn't think he'd 'ave the gall to show 'is face again.'

'It's a wonder Arthur didn't say anything in work,' Mary said. 'He has his dinner with Harry and Bill every day in the canteen.'

'Don't blame Arthur, I asked him not to tell anyone. And he doesn't know Danny came back on Monday 'cos I didn't tell him or the boys. They were angry and upset enough, it was no good making things worse.'

'And Colin stood up to 'im, did he?' Eileen chuckled. 'He'd get a shock seein' 'ow big his sons 'ave grown.'

'Well, it's all over now,' Vera said. 'We've seen the last of Danny Jackson.'

'I wouldn't bank on that,' Eileen said. 'He's got nerve enough for anythin'.'

'No, he'll not be back.' Vera twisted a lock of hair that had fallen across her face. 'When I think of it I feel real proud of meself the way I stood up to him. As cool as a cucumber, I asked him to leave because the very sight of him made me want to vomit, made my skin crawl.'

'That's tellin' him, kiddo!' Eileen touched her friend's shoulder. 'I'm proud of yer.'

'You've got more guts than me,' Mary said. 'I'd have run a mile from him.'

'It was seeing him and Arthur together that gave me the courage. Arthur would make ten of him, any day.'

'But yer won't marry 'im?' Eileen clicked her tongue. 'Yer want yer bumps feelin', Vera.'

Vera tilted her head to one side and her eyes locked with Eileen's. 'Me and Arthur had a good talk on Sunday, and I got a feeling someone had been telling tales out of school. Am I right, Eileen?'

Eileen had the grace to blush. 'Well, yer both me mates, aren't yer? An' if yer think I'm just goin' to sit back an' let two of me mates ruin their lives, yer've got another think comin'.'

'I'm not angry, Eileen, I'm glad you did. You were right about Arthur, and I was wrong. He's a good man and I'm counting my blessings.'

Eileen leaned forward, her heavy bust resting on the table. 'Yer mean yer goin' to marry 'im?'

'Yes. I've told Colin and Peter and they're over the moon.'

'Yippee! I can buy meself a big 'at now!' Eileen brought her clenched fist down on the table, her eyes lost in the folds of flesh on her chubby, smiling face. 'I'll get a good one so it will do for when our Billy gets married.'

Eileen's excitement was contagious and Vera felt happiness bubbling inside her. 'Hey, slow down, Eileen! We won't be getting married for ages. Don't forget there'll be seven of us with Arthur's two boys, so we'll need a bigger house.' Vera knew she sounded like a young girl instead of a forty-four-year-old woman, but she was so happy she wanted to share it with her friends. 'Anyway, Arthur said he's going to court me properly first.'

'Oh, my God, love's young dream.' Eileen was so excited her backside kept leaving the seat of her chair. 'A real Sir Galahad, is Arthur. All he needs is a white 'orse.' She opened her mouth and let out a roar of laughter. 'I can just imagine Elsie Smith's face if he trotted down the street on a 'orse and tethered it to the lamppost.'

Vera joined in her laughter. 'Arthur said he's going to knock on

147

Elsie's door and introduce himself. He's heard that much about her he can't wait to meet her, I'm sure he thinks I exaggerate when I tell him how nosy she is.'

Mary's eyes were all dreamy. 'We've all hoped this would happen, Vera, and I'm made up for you. Arthur's a lovely, kind man and he'll make you a marvellous husband.'

Vera's face became serious. 'You're both used to being spoilt by your husbands, but I've never known it before. I've never been treated as though I'm someone special. Never been waited on, had doors opened for me or been given presents of flowers and chocolates. But Arthur does all those things and it's boosted my confidence, given me back my pride.'

'Keep that up an' yer'll 'ave me bawlin' me eyes out.' Eileen sniffed up. 'Before I put the kettle on, just answer me one question. Do yer love the man?'

A blush covered Vera's face. 'Yes, I love him.'

'All the excitement,' Eileen laughed. 'Just like yer see on the films, only better like.'

'You're a sucker for a happy ending, aren't you, chick?' Bill had listened in silence, his face changing from surprise to pleasure as Eileen brought him up-to-date with the news. No one could tell a story as well as his wife, even if she did add little details of her own to make it more dramatic. 'I'm very pleased for both of them. In fact it's good news all round, because Arthur's two boys need a woman to look after them. They need a proper home where there'll be a fire lit when they come in and a meal on the table.'

The door burst open and Edna appeared. 'Mam, our Joan must have me new blouse on, I've looked everywhere for it.'

Eileen shook her head, tutting, 'She's a little flamer, that one.'

'It's not fair, Mam!' Edna said indignantly. 'I only bought it on Wednesday an' I haven't even worn it meself yet.'

'I'll 'ave a word with 'er when she comes in.' Eileen could understand Edna's frustration. She didn't earn much as a junior shop assistant and had to count every penny. 'When I've finished with 'er, she won't be borrowin' any more of yer clothes.'

'She had no right to take it without askin'.' Edna's face was flushed with the injustice of it. 'I had to save up for four weeks to buy it.'

'I'll have a word with her, love,' Bill said. 'She won't do it again.'

'I don't want it back, she can keep it.' Edna fled from the room and tears streamed down her face as she climbed the stairs. She'd had her eye on the pink satin blouse for weeks and was so proud when she'd walked out of Etam's with it. And when she'd tried it on in front of the mirror in the bedroom, she thought it really suited her.

Edna sat on the side of the bed, devastated. She'd meant what she said about not wanting the blouse back. Now Joan had worn it, it wasn't new any more, so her sister could keep it. But she'd make her pay for it, right down to the last penny.

Edna snuggled under the bedclothes in the darkened bedroom waiting for her sister. She was dead tired and only determination kept her from dropping off to sleep. The hands on the illuminated clock told her it was a quarter to twelve so she shouldn't have much longer to wait. Billy had not long come in and she could hear him moving around in the room next door. He was a smasher, their Billy, always happy and good humoured. What a pity their Joan wasn't the same.

Edna heard the key in the lock and raised her head from the pillow to listen for footsteps on the stairs. When the door opened and Joan crossed to switch the bedside lamp on, Edna closed her eyes and pretended to be asleep. Through half-closed lids she watched her sister take her coat off, revealing the dusky pink blouse with the lace collar.

Joan hung her coat in the wardrobe and turned to find Edna sitting on the side of the bed. 'I thought you were asleep.'

'You mean you hoped I was.' Edna's face was blazing. 'You can't keep yer hands off anything, can you? Greedy and selfish, that's what you are.'

Joan pulled the blouse over her head and threw it on Edna's bed, a sneer on her sulky face. 'Here, cry baby, take it.'

'Not on your life, I won't!' Edna was off the bed like a flash and shoved the blouse into Joan's face. 'You needn't think I'm wearing this after you.' Her nose wrinkled. 'It stinks of your scent.' Mindful of the sleeping household, she lowered her voice. 'I want the money for a new one and yer can keep this, seein' as you like it so much.'

'That's a laugh,' Joan spoke scornfully. 'Just try and get the money off me.'

'Oh, I don't have to, me mam will!' Edna watched the change of

149

expression on her sister's face and derived some satisfaction from it. 'Yes, I told me mam and dad.'

Joan's eyes narrowed. 'Running to Mummy to tell tales, eh? Why don't you grow up?'

'I didn't tell Mummy and Daddy,' Edna mimicked her sister's voice, 'I told me mam and dad.'

Joan dropped her head. All this fuss over a stupid blouse. But the last thing she wanted was trouble with her parents. So her face took on a look of penitence. 'I didn't think you'd mine me borrowing it, and I'm sorry. I'll wash and iron it for you.'

'Don't bother, I don't want the blouse, I want the money for it.' Edna turned her back in disgust and climbed into bed. 'And if you don't give it to me, I'll tell me mam.' She turned on her side and pulled the bedclothes up to her ears. She wouldn't have minded if Joan didn't have many clothes, but she had a wardrobe full of them. Anyway, perhaps this would teach her sister not to take something that didn't belong to her. 'Put the light out and let me get to sleep.'

Billy inserted the key in the lock, then turned his head to look at Mavis. 'I can't wait to see their faces.'

Her eyes shining with happiness, Mavis gave him a gentle push. 'Go on, hurry up.'

Eileen's greeting was one of surprise and pleasure. 'You're back early, aren't yer? Did yer mam throw 'im out, Mavis? I wouldn't blame 'er if she did 'cos she must be fed up lookin' at 'is ugly puss. He spends more time at your 'ouse than he does 'ere.'

Billy sat on the couch and pulled Mavis down beside him. 'Where's me dad?'

'Upstairs gettin' his clothes ready for work tomorrow.' Eileen's eyes narrowed. 'Is there somethin' up?'

'Me and Mavis have got something to tell you.' Billy grinned. 'We'll wait for me dad to come down.'

Eileen's heart missed a beat. Oh, Lord, was Mavis in the family way? Then she saw the twinkling in Mavis's eyes and knew she was wrong. She lumbered to her feet, silently calling herself a bad-minded so-and-so. 'I'll give him a shout.'

'Hey, Bill!' Eileen yelled from the bottom of the stairs. 'Get that bag of bones of yours down 'ere, we've got company.'

'Be right down, chick!'

Edna had been lying on top of her bed reading when she heard her mother call. She put the book down quickly and made a dash for the stairs, jumping them two at a time. 'Oh, it's you two! I thought it was someone important when me mam said we had visitors.'

'Ta very much.' Mavis's laugh was high with nerves. 'I suppose we're just a couple of tramps?'

'I should 'ave known you wouldn't miss anythin'.' Eileen pulled a face at Edna. 'It wouldn't be a show without Punch.' Bill came into the room then and Eileen said, 'Here's the man 'imself.'

'What's all the fuss?' Bill smiled a welcome. 'I thought at least it was the Lord Mayor.'

'Our Billy wants a word with us,' Eileen said. 'So sit down an' let 'im get it off 'is chest before he conks out.'

Bill sat in his chair and lit a cigarette before turning to his son. 'Right, we're all ears.'

Billy's adam's apple moved up and down as he tried to dislodge the lump in his throat. 'Yer remember the Bowers that lived opposite to us in the old 'ouse, don't yer? You know, Jean and Gordon and their children, Jane and David?'

'Billy, I'm not goin' forgetful in me old age, of course I remember Jean and Gordon.' Eileen looked puzzled. 'What about them?'

'They're emigrating to Canada. They've been trying for over a year and they've just heard they've been accepted.'

Eileen's mouth fell open. 'Yer not thinking of goin' to live in Canada, are yez?' She felt weak with fear. 'Oh, my God!'

'No, Mam, of course not.' Billy's face was creased in a huge grin. 'I wouldn't move that far from you an' me dad.'

Eileen looked up to the ceiling and put her hands together as though in prayer. 'Oh, thank you.'

'What's this leading up to, son?' Bill asked. 'Because it is leading to something, isn't it?'

Billy nodded, then prodded by Mavis, asked, 'Would you mind if we got married sooner than we intended? Yer see, we'd like to try and get their house when the Bowers leave. Mrs Radford said she'd have a word with the landlord, an' she thinks we'd be in with a good chance.'

'Yer mean yer'd be goin' back to Bray Street?' Eileen leaned forward so quickly she nearly toppled over. 'Ooh, yer lucky things!'

'It would be a good start to married life for you.' Bill threw his cigarette end into the fire. 'A nice little house, and near Mavis's family and all your friends.'

'We mightn't get it, but I wanted to ask you and me mam first, before I went after it.' Billy hung his head. 'I feel a bit mean about it really because I've never been able to give me mam much money for me keep. And just when I'm going on full wages and could give more, I up and get married.'

'Let that be the least of your worries, son,' Bill said. 'What your mam and I have never had, we'll never miss. All we want is for our children to be happy.'

'Mam, how d'you feel about it? D'you mind?'

Eileen's eyes were misty as she gazed at her son. He was always so thoughtful and considerate, and she loved him dearly. She wouldn't half miss him when he was gone. She straightened up. This was no time for tears. 'I'm over the moon. I'll be able to come to Bray Street for me holidays.'

Billy stood up and walked over to her. He put his arms around her and hugged her tight. 'Mam, I love you so much I could eat you.' He planted a kiss on her cheek. 'Thanks for being the best mam in the world.'

Edna hadn't spoken a word, just sat and taken it all in. Now she asked Mavis, 'What colour bridesmaids' dresses are yer havin'?'

Eileen roared with laughter. 'Practical Annie! If they get married too soon, we'll all turn up at the church in our nuddy.'

'We'll manage,' Bill said, moved by Billy's show of emotion. 'I've got enough put by, unless you want a big posh affair.'

'We'll have what we can afford.' Billy sat down again and took hold of Mavis's hand. 'We're not starting married life off in debt. As long as we've got two chairs to sit on, a table and a bed, that'll do until we can afford more.'

'Bring yer mam and dad down one day, Mavis,' Eileen said, 'and we'll put our 'eads together an' see what we come up with.'

'Let's wait and see if we get the house first, Mam. Everything hinges on that.'

After Billy and Mavis had left, Eileen went into the front room to Maggie who was listening to a play on the wireless. 'Yer've missed all the excitement, Mam.'

Maggie turned the volume down. 'Why, what have I missed?'

'Get yer coat on an' come up to Mary's with me. I'm not goin' through the whole story with you an' then again with Mary. So shake a leg, missus, and let's get the show on the road.'

Maggie folded her arms, 'I'm in the middle of listening to a play and I want to hear how it ends.'

Eileen made for the door. 'Okay, missus, if yer not interested in yer grandson gettin' married, then it's no skin off my nose.'

Maggie was out of her chair like a shot. 'I'll get me coat.'

Chapter Seventeen

Vera had never been one for having neighbours popping in for a natter, or perhaps to borrow something. Not because she didn't want to be friendly, 'cos heaven knows there were times when she would have welcomed company with open arms. But she was afraid of Danny. She never knew when he was going to be in one of his foul moods, insulting and sarcastic, so she kept herself to herself. And when he'd walked out on her, she'd felt so worthless she became more reclusive. The only real friends she had were the Gillmosses and the Sedgemoors, and the only neighbour who ever called in was Harry's mother, Lizzie Sedgemoor. So when a knock came on the door on the Thursday morning, Vera opened the door with a smile on her face, expecting to find Lizzie standing on the step.

'Hello, Vera.' Danny's spirits lifted, thinking the smile was for him. 'Is there a cup of tea in the pot?'

'What d'you want, Danny?' Vera half closed the door. 'I thought I made it plain the other day that I didn't want to see you again.'

'I've been down to the docks to ask for me old job back,' Danny said. 'I start on Monday.'

'I'm glad for you, but will you please go away now? I'm just getting Carol ready to go to the shops.'

'Surely ten minutes isn't going to make that much difference.' Danny's voice was sickly sweet. 'I've got so much time on me hands I don't know what to do with meself. Just a cup of tea and I'll be on me way.'

Vera's brain was ticking over like mad. She knew she shouldn't let him in, Arthur and the boys would go mad, but perhaps it would be quicker than standing at the door arguing with him. She pulled the door back. 'Ten minutes, Danny, no longer.'

Carol left her toys when she saw who their visitor was and ran to

155

put her arms around Vera's waist. 'Mummy?'

'It's all right, darling, we're going to the shops soon. Come to the kitchen and help Mummy make a cup of tea.'

Danny looked completely at ease as he sipped his tea, talking about the old mates he'd seen down at the docks. 'I'll be glad to start work and get a few bob in me pocket. You know I've never been work shy, don't yer, Vera?'

Vera nodded. It was true he'd never been out of work and also true he liked a few bob in his pockets. But what Danny seemed to have forgotten was that she saw very little of the money he earned. He kept most of it for himself, to buy booze and cigarettes while she had to eke out the meagre pittance he gave her.

'When I get meself organised I'll be able to slip you a few bob,' Danny said. 'You can buy yerself some clothes, and something for Carol.' He smiled at his daughter, who was half hidden behind Vera. 'You'd like a new dolly, wouldn't you, love?'

'Carol has enough toys, and anyway, you'll need all your money to get yourself fixed up with somewhere to live,' Vera said to remind him he was no longer part of her life.

Danny seemed not to hear. Instead, he stood up and put the now empty cup on the table. He'd thought out his plan of action very carefully, and that was to keep cool, take things slowly and not to put pressure on Vera. 'I'll be off and let you get on with what you 'ave to do.'

Surprised, Vera followed him to the door. He was as meek as a lamb today but she knew better than to trust him. 'Goodbye, Danny.'

'Thanks for the tea.' With a wave of his hand Danny was off down the street, leaving Vera with a puzzled expression on her face. What she didn't see was her ex-husband's smile of satisfaction. Things had gone just as he planned. Another couple of calls like today, keeping his temper and being pleasant, and he'd have his foot in the door.

'Where are you off to tonight?' Vera asked Colin as they sat around the table having their tea. 'Anywhere nice?'

'Glenda wants to go to the Empire to see Donald Peers.' Colin screwed his face up. 'I don't want to go, but Glenda thinks he's the last word.'

'Go on, yer big cissie,' Peter laughed. 'Fancy going to see him!' He started to warble, 'By a babbling brook.'

Colin smiled good naturedly. 'Wait till you've got a girlfriend, clever clogs, and see the things you'll be doing in the name of love.'

Vera gazed from Colin to Peter. They were good boys, never caused her a moment's heartache. Sighing, she pushed a potato around her plate. She really should tell them about their dad calling. If she didn't, and one of the neighbours did, they'd think she was underhanded. Taking her courage in both hands, she said, 'Your dad called today.'

The boys' mouths stopped chewing, the smiles left their faces. 'Aw, Mam, yer didn't let him in, did you?' When Vera nodded, Colin said, 'You should have chased him!'

'He only called to say he'd got his old job back. He wasn't here more than ten minutes.'

'Mam, he's trying to work his way back in,' Peter said softly. 'Don't you see that?'

'Yes, I do see that. But he is your father and one day you might feel differently about him.'

'No chance!' Colin said. 'I don't ever want to set eyes on him again and neither does Peter.'

'What about Arthur?' Peter asked. 'You're going to marry him soon, and he won't be very happy if me dad keeps popping up.'

'I'm not going to upset Arthur by telling him, and I don't want either of you to mention it. I don't want anything to do with your dad but I want to satisfy meself that you know what you're doing.'

'Mam, this has been a happy house since he went away, it certainly wasn't while he was here,' Colin said. 'Me and Peter haven't forgotten how he left you swinging to bring the three of us up on your own. Never once did he write to ask how you were managing or if we were all right. We could have been dead for all he cared.' Colin pushed his plate away. 'Me and Peter know what we're talking about and we don't want to see him again. We don't even think of him as our father.'

Peter nodded. 'Colin's right, Mam. When you marry Arthur he'll be our dad. He's been more of a father to us than our real one ever was.'

Colin picked up his plate. 'If he calls again, don't let him in. Tell him what we said and send him on his way.' He stopped halfway to the kitchen. 'Promise?'

Vera nodded. 'I promise.'

★ ★ ★

Elsie Smith was cleaning the inside of her windows with a chammy leather when Danny passed. Never one to hide her curiosity, she rested her clenched fists on the window ledge. She heard him knock at Vera's door and pressed her face against the glass pane waiting to see if he went inside. He was smiling and Elsie saw his mouth moving but couldn't hear what he was saying. Then she saw his expression change to one of anger and heard him shout, 'Let me in!'

There was silence for a few seconds, then Danny's arms started to flay as though he was shadow boxing. 'Fred's right,' Elsie spoke aloud, her teeth gnashing so hard her false dentures were dislodged. 'He's got a flamin' nerve coming round here throwing his weight around.'

Then Elsie saw Vera being pulled into the street and blows being rained on to her body. One arm of Vera's was covering her face while with the other she was trying to push Danny away.

Elsie threw the chammy leather down and ran to the kitchen where she picked up a long-handled sweeping brush. 'He's not gettin' away with that!'

Danny never knew what hit him. The first blow from the brush sent him reeling against the wall, a look of amazement on his face. When he saw Elsie brandishing the brush he roared with anger, 'Get back in yer house before I flatten yer, yer nosy faggot.'

By this time the noise had brought several women to their doors. Had it been necessary every one of them would have gone to Vera's aid. None would have stood by and let a man beat a woman. But one look at Elsie Smith's face told them their help wasn't needed. Only the size of six pennyworth of copper, she stood her ground, her thin lips pursed, her eyes blazing. Pushing the bristles of the brush in Danny's face, she taunted, 'Go on, flatten me, if yer dare.'

Danny made a grab for the brush but Elsie was too quick for him and side stepped. One of the women called out to ask if she should run up to the police station but Elsie shook her head. Although she looked fierce, she was enjoying every minute of it. Wait till she told Fred! This bit of news would get his nose out of the *Echo*. 'Well? Didn't yer say yer were going to flatten me?'

Danny looked at the group of women who had gathered, their arms folded, their faces telling him they meant business. He spread his hands out and spoke quietly, 'I only want to talk to me wife. What's wrong with that?'

Vera was leaning against the wall, her head dropped in shame.

She was rubbing her arms where Danny's punches had landed. It had never been known for Elsie Smith to show compassion, but seeing Vera's distressed face filled her with anger. Once more the brush was pushed into Danny's face. 'Speak with yer hands, do yer, eh?' Elsie jabbed the hard bristles into the now frightened man's neck. 'On yer way, Danny Jackson, before I let yer have it over the head.'

Danny made one more effort. He looked at Vera and pleaded, 'Tell them I only want to talk to yer.'

Vera met his eyes. 'You are not my husband and I do not want you in my house.' Her gaze swept from Elsie to the group of neighbours. 'We are divorced.'

A cackle left Elsie's mouth. 'There y'are then.' She lifted the brush as though to bring it down on Danny's head and he took to his heels and fled down the street with Elsie in hot pursuit, the jeers of the women ringing in his ears.

Arthur knocked on the door and smiled when it was opened by Elsie. 'I've come to thank you.' He held out his hand. 'My name's Arthur Kennedy and I'm a friend of Vera's.'

Elsie shook the outstretched hand, her eyes bright with curiosity. Now she'd find out what was going on between this man and Vera. 'Won't you come in?'

Arthur accepted a cup of tea and although he'd been told what had happened that afternoon, he listened attentively to Elsie's version. 'You were very brave and I can't thank you enough,' Arthur said. 'Vera's had enough troubles without Danny making more for her.'

Fred took an instant liking to Arthur and they got on like a house on fire. Over the next half hour Elsie was in her element listening to Arthur talking about his sons, and how he and Vera were getting married when they could find a bigger house.

A smile crossed Elsie's thin face. Fred had praised her no end when she'd told him what happened. Told her he was proud of her, and he'd never said anything like that to her for donkey's years. And the neighbours had made a fuss of her, too. Everyone said how brave she'd been, but Elsie knew it wasn't bravery that had set her on Danny. In fact, if she'd taken time out to think, she'd never have dared stand up to him. It was the anger that had surfaced so quickly that sent her out with the brush. Anger that a man should raise his hand to a woman. Her and Fred might have had their differences, but in all their married life he'd never once raised his hand to her.

'Guess who's comin' to see me tonight?'

'How many guesses do I get, chick?' Bill smiled. 'There's a helluva lot of people in the world.'

'Yer'd never get it in a month of Sundays.' Eileen passed the sheet of notepaper across the table. 'Jean Simpson.'

Bill raised his brows. 'The girl you've been writing to in America?'

Eileen nodded. 'I worked with 'er in the munitions factory. She married a Yank and went to live over there when the war was over. She's home on holiday to see her family.'

'It costs a few bob to come from there.' Bill handed the letter back. 'She must have married into money.'

'He didn't seem to be short when 'e was here, but then none of the Yanks were. Our poor buggers were on about a shilling a week and the Yanks were loaded.' Eileen folded the letter and grinned. 'Our boys used to complain because the Americans got all the girls. They had plenty of money to give them a good time, and they could get stockings and lipsticks and things that yer couldn't buy here for love nor money.'

Bill took a packet of cigarettes from his pocket. 'What time is she coming and do I have to get changed?'

'Seven o'clock and no, yer don't 'ave to change.' Eileen picked up his empty plate. 'I hope Billy and the girls are 'ome handy so I can get their dinners over with. I'd like the place tidy when Jean comes.'

Eileen had just washed the last plate when the knocker sounded. 'I'll go,' she shouted, wiping her hands on the end of the tea towel Maggie was using to dry the dishes.

Eileen stared open-mouthed at the slim, elegant woman smiling up at her. 'My God, yer look like a film star!'

'You haven't changed a bit,' Jean laughed. 'Still the same Eileen.'

'I don't know whether that's a compliment or an insult.' Eileen closed the door. 'Come in an' meet the family.'

Billy was on his way out but stayed long enough to shake hands. 'You might still be here when I get back.'

'He's a nice-looking boy,' Jean said when he'd gone. 'I wonder who he takes after?'

'Ay, none of yer lip, missus, or yer'll be goin' back to America with two broken legs.'

Joan and Edna came downstairs together, both ready to go out. Joan's eyes filled with envy when she took in Jean's clothes, make-up and hair style. Although her parents didn't know about Augie, she was still seeing him and wanted to question Jean about life in America. See if it really was as good as he said it was. Her face was animated as she listened and she would have stayed longer if Eileen hadn't interrupted.

'Ay, aren't you two goin' out? Me mate comes to see me after four years an' I can't get a word in edgeways.'

Reluctantly, Joan stood up. 'Are you coming again before you go back?'

'I sure am.' Jean spoke with a slow American drawl. 'I want to catch up on all your Mom's news.' She looked from one sister to the other. 'You look like twins.'

Edna was delighted because she thought her sister was very pretty, but not for the world would she let her know that. She was big-headed enough as it was. 'If I thought that I'd put me head in a gas oven.'

Joan gave a sneer. 'I'll give you the money for the gas.'

'We'll have less of that,' Eileen said. 'On yer way before there's skin an' hair flyin'.'

Edna smiled at Jean before leaving. 'I'll probably see you later. I'm only goin' to the Palace with Janet to see Larry Parkes in "Jolson Sings Again".'

Bill chatted with Jean for a while, then said he felt like a pint. 'I'll leave you two girls to catch up on the news.'

After Maggie had retired to her room, Eileen made herself comfortable on the couch. 'Well, how's life in America? Is it like yer see on the pictures?'

Jean laughed. 'For some it is. I'm lucky, Ivan's people have money and we want for nothing. But some of the English girls were in for a shock when they got there. There's a lot of slums, and when I say slums, honey, I mean slums. Far worse than anything we've got over here. And some of the girls I travelled over with found themselves living in houses little better than huts. In fact, hundreds of them have come home again.'

While Jean was talking, Eileen weighed her up. Gone was the bleached hair with an inch of dark root showing, and the eyebrows which she'd always shaved off had grown again and were now nicely arched.

'Well, you seem to 'ave done all right for yerself,' Eileen said. 'Yer look proper glamorous in yer nice clothes.' Her body started to shake with laughter. 'Yer look like that ugly ducklin' that turned into a swan.'

Jean joined in the laughter. 'It was Ivan's mother who waved her magic wand. She nearly had a fit when she saw what her beloved son had married. She didn't say it, but I knew she thought he'd lost the run of his senses. The day after I arrived she tactfully said she'd show me around the shops. By the time she'd finished with me, even Ivan didn't recognise me. My hair had been dyed back to its natural colour and she'd bought me a whole new wardrobe. Everything to her taste, of course, I had no say in the choice of clothes she bought. When she finally decided I was fit to be seen, and not before, I was introduced to the rest of the family and their high-falutin friends.'

'Ah, one of those is she?' Eileen nodded knowingly. 'An' what did Ivan 'ave to say?'

'If you knew his mother, you wouldn't have to ask that. When she cracks the whip, everybody jumps.'

'Yer get on all right with Ivan, don't yer?'

'Yes, he's a good husband and we get along fine. But he's under his mother's thumb and what she says goes.'

'Come in the kitchen while I make us a cuppa.' Eileen heaved herself off the couch. 'We can talk out there.'

While they waited for the kettle to boil, Jean talked of the house she shared with Ivan, the swimming pool in the large garden, the cocktail parties and the daily woman she had to do her cleaning.

Eileen poured the boiling water into the brown earthenware teapot. 'Yer've landed on yer feet by the sound of things.'

Jean wrinkled her nose. 'It's all right if you like that sort of thing.' She turned the conversation to Eileen. 'You've got a nice house here.'

It was Eileen's turn to wrinkle her nose. 'Kid, I'd go back to me old house any day. The people were more friendly. It's too quiet round 'ere for my likin'. All yer ever get from the neighbours is "Good morning, Mrs Gillmoss". I've been 'ere four years an' 'ave never 'ad a proper conversation with any of them, except Mary of course, and Doris next door.'

They carried their tea through and began to reminisce about the days they worked together. 'I still miss it, yer know,' Eileen said. 'I often think about Maisie Phillips and Ethel Hignet. And poor Willy

Turnbull, the way I used to pull the poor sod's leg. I'd love to see them all again.'

'You're going to.' Jean laughed as Eileen's mouth dropped. 'I've been writing to Maisie Phillips and I've arranged a little get-together for next week. Maisie, Ethel, you and me. And Mary if she'd like to come.'

'Well, I'll be blowed! You live thousands of miles away an' yer know more than I do!' Eileen rubbed her hands together with glee. 'Ooh, I'm made up, honest. It'll be smashin' seein' them again. I wonder if they've changed?'

Jean tapped the side of her nose. 'You'll have to wait and see.'

Edna came home with her eyes and nose red from crying. 'It was a lovely picture, Mam, but awful sad.' Her eyes landed on Jean. 'Does Larry Parkes live anywhere near you?'

Jean laughed. 'Honey, America is a very big country. I'd say Hollywood was about two thousand miles away.'

Edna looked disappointed. 'He's lovely.' She said goodnight and made her way to bed to dream of the handsome man who blacked his face, loved his wife but loved singing more.

Eileen and Bill had just climbed into bed when they heard Billy's voice as his footsteps pounded up the stairs. 'Mam, are yer asleep yet?'

'What a bloody stupid question!' Eileen grinned at Bill as their son burst through the door. 'In the name of God, Billy, is the place on fire?'

'Mam, we've got the house!' Billy was so excited he could hardly get the words out quickly enough. 'Mrs Radford saw the landlord today and he said we could have it when the Bowers leave.'

'Oh, son!' The bed springs creaked in protest as Eileen rocked back and forth. 'That's marvellous news!'

Billy grinned, running his fingers through his hair. 'I haven't seen the Bowers yet, but I'll call tomorrow and find out if they've got a date for sailing.' He sat on the side of the bed, his heart thumping so loud he thought it would burst out of his body. 'I can't believe it, it seems too good to be true.'

'You're very lucky, son,' Bill said. 'There's not many couples have a house ready to move into when they get married.'

'I've told Mavis there's no more nights out for us, we'll have to save every penny. If I walk to work every day, that'll save a few bob a week and it all mounts up.'

'Have you an' Mavis decided where yer gettin' married?' Eileen asked. 'And is it goin' to be a quiet affair?'

'We're gettin' married at the Blessed Sacrament and I'm goin' to see Father Murphy tomorrow night so he can arrange to have the banns read out.' Billy started to blush. 'Mavis wants a white wedding an' I was wondering if Auntie Mary would make her dress?'

'I'm sure she'd be glad to.' The bed shook when Eileen burst out laughing. 'Mary's goin' to 'ave her work cut out over the next few weeks 'cos she's makin' my dress as well, an' with my size it's once round me an' twice round the gas works.'

'What about the bridesmaids, son?' Bill asked. 'Or aren't you going to have any?'

'We've talked about it, but haven't decided yet. We'll have to go careful 'cos we don't have much money.' Billy eased himself off the bed. 'We'll sort it all out when we know for sure when the Bowers are going. Anyway I'm off to bed. Not that I'll be able to sleep 'cos me nerves are as taut as a violin string.'

'You an' me, too, sunshine!' Eileen said. 'I'm wide awake now.'

'Goodnight and God bless, Mam. Goodnight, Dad.'

'Ooh, I won't 'alf miss him.' Eileen picked at the sheet. 'I love every hair on 'is 'ead.'

Bill lay down on his side and pulled the clothes up to his chin. 'Your husband has got to go to work tomorrow and needs his shut-eye. So if you intend staying awake all night, chick, don't hold a conversation with yourself, please?'

'Don't worry.' Eileen patted his shoulder. 'I'll talk in a whisper an' I won't argue with meself. If I get on yer nerves, just clock me one.'

Bill suddenly remembered what Arthur had told him about Danny fighting with Vera. What with Jean staying until it was time for them to go to bed, he hadn't had the chance to talk to Eileen. He half turned, intending to tell her, then changed his mind. She had enough to think about as it was, and if he gave her anything more to worry about she'd never close her eyes. He'd tell her in the morning. 'Goodnight, chick, try and get some sleep.'

Chapter Eighteen

'Mam, I've got a hot-pot cookin' in the oven on a low light, so will yer keep yer eye on it for me? I'll be 'ome before the gang get in from work.' Eileen, standing in front of the mirror on the wall in Maggie's room, gave her hair a pat. 'I've been in bloody agony all night sleepin' in me dinky curlers, and for all the good it's done I needn't 'ave bothered 'cos me hair still looks a mess.' She winked at Maggie through the mirror. 'Still, we can't 'ave brains and beauty, can we?

'Well, I'm off to see me old mates.' Eileen waddled into the hall where Jean Simpson was waiting. 'Ta-ra, Mam!'

Eileen banged the door behind her and fell into step beside Jean. 'Where are we meetin' them?'

'In the St George Hotel on Lime Street.' Jean slipped her arm through Eileen's. 'It's a pity Mary couldn't come.'

'She meets the children comin' out of school so she wouldn't 'ave been back in time.' They reached the corner of the road and Eileen spotted a bus coming. 'Run on, kid, an' ask the conductor to wait for me.'

Eileen took the seat by the window, leaving about six inches for Jean to balance her bottom on. And when the bus lurched to one side as it went round the dangerous bend by Orrell Park Station, Jean had to hang on like grim death to the seat in front.

'The Americans have no idea what we went through during the war.' Jean had forgotten how much damage had been inflicted when the May blitz was at its height, and as the bus made its way into the city she surveyed with sadness the open spaces where houses and shops had once stood. 'I know they lost a lot of men and we probably wouldn't have made it without their help, but they didn't have the bombing to worry about.'

'My Bill says it'll take twenty years to build the city up again,'

Eileen said. 'We're givin' money to the countries we were fightin' so they can rebuild their countries when we're skint ourselves.'

'Ah, look at the poor old Rotunda,' Jean said, pointing a finger. 'I can't see them doing much with that.'

The bus drew to a stop in Lime Street where the two friends alighted. They waited for a lull in the traffic before darting across the busiest street in Liverpool city centre. Eileen paused for a second outside the hotel to smooth the lapels of her coat before following Jean through the doors. Her gaze swept over the people sitting at tables, seeking out her old friends.

'They're not 'ere yet.'

'Yes, there they are.' Jean pointed to a table near the back of the room and started to make her way towards it when Eileen's arm stopped her in her tracks.

'It's not them.'

'Yes it is. Look, they're waving.'

Eileen studied the two grey-haired women sitting at the table and shook her head. 'My God, they 'aven't 'alf changed.'

Jean pulled Eileen forward. 'They're probably thinking the same about us.'

'I wouldn't 'ave known yez!' Eileen dropped into the seat, her eyes on Maisie Phillips. The bleached blond hair was now a silver grey, and instead of the heavy make-up Eileen used to say she put on with a trowel, Maisie's face was just lightly dusted with powder. And her old trade mark, the bright orange Tangee lipstick, had been replaced with a soft rose pink. No one had ever known Maisie's true age, she'd been thirty-nine all the years Eileen had worked with her. But looking at her now, Eileen guessed she mustn't be far off sixty.

'Oh, it's lovely to see you again.' Ethel Hignet's ill-fitting false teeth left her gums for a second, then clicked back into place. 'You look very well, Jean, proper posh. And Eileen hasn't changed at all.'

'Yer mean I'm just as fat an' untidy as ever?' Eileen grinned. Ethel was still as thin as a beanpole, and her face as pale as ever. The only difference Eileen could see was the hair. It used to be black and frizzy, now it was almost white and dead straight.

'How's life treatin' yer both?' Eileen asked. 'Are yer still women of leisure, like meself?'

'Worse luck,' Maisie said. 'I couldn't wait to get out of that

166

blasted factory when the war was over, but I'd give anything to be back. Not that I wish the war was still on, but I miss the company.'

'Yeah, me too,' Ethel said. 'Me an' Maisie are always talkin' about the old times, aren't we, Maisie?'

Ethel hasn't changed, Eileen thought. She still hangs on to every word Maisie says. Probably still follows her round like a lap dog. 'See each other often do yez?'

'Every day,' Maisie answered with a laugh. 'We live in the same road now. I got a transfer to Huyton not long after the war finished.'

'D'yez ever hear of Willy Turnbull?' Eileen asked. 'I often wonder what became of 'im.'

'He got married, yer know,' Maisie told her. 'Married a woman whose husband was killed in the war.'

'Go way!' Eileen sat back in surprise. 'I never thought that poor bugger would ever get 'imself a wife, although, God knows, he tried hard enough.'

'Got a ready-made family he has,' Ethel said. 'Took on a woman with three kids.'

'Let's go downstairs to the restaurant.' Jean stood up. 'We can talk while we're eating.' She saw the anxious glances exchanged between Maisie and Ethel and quickly added, 'It's my treat.'

When they'd chosen from the menu, Jean called the waiter over and added two bottles of wine to the order. Then she answered the questions that came thick and fast about life in America. She was full of praise for the country and its people, but as Eileen listened she had a gut feeling that everything in Jean's garden wasn't as rosy as she made out. You don't work with a person for four years without getting to know them inside out, she told herself, and unless I'm much mistaken, there's a bit of sadness behind Jean's laughter.

As the wine flowed, so did the conversation and laughter. Memories of the tricks Eileen had played on them all, especially Willy Turnbull, were talked about with hilarity, causing Ethel's clicking teeth to work overtime. 'Yer gave us many a laugh,' she said. 'Yer were as mad as a flippin' hatter.'

'It was her table manners I remember most,' Maisie laughed. 'The dockers' sandwiches she used to make with the chips in the canteen.'

'Eileen lives in a nice house now,' Jean told them. 'She's gone up in the world.'

'Don't kid yerself,' Eileen huffed. 'If goin' up in the world means bein' miserable, then I'd rather be a ruddy tramp.'

Maisie looked surprised. 'Don't yer like yer new house?'

'Oh, the house is all right,' Eileen said. 'It's the miserable flamin' people in the road.' Then she adopted her posh voice and proceeded to imitate some of her neighbours. With her hand in the air, her little finger crooked, she had them off to a T. Her three friends roared with laughter, causing heads to turn in their direction. Those sitting at nearby tables did their best to look as though they weren't listening, but their smiling faces betrayed them. When Eileen was in full flow, on top form, it was impossible not to laugh.

Jean wiped her eyes and took a deep breath. 'Just like old times. I haven't laughed so much since the war finished.'

'It's done me a power of good, too,' Eileen said. 'It's not often I get a chance these days to show off me talents.' She squinted at the watch Bill had bought her the first Christmas he was home after the war. She only wore it on high days and holidays. 'I'd better be makin tracks or me mam'll 'ave her knickers in a twist thinkin' I'm not goin' to be home in time to put the dinner out.'

'Can we meet again before yer go back, Jean?' Maisie asked. 'I'd be made up if we could.'

'Yeah, sure,' Jean said. 'I'll drop you a line and make a date.'

Eileen was grinning as she stepped from the bus. It had been lovely seeing her old mates again. She'd have to ask for Maisie's address next time they met, then she could invite her and Ethel down one day. The laugh they'd had today had cheered her up no end, it was as good as a tonic. She looked at her watch as she turned the corner of her road and quickened her pace. The family would be in by now and wanting their dinner. Still, it didn't happen often so they couldn't moan. A mischievous smile crossed her face. They could moan all they liked, it wouldn't spoil the pleasure she'd had.

Eileen took the key from the lock and opened the door. 'I'm home!' Her brow furrowed as she walked down the hall. It was as quiet as a graveyard; where was everybody?

Eileen pushed the living room door open and froze. Edna was sitting at the table with her head in her hands, her shoulders shaking as quiet sobs racked her body. Bill, young Billy and Maggie were standing like statues by the fireplace, their faces grim.

'What's up?' Eileen croaked, her heart doing somersaults. Then she noticed Joan was missing. 'Where's our Joan?'

'That's what we're trying to figure out,' Bill said. 'She went into the shop to see Edna this afternoon and said she wasn't coming home. Told her she was going to live with a friend.'

'Oh, she's pullin' her leg.' Eileen let out a sigh of relief. 'She's probably gone to the pictures straight from work.'

Edna lifted her head, her eyes red-rimmed. 'She wasn't pulling me leg, Mam, she meant it. I asked where her friend lived, but she wouldn't tell me.'

'No, I don't believe it,' Eileen said. 'What would she leave 'ome for? All her clothes an' things are 'ere.'

'There's a lot of her things gone, lass,' Maggie said quietly. 'The first thing I did when Edna told us, was to look in her room. There's only some old things left in the wardrobe and drawers, all her good clothes have gone. She must have been taking them out on the quiet over the last few weeks.'

'I can't make head nor tail of it.' Bill looked anxious. 'You haven't had a row with her, have you, chick?'

'Not a wrong word,' Eileen said, 'I just don't understand it.'

'Well, there's not much I can do tonight, but I'll take an hour off tomorrow and go down to Vernons. I'll see the personnel officer and find out what's going on.'

'She doesn't work there any more.' Edna held an already sodden handkerchief to her screwed-up eyes as a fresh burst of sobbing threatened. 'She said she left there weeks ago and has got another job, but wouldn't tell me where.'

Her face drained of colour, Eileen appealed to Bill. 'Why would she do that to us? She's got a good 'ome here.'

Maggie, unable to bear the look of distress on Eileen's face, turned to the kitchen. 'I'll make you a cup of sweet tea.'

'Bill!' Eileen was becoming hysterical. 'We've got to do somethin'! She can't leave 'ome, she's not old enough.'

'There's not much we can do, chick, if that's what she wants.' Bill sat beside Eileen and took her hand. 'She's nearly nineteen now and we can't stop her doing anything she wants. We've no say in the matter.'

Edna's cries grew louder and Billy went to put an arm across her shoulders. 'Don't cry, Sis, it's not your fault.'

'But she's me sister! Why didn't she tell me what she was going to do an' I could have stopped her?'

Eileen closed her eyes and took two deep breaths before asking, 'Tell me exactly what happened, sunshine?'

Edna wiped her nose on the back of her hand. 'She came up to me in the shop an' said she wouldn't be coming home any more 'cos she's gone to live with a girl she works with. I thought she was having me on at first, but when I saw she meant it, I said you'd find out where she'd gone by asking at Vernons. She just laughed at me and said you'd have a job because she'd left there.'

'The hard-faced little madam.' Despite being worried to death, Eileen felt angry that her daughter would cause them such anguish. 'And that's all she said?'

'Told me to tell you not to worry, that she'd be all right. And she said she'd come and see me again in the shop.' Tears ran down Edna's cheeks and her voice was choked with emotion. 'I asked her to come an' see you, Mam, but she said you'd try and stop her and she'd made up her mind.'

'Didn't she give you a reason?' Bill asked.

Edna shook her head. 'Just said she was old enough now to do what she wants.'

'She deserves a damn good hiding.' Young Billy was beside himself with anger. How dare she upset his mam and dad like this! The trouble was, their Joan had never appreciated how lucky she was. 'She'll be back, never fear. When she realises what side her bread's buttered, she'll be home like a shot.'

Bill could feel Eileen's hand shaking and he squeezed it gently. 'Billy's right, chick. If she's sharing a house or a flat, then she'll have to do half the housework and cough up enough money to pay half the rent and all the bills. And knowing our Joan, she won't like that one little bit.'

'I don't want 'er to come back for those reasons, Bill! She's left 'ome because she obviously doesn't like it 'ere, so let her stay away. If she 'asn't got the decency to face her own family, doesn't care about 'ow much she hurts us, then she needn't bother comin' back.' Even as she spoke, Eileen knew she didn't mean a word of it. But she hurt so much inside she needed to relieve the pain, and the only way she knew how was to get angry. 'Next time yer sister comes in the shop, tell 'er what I said.'

Billy watched his mother walk through to the kitchen and her grief-stricken face filled him with sadness. For all her brave words, he knew she was devastated. 'If I had our Joan here, I'd strangle her with me bare hands,' Billy whispered across the room to his father. 'How could she do this to me mam?'

170

'Sshh!' Bill put a finger to his lips. 'Don't say too much, son, least said, soonest mended.'

Bill stopped at the kitchen door and with a heavy heart watched as Eileen sobbed on Maggie's shoulder, 'Why, Mam? Why 'as she done this? I 'aven't been such a bad mother, 'ave I?'

'Of course not!' Maggie motioned with her head for Bill to leave them be. To let her daughter cry away some of the sadness and hurt she felt. Maggie stroked Eileen's hair. 'One of her friends has probably talked her into it and Joan's been easily led. But it won't last long, the novelty will soon wear off, lass, and she'll come running home.'

Joan walked out of George Henry Lees biting on her bottom lip to keep the tears back. It had been much harder than she'd thought it would be. The look of distress on Edna's face had almost made her change her mind. But it wasn't the end of the world, she told herself. She could keep in touch with her sister and in a few weeks she'd go and see her mam and dad.

As Joan made her way towards C and A, where she was meeting Valerie, for once she was truthful with herself. It was her own fault she'd had to leave home. If she hadn't lied to Augie it need never have happened. But she'd never had the courage to tell him she'd lied. And every time he'd asked to meet her family, instead of being honest with him, she'd told him she didn't get on with her parents. It was Augie who'd suggested she went to live with his friend's girlfriend, Valerie, and it had seemed a marvellous idea at the time. She'd be able to see him every night without worrying what time she got home or making excuses about where she was going.

Joan saw Valerie and waved. She fixed a smile on her face and banished her misgivings from her mind. Everything was going to be all right. She got on well with Valerie and had been to her three-bedroomed semi in Woolton several times with Augie.

'Well, how did it go?' Valerie asked. She was four or five years older than Joan and much more experienced in every aspect of life. She wasn't pretty in the usual sense, her mouth and nose were too wide, but she was very attractive and sophisticated. Dark haired, slim, always well dressed and very sure of herself – Joan thought she was the bees' knees. 'Was your sister surprised?'

'That's putting it mildly,' Joan laughed nervously. 'She was speechless.'

'You can tell me about it later.' Valerie waved a bag in the air. 'I've bought the food, so let's get home and start on the dinner. I want to make a really special meal for Richie and Augie tonight and you can help.'

Valerie glanced sideways at Joan and was about to say something when she changed her mind. She wasn't very happy about the arrangements but it wasn't up to her to interfere. The kid, and she was only a kid, would find out for herself soon enough.

When sleep wouldn't come the first night at Valerie's, Joan put it down to being in a strange bed. And all the other nights when she tossed and turned, she wouldn't let herself waver from that excuse. Whenever a doubt crept into her mind she banished it, telling herself how much better off she was now. Wasn't she able to see Augie every night when he could get away from the Burtonwood base? And didn't he treat her like someone special, taking her to places she'd never been to before because she couldn't afford it?

But the night came when Joan lay awake, staring at the bedroom ceiling and letting her thoughts run their true course. She dropped the cloak of pretence and admitted to herself she was homesick. She missed her own bed and her nightly chats with Edna. She even missed their rows, because she realised now it was all part of being sisters. And she missed their Billy's smiling face and his cheery disposition. She'd never appreciated how lucky she was to have a brother like him until now, when it was too late. And her Nan. Dear, sweet Nan, with her infinite patience and willingness to help. In her own quiet way, it was Nan who was always there to placate and keep the peace.

For the first time since she'd left home, Joan allowed her thoughts to run free. Images of her mam and dad flickered across her mind like a silent movie. She could see, as clear as a picture, her dad smiling as he watched her mam perform one of her funny antics, his devotion to his wife written on his face for the whole world to see. Then her mam appeared, standing in the middle of the room with her hands on her wide hips and her head thrown back as she roared with laughter.

Joan turned her head on the pillow and allowed her tears to run unchecked. She missed them all so much, it hurt. If only she was back with them to share the warmth and love they wrapped around each other, to hear her dad's gentle voice and her mam's throaty chuckle, to be the butt of one of Billy's jokes and fight like cat and dog with their Edna.

Joan pulled the sheet over her head to muffle the sound of her sobs.

Valerie slept in the next room and if she heard Joan crying she'd be in like a shot, thinking she was the cause of it. But what had happened that day wasn't the reason Joan had allowed her fears and unhappiness to surface. It had been festering since the day she'd walked out on her family. Today's incident had just been the straw that broke the camel's back.

Since she'd moved in, Joan and Valerie had got into a routine of doing household chores on certain days. And Sunday was the day they stripped their beds and vacuumed and dusted the bedrooms. This morning Joan had finished her room, and as she could hear Valerie talking to Richie on the phone in the hall, she decided to help by starting on Valerie's room. She pulled the bedclothes from the bed, threw the sheets and pillowcases to one side for washing, then opened the drawer in the tallboy where she knew Valerie kept her clean bed linen. She pulled two slips out and was about to close the drawer when she saw some photographs of a soldier in uniform. Without thinking, Joan took the photos out and was looking through them when Valerie came into the room.

'Nice-looking man,' Joan said. 'Is he your brother?'

Valerie snatched the photos from Joan's hands, her face blazing. 'What the hell are you doing, snooping through my things? You have no right to be in here.'

'I was only trying to help,' Joan protested, wondering what she'd done wrong.

Valerie noted the bedclothes on the floor and the two clean pillow slips and her temper evaporated. 'Take no notice of me.' She threw the photos in the drawer. 'I must have got out of bed on the wrong side this morning.'

Joan said, 'I'll give you a hand.' While she waited for Valerie to shake out the sheet, she asked, 'Is the man your brother?'

Valerie let the corners of the sheet drop and looked across the bed. For seconds she just stared, then shrugged her shoulders. 'He's not a soldier any more, he works abroad. And he's not my brother, he's my husband.'

'But, then . . .' Joan stuttered.

'Look, let's get one thing straight,' Valerie said. 'What I do is my business and has nothing to do with you. I love my husband, but he works away for six months at a time and I get lonely. Richie knows I'm married and when my husband comes home our affair will be finished. Now you know, but as I said, it's none of your business.'

There'd been a coolness between them for the rest of the day, and Joan was glad when Augie came to take her out. But as he drove the jeep towards the city centre, Joan found herself looking sideways at him. Did he know what was going on? If he did, and condoned it, he was as bad as Valerie and Richie.

Joan's thoughts ran on. If he saw no wrong in them cheating on Valerie's husband, then he wouldn't be beyond cheating on someone himself, would he? She took a deep breath. 'Augie, are you married? Tell me the truth.'

Augie took his eyes off the road for a second, surprise written on his face at the unexpected question. 'No, honey, of course I'm not!'

He turned his head away quickly, but not quickly enough for Joan to miss the colour rising from his neck, or the look of guilt in his eyes. She didn't question him any more, she didn't need to.

Now Joan punched the pillow, the blow containing all the emotions she'd kept at bay for so long. What a stupid, naive fool she'd been! Why had she never asked herself how Valerie could keep such a nice house going, and have a wardrobe full of clothes, on the wages she earned?

Then anger took over. I've often told me mam lies, Joan thought, and right now I regret every one of them. But mine have never hurt anyone, not like Valerie, who was not only cheating on her husband, but in not wearing a wedding ring, was living a lie. There was no excuse for her or for Richie. And as for Augie, well she never wanted to set eyes on him again. He was, as her Nan would say, too sweet to be wholesome.

'Oh, Mam,' Joan cried softly, wishing she could feel the big, soft warm body holding her close. 'I want to come home, but would you have me after what I've done? I do love you, Mam, but I don't know if you still love me.'

Chapter Nineteen

'I think that's about right,' Mary said, holding the material against Eileen's leg. Her friend had come for a final fitting of the dress she was making for Billy's wedding, and all that it needed now was the hem turning up. 'It's about four inches below your knees.'

Eileen, trying to see over her mountainous bust, grunted in disgust. 'I can't see a thing, kid! As long as I'm not showin' the leg of me knickers, then it'll do.'

Mary filled her mouth with pins and began the task of getting the hem straight. It wasn't easy with Eileen being so big in the front. 'Keep still, will you? Otherwise it'll be all cockeyed.' She crawled round on her knees, leaning back occasionally to make sure she was keeping the hem even. 'Move nearer the window and turn around slowly so I can see it at a distance.'

'Bloody 'ell, all this just to look glamorous.' Eileen twirled slowly, then did a quick spin. 'Will I outshine the bride?'

Mary struggled to her feet. 'I can't promise that, but it really suits you.' She surveyed the dress with a critical eye. It was a crepe material in sage green, with three-quarter sleeves and a sweetheart neck. 'I'm glad you didn't get a dark colour like you usually do. That green looks great on you, brings out the colour of your eyes.'

'Help me off with it, kid, or I'll be stickin' pins in meself.'

Mary folded the dress and draped it over the back of a chair. 'I'll sit and finish it off tonight.'

'We've kept yer busy the last month, haven't we, kid? Yer've been a real angel doin' all those dresses. Saved our Billy an' Mavis a lot of money. In fact, let's face it, they wouldn't be 'aving any bridesmaids if it wasn't for you.'

'It's been hard going, but I've enjoyed doing them,' Mary said. 'I'm very fond of your Billy and I was glad to help.'

'He's a real cracker, my son, even if I say it as shouldn't. Got a heart of gold. I was made up when 'e asked if Carol would like to be a bridesmaid. There's not many lads his age would 'ave done that, now, is there?'

Mary gazed at her friend with fondness. Behind all the bluff, Mary knew she was heartbroken that Joan wouldn't be here to be a bridesmaid at her brother's wedding. 'No word from Joan?'

Eileen's eyes clouded. 'No. She's been in the shop to see Edna, and she knows the wedding's in two weeks, but we've not 'eard a dickie bird from her. I'll never forgive 'er for lettin' our Billy down.'

Mary sighed as she pressed back the cuticles from her nails. 'She's a very silly girl. One day she'll need her family.'

'In the beginnin' I expected 'er back every day. Never thought she'd stay away a month,' Eileen said. 'If she walked through that door now, I wouldn't know whether to hug 'er or break her flamin' neck. She's been very naughty not gettin' in touch with me an' Bill, but for all that she's me daughter an' I love her.'

'Is everything fixed up for the wedding?' Mary asked, to get Eileen's mind away from her wayward daughter.

'Yeah, we've sorted it all out with the Radfords. We were goin' to pay for everything between us, but young Billy wouldn't hear of it. He said it's the bridegroom's job to pay for certain things, and he wanted to do things properly. So we're all givin' 'im money as a weddin' present and they can buy furniture with it. Me an' Bill are scrimpin' and scratchin' to give as much as we can. I've got a few pound to come in Co-op divvy, so I'm nippin' to Byrom Street temorrer to pick it up. It's not much, but every little helps, as the old woman said when she did a jimmy riddle in the river.' Eileen laughed at the look on Mary's face. 'If all else fails, kid, I'll 'ave to pawn me weddin' ring.'

'Don't you dare!' Mary said. 'I can lend you a few pound . . . it's unlucky to pawn things.'

'Ah, that's an old wives' tale, kid! This ring of mine was in an' out of pawn that often when the kids were little, it's a wonder it isn't worn out. My Bill didn't know, mind yer, or there'd 'ave been blue murder. But when we got married and moved into Bray Street, we didn't 'ave much furniture. We were goin' to save up an' buy when we could afford. But we 'adn't reckoned on 'aving three kids in four years, an' it put a halt to our gallop. It was hard goin', tryin' to make ends meets, I can tell yer. Sometimes it was a case of starvin or goin' to the pawn shop. Yer know Pobjoys, at Everton Valley? Well, I used to trot along there every Monday mornin' with me weddin' ring an' I'd get enough on it to keep us in food till pay day.'

'But Bill must have noticed you weren't wearing your ring,' Mary said. 'He's not blind.'

'Ah, well, yer see, kid, I was very crafty. I bought meself a tanner ring from Woolies and Bill never knew the difference.'

'You're a case, you are.'

'As the sayin' goes, kid, what Bill never knew never 'urt him.'

'Has young Billy got the key to his house yet?'

'He's hopin' to get it today. If he does, we're goin with 'im tonight to see it.' Eileen laughed, 'Honest, he's so happy he's like a kid with a new toy.'

'He deserves to go through life being happy,' Mary said. 'He's one helluva nice boy. I only hope our Tony grows up to be as nice as him.'

Billy couldn't hide his impatience. 'I'll go on ahead, Mam.'

Eileen, her arm linked through Bill's, nodded. 'Okay, son, but don't go in yer new 'ouse till we get there. I want to see yer face.'

'I don't think I've ever seen anyone so happy,' Bill said, watching Billy racing up the street. 'It does my heart good to see the pleasure on his face.'

'Ay, mister!' Eileen squeezed his arm. 'What about the day we got married? Are yer tryin' to tell me yer weren't as happy then as our Billy is now?'

'Of course I was! But I was more nervous than him. I was walking round like a headless chicken for weeks before we got wed. Our Billy doesn't seem to have any nerves.'

'It's like history repeatin' itself,' Eileen said. 'The day we got married we moved into our own little 'ouse in the same street.'

Bill glanced sideways. Was Eileen still hankering after the old house after all this time? Mind you, women were more sentimental than men.

Billy was standing with Mavis outside the house the Bowers had moved out of last week. He was hopping from one foot to the other. 'Put a move on, Mam!'

'Hold yer 'orses, son! Give us a chance to get me breath back.'

Billy put the key in the lock, his face glowing with pride. He stepped back to let Eileen go in first, and caught her gazing at their old house opposite with a funny look on her face. 'In you go, Mam.

You can be first to set foot in our new house.'

Mavis was giggling with nervous excitement as they toured the small two-up two-down. 'It's not in bad nick, son,' Bill said, looking around. 'The decorating will do you for a while.'

'I won't be doing any papering until we've got some furniture in,' Billy laughed. 'It's no good havin' nice walls when you've no chairs to sit on.'

'Give it time, son.' Bill would have liked to say that with the money they were getting as a wedding present, things would be coming quicker than the young couple thought. But that would spoil the surprise. And anyway, as half the money was coming from Mavis's parents, it wasn't up to him to let the cat out of the bag. 'In no time at all you'll have the house as you want it.'

'Course yer will!' Eileen said. 'In a couple of months yer'll 'ave the place like a little palace an' be as snug as two bugs in a rug.'

'You know, I never knew that palaces had bugs.' Billy fended off a blow from his mother. 'I thought the King and Queen were too posh to have such common things as bugs.'

Eileen pushed him playfully against the wall. 'Watch it, big boy, or yer'll be walking down the aisle on crutches.'

'Help, Mavis, I'm being attacked.'

'You're on your own, Billy Gillmoss.' Mavis winked at Bill. 'I'm keeping on the right side of me mother-in-law.'

'Yer know, I always knew we were goin' to get on well together.' Eileen put her arms around Mavis. 'Welcome to yer new 'ome, sunshine, an' welcome to the family.'

'What time's Harry pickin' yez up?' Eileen was pacing up and down the living room, looking at the clock every few seconds. She had a fixed smile on her face, telling herself to look cheerful even if she didn't feel it. After all, it was Billy's big day and she mustn't spoil it for him. But her heart was heavy. In a few minutes her only son would be walking out of the door and not coming back. What with Joan leaving, and now Billy, the house just wasn't going to be the same. 'I 'ope he won't be late gettin' yez to the church.'

'Mam, will you relax?' Billy showed no sign of nerves as he sat next to his best man, the boy who'd been his friend since school-days. 'You'd think it was her getting married, wouldn't you, Jacko?'

'You mam isn't the only nervous one,' Jack replied. 'My tummy is tied up in knots.'

'Yer've got the ring, haven't yer?' Eileen stopped her pacing and stood in front of Jacko. 'I'll kill yer if yer drop it.'

The knocker sounded and Eileen jumped. 'I 'ope this is Harry.'

Harry breezed in, a smile creasing his face. 'I've delivered Edna and Carol to Mavis's, and while I was there Rene turned up with Victoria. So everything is organised at that end. I'll run you and Jacko down now, Billy, then come back for the rest.'

'What about Arthur?' Eileen fussed. 'How's he gettin' to the church with the boys?'

'On the bus.' Harry ran his eyes over Eileen, the cleft in his chin deepening when he grinned. With her green dress she was wearing a wide-brimmed black hat with matching shoes, gloves and handbag. 'You look very fetching, Mrs Gillmoss, if I may say so.'

'Oh, go way with yer.' Eileen blushed. 'Flattery will get yer nowhere.'

'You do look nice, Mam,' Billy said, while his father nodded in agreement.

'Will yer get goin'?' Eileen shooed them out. She was getting more emotional with every passing minute and it didn't help to keep reminding herself that every mother felt the same when one of her children flew the nest. Because deep down in her heart she knew the root of her sadness lay in the fact that Joan wouldn't be there to see her brother married. It just wasn't right, and although no one had said a word, she knew it had marred the happiness of the whole family.

Eileen held on to her hat as she swung her legs round to get out of Harry's car. She heard people clapping and looked with surprise at the people standing inside the gates of the Blessed Sacrament Church. All the old neighbours had turned up from Bray Street and Eileen could feel tears stinging the backs of her eyes. 'All me mates are 'ere.'

Bill gave her a hand and pulled her to her feet. 'Yes, I know, chick.'

'Yer look smashin', Eileen,' Cissie Maddox called.

'Like a mannequin,' Milly Knight said, while her husband winked his agreement.

Ada and Tommy Wilson smiled as she passed. 'I could fancy yer in that outfit,' Tommy said, then feigned a look of pain as Ada dug him sharply in the ribs.

'Behave yerself,' Ada said, a grin on her face. 'A man of your age, yer should be ashamed of yerself.'

'It's lovely to see yez all,' Eileen said, standing on the church step, overcome by the reception. 'I'll see yez later.'

Eileen linked Bill's arm as they walked down the aisle and took their seats in the bench behind Billy and Jacko. She nodded to Mrs Radford, sitting in the pew opposite, before whispering to Jacko, 'Yer've got the ring, 'aven't yer?'

Billy turned around and tutted. 'It's in his top pocket, I've checked half a dozen times.'

Eileen felt like hugging her son, he looked so handsome in his dark grey suit, white shirt and pale blue tie. And he was so relaxed, completely at ease.

The church was filling up. Maggie arrived with Rene and Alan, all dressed in their best, then Arthur and his two sons. Friends, neighbours and work mates of the bride and groom all slid into the pews on both sides of the aisle. Eileen kept turning her head to wave and smile, while all the time her eyes were peeled for a sign of Joan. Even at this late hour, she hadn't given up hope.

The organ began to play 'Here Comes The Bride', and Eileen forgot everything at the sight of Mavis, her hand on her father's arm, walking down the aisle. Her white satin dress was close fitting to the waist, then billowed out into a full skirt which reached to the floor. It had a square-shaped neck and leg-of-mutton sleeves tapering to fit tightly around her wrists. A long white veil was secured with a spray of orange blossom and her bouquet was a mixture of pink and white carnations.

'Oh, doesn't she look beautiful?' Eileen said, before nudging Bill as the bridesmaids followed Mavis to the altar. Edna led the way followed by Carol and Victoria. Their dresses were in pale blue satin with full skirts, crowns of flowers adorned their heads and their posies were made up of pink and white flowers.

It was all too much for Eileen and the tears rolled down her cheeks. 'Have yer got a hankie, Bill?' She blew her nose and managed to control her emotions until she heard Billy's voice, strong and steady, saying, 'I do.' After that Eileen saw everything through a haze and only regained her composure when they were outside the church once again posing for the photographer.

'Where's me Nan?' Billy left his bride to fetch Maggie who was standing shyly to one side. 'Auntie Rene and Uncle Alan, come on,' he urged, 'we want all the family on this one.'

When the photographer had finished and folded away his tripod, everyone crowded around to congratulate the newly-weds and throw confetti. There was so much laughing and so many jokes flying, nobody noticed the lone figure of a slim girl standing looking through the railings at the side of the church. She was wearing a long coat fastened up to her chin and her long hair was hidden under the scarf which was pulled low over her forehead.

Joan feasted her eyes on the happy crowd, lingering for a while on Billy, then finally coming to rest on Eileen. She could feel the rivulet of tears rolling down her cheeks on to her neck but made no effort to wipe them away. Oh, Mam, she cried silently, what have I done? You'll never forgive me now, I know you won't.

Mary and Vera had stayed behind to see to the tables and when they'd finished, they stood back to survey their handiwork. Eileen had borrowed two trestle tables and space had been made for them by moving all the furniture into Maggie's room. They were covered in spotless white sheets, and groaning under the weight of food. Pride of place on one of the tables had been given to the one-tier, square wedding cake, which Maggie had made and Vera had iced. Vera had made a good job of it too, decorating it with little silver shoes, bells and white ribbon. Around it were plates of sandwiches, sausage rolls, meat pies cut in half and two large glass bowls filled with trifle decorated with hundreds and thousands. Lending a splash of colour were four cake stands filled with jelly creams in their stiff, white pleated cases. And where it was possible on the crowded tables, there were small vases filled with purple button daisies.

'We've done a good job, even if I do say so meself,' Mary said. 'Not bad for beginners, eh, Vera?'

'The tables look a treat.' Vera's eyes widened when a knock came on the door. 'We cut that a bit fine, didn't we?'

She hurried along the hall, untying her apron as she went. When she saw Billy sweep Mavis off her feet, she called over her shoulder. 'Quick, Mary, you can't miss this.'

The sheer bliss on Billy's face was a joy to behold. 'Before you say anything, I know it's me own threshold I should be carrying me bride over, and I'll be doing that later, all right and proper. But me mam's house will always be a second home to me, and Mavis feels the same.' With exaggerated groans, Billy staggered along the hall

181

with his blushing bride giggling in his arms. But when he entered the room, he took one look at the tables and lowered Mavis to the floor. He struggled for the right words as he glanced from Mary to Vera. 'I'm speechless.' He gazed at the attractive way the food had been laid out, then gathered them both in his arms and held them close. 'The Adelphi couldn't have done us prouder! What do you say, eh, Mrs Gillmoss, Junior?'

'Oh, lord, aren't we the fine ones?' Mary ran to Mavis and kissed her. 'We were so busy congratulating ourselves, we forgot about congratulating you.'

Vera was pumping Billy's hand when the first of the guests started to arrive and after that the peace of the house was turned into bedlam. Bill was the first to make a short speech and toast the happy couple, then it was Mr Radford followed by a very nervous Jacko. As he told his mates the next day, it was worse being a best man than it was to be a groom. More responsibilities, like, you know.

Then it was Billy's turn. With a glass in one hand and an arm around his bride, he thanked everyone, leaving out not a soul. He looked so tall and handsome, every inch the gentleman, Eileen felt so proud she thought her heart would burst. And when he lifted his glass and asked everyone to drink to his mam and dad, the best parents anyone could ask for, she couldn't hold back the tears, or her feelings.

She rushed to throw her arms round her son's neck, knocking his glass flying and spilling beer on those unlucky enough to be standing near. With her hat pushed precariously to one side of her head, she cried, 'I'm not 'alf goin' to miss yer, son.' She glanced sideways at Mavis. 'Yer will look after 'im won't yer? An' make sure he gets enough to eat?'

With that, everyone burst out laughing and the festivities began.

'Your Carol is so happy she doesn't know what to do with herself.' Arthur was standing next to Vera, a glass in one hand, a plate in the other. 'She looks very grown up today.'

'I'm keeping me eye on her. She's stuffing herself with those jelly creams and she'll be sick if she's not careful.'

'She can be a bridesmaid when we get married,' Arthur said. 'She'll like that.'

Vera lifted her brows. 'In a register office?'

'What's the difference?' Arthur smiled. 'I don't care if we get married in a coal yard as long as you come out wearing my ring.'

Mary pushed her way through the crowds towards them. 'It's like St John's market on Christmas Eve.'

'Or the Grafton on a Saturday night.' Arthur grinned.

'Vera, I've just remembered the parcel that came for Billy,' Mary said. 'Did you give it to him?'

'Oh, lord, I forgot.' Vera put her plate down. 'I'll go and get it.'

She disappeared into the kitchen, returning with a square parcel in her arms. 'Billy, this came for you.'

Billy looked puzzled. 'What is it?'

Talking stopped as everyone's gaze focused on the parcel. 'Where did it come from?' Billy was tearing at the wrapping. 'I thought we'd had all our presents.'

'We don't know who left it,' Vera said. 'Me and Mary were busy in the kitchen when we heard a knock. It only took me a few seconds to dry me hands, but when I opened the door there was no one there, just the parcel on the step. I looked up and down the road but I couldn't see anybody.' Billy threw the wrapping paper to the floor and with everyone gathered round, opened the cardboard box. Inside, packed in straw, was a six-piece tea service. Billy lifted out one of the cups and held it aloft. 'This'll come in handy, save us drinking out of jam jars when we have visitors.'

Eileen peered into the box. 'Isn't there a card with it?'

Billy handed the box to Mavis while he searched inside. After a few seconds he waved a white envelope. 'Mystery solved,' he grinned as he took out the greetings card. But his smile faded when he started to read the message inside. Mavis was looking over his shoulder and her gasp of surprise brought Eileen forward. 'Who's it from?'

Billy handed her the card. 'Our Joan.'

Bill rested his chin on Eileen's shoulder and read the words aloud.

'Dear Billy, Sorry I can't be with you today but I wish you and Mavis all the luck in the world. Joan.'

Without a word Eileen handed the card back to Billy and left the room. Bill saw all eyes in the room follow his wife and he shrugged his shoulders as though apologising. 'She'll be all right, you just carry on enjoying yourselves.'

Bill found Eileen standing by the bedroom window, crying softly. 'Come on, chick.' He held his arms out and Eileen walked into them. 'Don't cry, love,' he whispered. 'You know how it upsets me.

And you don't want to spoil things for our Billy on his wedding day. he should be able to look back on today as the happiest of his life.'

'Just give me five minutes to calm meself down, then I'll be all right.' Eileen looked up into his face. 'I'm glad Joan didn't forget Billy's weddin', it'll mean a lot to him. But if she could come to the 'ouse with 'is present, it wouldn't 'ave hurt her to come to the church. What 'ave we done to 'er that she doesn't even want to set eyes on us?'

'I can't even pretend to understand,' Bill sighed. 'But you know how young people do things they're sorry for afterwards but wouldn't for this world admit it. Perhaps that's the way it is with Joan, she doesn't want to eat humble pie.'

Eileen left the shelter of his arms to look at her reflection in the dressing table mirror. 'I'll swill me face and make meself presentable, then I'll go down.'

'Are you all right, Mam?' Billy's head appeared round the door. 'You're not upset over our Joan, are you?'

'Not at all, sunshine,' Eileen lied. 'All mothers are entitled to a little weep when one of their children gets married an' leaves 'ome. No, I'm very glad our Joan didn't forget 'er brother on 'is big day.' She picked up a comb and ran it through the fine, mousy hair. 'You go an' see to yer guests while I titivate meself up. I'll be down in two shakes of a lamb's tail to liven the place up. Give yer a party yer'll remember all yer life.'

Chapter Twenty

'Blimey! I thought you'd be back in America by now.' Eileen stood aside and pulled her tummy in to let Jean pass. Closing the door behind her, she said, 'I've been callin' yer all the names under the sun for not comin' to say ta-ra.'

'As though I'd do that to you!' Jean put her carrier bag on the floor and sat down. 'You know what it's like, going to visit all the relatives and God knows who else. Me mam's had me visiting aunties I've never seen in me life before. Florrie, Maggie, Lizzie, Nellie, Fanny . . . you name them and I've visited them.'

'Terrible name that.' Eileen dropped heavily on to the couch. 'Fancy lumberin' a child with a name like Fanny.'

'She was christened Frances, and that's a lovely name. But her Mum started to call her Fanny when she was a baby, as a pet name, and it stuck.'

'How's life treatin' yer, anyway?' Eileen asked. 'Yer've been 'ome over a month now, aren't yer missin' yer 'usband?'

'I'm missing Ivan, yes.' Jean grimaced. 'But I'm dreading leaving me family again. I wish America wasn't so far away, then I'd be able to see them more often. I never thought I'd miss them, or Liverpool, so much.'

'Well, yer would marry a Yank, kid, so yer stuck with it . . . like Fanny is with 'er name.'

'To tell you the truth, Eileen, I've been seriously thinking of not going back.'

Eileen's eyes opened in astonishment. 'Yer can't do that! Yer can't just walk out on Ivan! That would be a lousy trick, kid, an' I'm surprised at yer for even thinkin' of it. You love 'im don't yer?'

Jean nodded. 'Very much. But sometimes I feel so homesick it makes me ill. I thought I'd get over it, but after five years I still feel the same.'

'He's a good 'usband, isn't he?' Eileen leaned forward, her chubby hands clasped between her knees. 'Looks after yer well?'

'He's a smashing husband. Kind and gentle, and spoils me soft.'

'An' yer thinkin' of walkin' out on 'im? Well, I think yer want yer bumps feelin'. When the novelty of bein' 'ome wears off, yer'll be cryin' yer eyes out for 'im, and it'll be too late.' Eileen clicked her tongue. 'Listen to me, kid. If yer heart's with Ivan, then that's where yer home is. Yer've heard the old sayin', "home is where the heart is", well it's true. So get back to 'im as quick as yer can an' count yer blessings.' She patted Jean's knee. 'Yer know the best thing for curing yer homesickness, kid? Start a family. Then yer'll 'ave no time to sit an' mope.'

Eileen remembered the times during the war when Ivan had helped out their meagre rations with weekly gifts of sugar and meat. 'Tell 'im next time yer come over on holiday, I expect to see 'im with yer. He was a good mate to me, was Ivan, an' I don't forget me mates.'

'You and Ivan think alike,' Jean said. 'He wants to start a family.'

'Then get the next boat 'ome, kid, an' get crackin'.' Eileen grinned into Jean's face. 'You are goin' home, aren't yer?'

Jean nodded. 'If you'll come over and be godmother to our first.'

'Not bloody likely! Bring it over here to be christened.' Eileen wriggled to the edge of the couch. 'I'll put the kettle on.'

Jean bent to take a Sayers cake box from her carrier bag. 'I've brought us some fresh cream cakes to have with a cup of tea.'

'Ooh, no thanks, kid! I ate enough food at our Billy's weddin' on Saturday to sink a ship. I can't walk through the flippin' door now without turnin' sideways.'

Jean lifted the lid of the cake box to reveal four chocolate eclairs oozing with fresh cream. Her face fell and there was disappointment in her voice. 'You mean you won't have one?'

At the sight of cakes Eileen could feel her mouth watering. She snatched the box from Jean's knee. 'To hell with it, yer only live once!' She patted her tummy and grinned. 'What's a pound or two between friends, anyway? Two each, is it, kid?'

Edna raised her brows in surprise when she saw Joan approaching the counter. Her sister had been coming in on a Wednesday to see her, but today was only Monday. Edna glanced down the long counter to where the senior assistant, Miss Connelly, was serving, and hoped the customer would take her time choosing the coloured braid. 'You'll have to pretend you're buying something.' She slid one of the shallow drawers out of the cabinet behind her and placed it on the counter. 'These are very nice buttons, madam.' She raised her voice for the benefit of Miss Connelly, who was now writing the bill for her customer. 'For heaven's sake, look as though you're interested,' she hissed, 'otherwise you'll get me the sack.'

Joan inspected the variety of buttons, saying, 'I will buy some, they'll come in handy for a dress or jacket.'

Edna's eyes narrowed. Joan looked pale today and her nose was red as though she had a cold. 'It's not like you to come in on a Monday, what's up?'

'Nothing.' Joan put a grey button back and picked up a gilt one to hold against her blue coat. 'I just thought I'd ask how Billy's wedding went off.'

'If you were that interested, it's a pity you couldn't be bothered coming along to see it.' Edna's voice was sharp. 'But then, he's only your brother, nobody important.'

'I did come,' Joan said softly. 'I stood in the side street.'

'You what!' Edna realised she was shouting and her eyes flicked the length of the counter. But, thank goodness, Miss Connelly was busy serving again. 'You mean you went all that way and didn't even have the decency to congratulate our Billy and Mavis? That's lousy, that is.'

'I didn't think I'd be welcome.' Joan handed the gilt button over. 'I'll take four of these, please.' She kept her eyes averted but her tone of voice puzzled Edna. There was definitely something amiss here. Usually her sister looked cocky and full of herself, but today she was very subdued.

'Have you got a cold or something?' Edna asked as she dropped the buttons into a bag. 'You don't look well.'

Joan was about to say something when Miss Connelly appeared at Edna's elbow. 'Everything all right, Miss Gillmoss?'

'Yes, thank you.' Edna stepped aside. 'Would you like to write the receipt out, Miss Connelly?'

There was no excuse for lingering and Joan had to leave the shop without asking the questions she'd been rehearsing all morning, and with four gilt buttons she had no use for.

Eileen laid down the knife and fork and picked up the remains of her lamb chop. She could feel gravy running down her chin as she nibbled at the meat left on the bone, but she wasn't in the mood to care. The silence around the table was getting on her nerves. The only sounds she'd heard in the last ten minutes had been the steady ticking of the clock on the mantelpiece and the occasional splutter from the coal fire. Tea time used to be such a happy occasion, with all the family round the table laughing and joking. Tonight it was like eating in a graveyard.

With a look of disgust on her face, Eileen threw the bone on to the plate and lifted the corner of her pinny to wipe the gravy from her chin. She gazed from Bill to Edna thinking how her family had shrunk in just a few weeks. There were only the three of them now, but surely to God that didn't mean they had to behave like monks who had taken a vow of silence? She was used to Bill being quiet, he'd never been the talkative type. But not so Edna. Usually you couldn't shut her up, yet tonight there was no getting a word out of her. Eileen had tried a few times to get them talking, telling them about Jean's visit, and the cream cakes. Since then, though, there'd been no attempt at conversation.

'What's the matter with you tonight, sunshine? Have yer been gettin' told off in work?'

Edna jerked her head round. She'd been miles away. 'What did you say, Mam?'

'Ye gods, she's goin' deaf as well as dumb!' Eileen pushed her plate away and rested her bust on the table. 'I asked if yer'd been gettin' told off in work? Yer 'aven't opened yer gob in the last half hour, an' that's never been known before.'

A battle had been raging in Edna's head about whether to tell her Mam about their Joan. She'd told her all the other times, but there'd been something different about her sister today and Edna didn't know whether she'd be doing the right thing in mentioning it. Better not, she decided. It was probably only her imagination anyway. She'd wait till Wednesday and see if her sister came in again. She smiled at Eileen. 'I was just thinking.'

'Well, stop thinkin' an' talk to me. Tell me somethin' funny, I could do with cheerin' up.'

Edna put her elbow on the table and cupped her chin in her hand. 'There's not much happened today, it's been very quiet. Except that a woman brought some ribbon back and wanted Miss Connelly to exchange it.' Her face lit up. 'I thought it was hilarious but Miss

188

Connelly didn't see the funny side at all. In fact it put her in a bad temper all day. The ribbon had been used to make a bow, anyone with half an eye could see that 'cos it was all creased, and Miss Connelly said she couldn't exchange it. But the customer brazened it out, saying the ribbon hadn't been used and was Miss Connelly calling her a liar? It ended up with the floor manager coming over to see what the fuss was, and he told Miss Connelly to exchange the ribbon.' Edna picked up her fork and speared a potato. 'So you see, Mam, in George Henry Lees the customer is always right.'

'An' has Miss Connelly been takin' her temper out on you?' Eileen asked, ready to defend her daughter.

'No, but I think she felt like punching the floor manager on the nose for making a show of her in front of the customer.'

'Who was in the right?'

'Miss Connelly was, but you don't argue with the boss. If he says jump, then you jump.' Edna raised her eyes to the ceiling. 'It wouldn't have been so bad if the customer had been nice about it, but she wasn't. She gloated over Miss Connelly's embarrassment and walked out of the shop with a smirk all over her face.'

'Cheeky bitch!' Eileen said.

Bill had been watching and listening with interest. He knew what was wrong with Eileen, she was missing the two chicks who had flown the nest. It was a while since Bill had thought about the baby they'd lost, but he did so now with sadness. If things had turned out differently, Eileen would have had a youngster to lavish her love on and wouldn't be missing the other two so much. 'Is that me Nan knocking on the wall?' Edna asked. 'It's either her or next door.'

'It'll be next door, but I'll check to make sure.' Eileen scraped her chair back. 'Be an angel an' clear the table for us.'

Maggie was holding on to the chest of drawers for support, her face grey. 'I don't feel well, lass.'

One look at her mother's face and the blood in Eileen's veins turned to ice. She'd never known her mam to be sick, ever. But she was now, you could see that by just looking at her. Eileen's mind was telling her to move, to do something, but her feet were rooted to the spot with fear.

'I think you'd better call the doctor, lass.' Maggie clutched at her side as a sharp pain cut into her like a knife.

'Oh, my God!' The sight of her beloved mother's face creased in agony galvanised Eileen into action. She stuck her head out of the door and yelled for Bill. He was beside her in seconds, spurred by the urgency in her tone. He took one look at Maggie and rushed to her side. 'What is it, Ma?'

'Terrible pains here, son.' Maggie's hand moved across her tummy. 'I've been having pains for a few days now, but I thought it was constipation. They were nothing like this though, I'm in agony.'

'Who's our doctor?' Bill turned to Eileen. 'I'll ring him from Mary's.'

'We haven't got a doctor.' Eileen was telling herself to be calm, her mam needed her, but it was hard. 'We 'aven't needed a doctor since we moved 'ere.' Her eyes met Bill's. 'D'yer think Dr Greenfield would come?'

'We're not on his panel now. It's too far to ask him to come. I'll get Mary to ring her doctor.'

Eileen followed him along the hall. 'Ask Mary to tell 'im it's urgent. An' will yer ring our Rene while yer there, I think she should be told.'

Dr Gray came out of Maggie's room and walked to the bottom of the stairs where Eileen and Bill were waiting. 'I think it's appendicitis, Mrs Gillmoss, and I want your mother in hospital right away. Can I use your phone to ring for an ambulance?'

Eileen was biting on her knuckles, fear written all over her face. It was left for Bill to explain they didn't have a phone. 'But I'll take you up to the Sedgemoors', it's only two doors away.'

As the doctor walked down the hall, Bill pressed Eileen's arm. 'Snap out of it, chick, for Ma's sake. Go and sit with her but don't let her see you're worried.'

Eileen couldn't move. If it was anyone else's mother, she'd run to hell and back to help. But this was her mam and her courage had deserted her. Edna was hovering near the living room door, the dirty dishes in the sink forgotten as she studied her mother's face. 'Don't worry, Mam, me Nan's going to be all right.'

'Do us a favour, sunshine, an' come in with me to sit with 'er? The state I'm in, I'll only make 'er feel a damn sight worse. I can't 'elp it but I'm worried sick. So will yer talk to 'er and try an' cheer her up?'

Edna took Eileen's hand. 'Course I will. Come on, Mam.'

For the umpteenth time, Bill went to the front door to see if there was any sign of the ambulance. Maggie was writhing in agony and although he tried not to show it, Bill was very concerned. He looked up and down the road and clicked his tongue with impatience. What the hell was keeping them so long? He closed the door and turned to find Eileen beside him. 'You stay in with Ma, I'll keep an eye out for the ambulance.'

'I can't bear to sit and watch 'er in pain when I can't do anythin' about it. I feel so helpless, Bill! I'd take the pain meself if I could, to stop her sufferin'.' Eileen grabbed his arm. 'She's not goin' to die, is she? Tell me she's not goin' to die, Bill, please?'

But Bill couldn't give Eileen the assurance she needed because things didn't look good to him. And the doctor must have thought it was serious to send Maggie to hospital right away. It would be wrong to build up Eileen's hopes. 'I don't know what to think, chick, I really don't.' He brushed a lock of hair from her eyes. 'We'll have to wait and see what the hospital say.'

'It's this bloody 'ouse, that's what it is. It's got a jinx on it. We've 'ad nothin' but bad luck since we moved 'ere.'

'Don't be so childish.' Bill didn't mean to speak sharply but he was too worried to listen to a load of mumbo-jumbo. 'I've no time for silly superstition and I'm surprised at you.'

Eileen's mouth opened, her face angry, but the words died on her lips when they heard the ambulance pull up outside. She shot Bill a withering look, then hurried into Maggie's room. 'They're 'ere, Mam. Once yer in 'ospital, they'll soon have yer sorted out. You mark my words, yer'll be as right as rain in a few days.'

Eileen bit on her lips so hard she could taste blood on her mouth, but she managed to keep the tears back until she saw her mother being lifted on to the stretcher. Then she broke down and it was Maggie who became the comforter. 'Don't cry, lass, there's a good girl.'

Bill was rough as he pulled Eileen out of the way of the ambulance men and bundled her into the back room. 'I'll go in the ambulance with Ma, you stay here.'

'No!' Eileen cried. 'She's me mam an' she needs me.'

'The last thing Ma wants is someone crying over her. And the state you're in, you'd be neither use nor ornament at the hospital. I'll stay as long as they'll let me, to see if I can find out anything tonight. So pull yourself together until your Rene gets here.'

It wasn't often that Bill used that tone of voice to her and it had an immediate effect. 'Yer right,' Eileen sniffed. 'I'm actin' like a baby.

You get off in the ambulance and look after me mam.' By this time Bill was running down the hall, Eileen in his wake. 'Tell 'er I love 'er, don't forget now.'

Rene arrived half an hour after the ambulance had left. She'd driven herself up in the secondhand Morris she'd bought six months ago after passing her driving test. She found Eileen sitting on the couch, her body hunched up, her face puffed with crying.

'Bill didn't say much on the phone, so tell me what's going on? What's wrong with me mam?'

Every question brought a fresh outburst of tears from Eileen and in the end it was Edna who had to relate what had happened. 'Me dad said he'd stay at the hospital until the doctor has examined me nan, that's if they'll let him.'

Rene gazed at Eileen. She felt like crying with her sister but knew that would do no one any good. 'You'd better buck yourself up, our Eileen, or you'll end up in hospital as well. It could be something minor, perhaps me mam's eaten something that doesn't agree with her.'

Eileen peered through swollen lids. 'Appendicitis isn't somethin' minor, is it? The doctor's not daft, he wouldn't have sent her away so quick if he hadn't thought it was serious.'

Rene jerked her head at Edna. 'Put the kettle on, love, there's a good girl. I'll stay till your dad gets home, see if he's been able to find out anything.'

Eileen made an effort at normal conversation. 'Did you put Victoria to bed before yer came out?'

'I was getting her ready for bed when Bill rang. Alan said he'd make her a drink, then take her up.'

But when it got to eleven o'clock and there was no sign of Bill, Rene grew uneasy. Alan would be worrying himself sick, as he always did when she was out in the car. If only Eileen had a phone, she could ring him and put his mind at rest.

It was just on twelve o'clock when they heard Bill's key in the lock. All eyes were on the door when he walked in, and from his face they knew he didn't have good news.

'Ma's got a burst appendix.' Bill ran a hand through his mop of white hair. He looked completely worn out and had been dreading having to tell them the news. 'They're operating on her tonight.'

★ ★ ★

Eileen stretched out on the couch, a cushion under her head and her old swagger coat covering her knees. Bill had tried to persuade her to go to bed but she wouldn't budge. How could she sleep when she didn't know how her mam was? And there was no point in keeping Bill awake with her tossing and turning, he needed as much sleep as he could get before facing a day's work.

It was getting cold in the room now the fire had gone out, and Eileen tucked the coat around the sides of her legs. 'I should 'ave banked the fire up, it would have kept the chill off the room.' She folded her arms under her bust and sighed. 'Bill was right, I suppose, when he said life must go on. But it's not knowin' 'ow me mam is that's worryin' me.'

Eileen plumped the cushions, then lay staring at the ceiling. 'You know, God, me mam's a good woman. She never misses Mass on a Sunday or Holy Day, never swears or tells lies, and I've never 'eard 'er speak ill of anyone in me whole life. But I don't need to tell You all this 'cos You know everything that goes on.' A lone tear trickled down Eileen's cheek and she could feel the warmth of it on her lips. 'I know I'm always askin' You favours, but this time it's for me mam, and I'm beggin' You, please don't let anythin' bad happen to her. Make 'er better, God, an' send her 'ome to me 'cos I love her so much.'

Chapter Twenty One

'Did you manage to get any sleep?' Bill asked when he walked through the door and saw Eileen sitting at the table, a slice of toast in her hand. 'I was that tired I don't even remember me head touching the pillow.'

'Yeah, I dropped off a few times.' Biting on her toast, Eileen rolled her eyes. Don't count that lie, God, she said silently, 'cos it was only a little white one to stop Bill from worrying.

'I wonder how Ma is?' Bill reached for the marmalade. 'At least no news is good news.'

'That's a daft thing to say! If yer've 'ad no news, 'ow d'yer know whether it's good or bad?'

'Because the police would have been here if there'd been bad news.' Bill spread a thick layer of butter on a fresh piece of toast. 'The hospital always notify the police if they need to contact the family.'

'I'll give Harry time to 'ave 'is breakfast, then slip up an' ask Mary to ring the 'ospital for me. They might let me in to see me mam this afternoon.'

'Go now, chick, before I go to work. Set me mind at rest.'

Eileen had her hand on the knocker when the door was opened by Mary, a dressing gown wrapped around her slim body, her hair all tousled. 'I was just coming down to yours. I rang the hospital because I knew you'd be on pins to know how your mam was.'

'What did they say, kid?'

'You know what hospitals are like, they never tell you anything except the patient is comfortable.'

'Did they say if I can go in an' see 'er this afternoon?'

Mary shook her head. 'I asked that, but the nurse I spoke to said no visitors until the doctor's been on his rounds. She said to ring again at four o'clock.'

'That means sittin' worryin' all day.' Eileen let out a deep sigh. 'I've a good mind to go in this afternoon and pretend I didn't know. Act daft, like.'

'You can ring later if you like. With you being her daughter, they may tell you more.'

'Our Rene will be 'ere about nine, so I'll wait an' see what she thinks.' Eileen backed down the short path. 'I'll have to get back to Bill, but thanks, kid. I'll see yer later . . . ta-ra.'

'I got the same as Mary at first,' Rene said. 'But I wasn't prepared to be fobbed off. I blew my top with the nurse, said it wasn't good enough and I was coming down to see the doctor.'

Eileen looked at her sister with admiration. Rene was so efficient and full of confidence, unlike herself who was as thick as two short planks. How could two sisters be so different in looks and intelligence? 'I bet yer didn't swear once, did yer, our kid?'

'No, but I was damn near it.' Rene huffed. 'I really gave her down the banks. Asked her how she would feel if her seventy-year-old mother had undergone a serious operation and someone tried to fob her off with the usual "the patient is comfortable".'

'What 'appens now?' Eileen asked.

'You're going to get yourself dressed up and we're going to the hospital. We might not be allowed to see me mam because she's bound to be knocked out after the operation, but at least we can see someone in authority who'll tell us how she is.'

'You're on, kid.' Eileen heaved herself up. 'Anything's better than sittin' here worryin' meself sick.'

They knocked at Mary's to let her know where they were going, then called at the florist's in Orrell Lane to buy an armful of colourful flowers. It was a tight squeeze getting Eileen into the small car, but Rene didn't stand on ceremony and pushed her sister none too gently into the confined space.

'Me nerves are shattered,' Eileen said as they walked from the car to the main entrance of Walton Hospital. 'I want to see me mam, but at the same time I'm terrified.'

'Leave all the talking to me,' Rene said, walking briskly down the corridor towards the ward and matron's office. Before knocking on the door, she passed the flowers over to Eileen. 'Here, you hold these.'

'Enter.'

That one word was enough to make Eileen's eyes roll. And when she saw the stern face of the matron she felt her tummy had suddenly been invaded by hundreds of fluttering butterflies.

'I can tell you no more than you were told on the telephone,' the matron said, tapping her desk with the rubber end of her pencil. 'Your mother is as comfortable as can be expected.'

'I think we are entitled to know if the operation was a success.' Rene spoke calmly, even though she was trembling inside. 'I am sure you understand, Matron, we are very concerned.'

Matron gazed from one to the other, her eyes finally resting on Eileen. 'The operation was a success, but I'm afraid your mother's age is against her. If she were a young person I'd have no hesitation in saying she would make a full recovery. But she is over seventy, and a serious operation at her time of life is always dangerous. The doctor was in to see her an hour ago, and he'll be keeping a close check on her progress.'

'When can we see her?' Rene asked.

'I'll have a word with the doctor after he's seen her again, so if you ring about four I'll let you know if he thinks she's well enough to have visitors. She isn't in the big ward yet, we've got her in a side ward where we can keep an eye on her.' The matron stood up to indicate the interview was at an end. 'Give the flowers to one of the nurses and she'll see they are taken to your mother's room.'

Eileen cleared her throat. 'Can we just take a peek at 'er?' She saw the slight hesitation on Matron's face and took advantage. 'Please? It would mean so much to us. We wouldn't let 'er see us.'

'My dear, your mother wouldn't see you even if you went in the room.' The stern face relaxed a little. 'She hasn't come round after the operation yet.'

'Please?' Eileen begged. 'Just a peep.'

Matron led them to a door which was half open. 'Just two minutes.'

Eileen gazed at the still form in the bed, and when she saw all the tubes attached to her mother her legs buckled under her. She fell back against the wall and would have fallen if Rene hadn't caught her in time.

'Come on, Eileen, out!' Rene took a firm grip of her sister's arm and led her to a bench in the corridor. 'Sit there for a minute and calm down.' Rene walked back a few yards. 'Thank you, Matron, I appreciate your kindness.'

197

'Would your sister like a drink of tea? I can arrange it.'

'No, thank you, she'll be all right. I've got a car outside and I'll have her home in five minutes.'

Mary had been at the window watching for Rene's car and was outside the passenger door in time to help pull Eileen from the restricted space. 'Come on now, all together . . . one . . . two . . . three!'

'Phew! Now I know what a sardine feels like.'

'I expected you home ages ago,' Mary said, taking Eileen's arm. 'I've been worried to death. How is Maggie?'

'We'd have been home long ago,' Rene said, 'but out Eileen was hysterical and we had to sit in the car park until she'd calmed down.'

'Let's get inside.' Eileen pulled her arm free to unlock the door. 'We'll tell yer about it over a cuppa.'

'I tried to tell her that everybody has tubes and things attached to them after an operation, but there was no getting through to Eileen.' Rene held her cup between her hands and blew on the piping hot tea. 'I was upset meself, because me mam did look terrible, but carrying on the way Tilly Mint here did, doesn't help anyone.'

'Honest to God, kid, I got the fright of me life.' Eileen shuddered at the memory. 'She looked so still, her face as white as a sheet, I thought she was dead.'

Mary could understand how her friend felt. Hadn't she been the same when her mam had the stroke? And if she hadn't had Eileen to help her through that bad patch, Mary would never have coped. With her strength and her humour, Eileen had kept her going. Now her friend was in need of the same support. 'You're expecting too much, Eileen! Just wait a few days and I bet you'll see a difference.'

'Will yer ring up at four o'clock for us, kid? I'm 'opeless on a telephone, the things scare the life out of me.'

'I'll leave Victoria with Irene next door, and me and Alan will go in tonight,' Rene said. 'We'll call in on the way back and let you know how she is.'

'Not on yer life!' Eileen banged her cup down. 'She's my mam, as well.'

'All right, don't bite me head off! We'll pick you up on the way.'

'What! Me get in that contraption again? No, thanks, sis, me an' Bill will get the bus.'

'You'd be better off ringing first,' Mary said. 'You may make that journey down there just to be told you can't see her.'

'I'm still goin', kid.' Eileen sounded determined. 'I'm not sittin' here twiddlin' me thumbs, worryin' meself to death.'

Only Eileen and Rene were allowed in the small side ward, and were told they had ten minutes only. Maggie looked exactly as she had that morning, her face white and drawn, her body perfectly still. Eileen, careful to avoid the tubes and drips, bent to kiss her cheek and whisper in her ear, but there was no response. Maggie didn't even know they were there.

In the meantime, Bill and Alan went in search of the matron to try to get some information. They were not encouraged by what she had to tell them. The doctor had placed Maggie on the critical list. She could have visitors at any time. But only close family, and only two at a time.

'I think we'll keep that under our hat,' Bill said, when the matron had bustled away, her starched uniform making a soft crackling noise. 'I'm going to bend the truth a little.'

When Eileen and Rene appeared, their eyes red with crying, Alan made a motion with his head to tell Bill he agreed. They were upset enough without burdening them with the extra worry.

'We've had a word with the matron,' Bill told them. 'And with Ma being in a side ward, you can come in any time you like. But once she's moved to the big ward you'll have to keep to the regular visiting hours.'

Maggie was taken off the critical list after a week and moved into the big ward. She was still very poorly, but the doctor said he was pleased with her progress so far. It was the longest week of Eileen's life. Each day she sat by her mother's bed talking and trying to be cheerful, while inside she cried. Maggie was a shadow of her former self, her skin didn't fit her face any more, but hung in loose folds, and her eyes were dull and lifeless.

'She tryin',' Eileen told Bill one night after Maggie had been in the big ward three days. 'Yer can see her makin' an effort to talk and smile, but it's as if she 'asn't got the heart.'

'Honestly, Eileen, I don't know what you expect! Isn't it enough that Ma's getting a bit better every day? Another week will see a big difference, just wait and see.'

'The woman in the next bed is nice, very friendly. She said she'll keep an eye on me mam for us.'

'Can't I go in and see her?' Edna asked. 'I could go tomorrow, it's half day closing. I want to see me nan, and it would give you a break.' Eileen was thoughtful for a while. She could do with an afternoon off, there was all that washing to be done. And the house could do with dusting and tidying, she'd let it go to pot over the last ten days. 'Yeah, okay, sunshine, I could do with getting stuck into some housework. But tell yer nan I'll be in at half seven.'

'I'll get her some nice flowers from one of the stalls by Central Station.' Edna munched on a chip dangling from the prongs of her fork. 'I'm dying to see her, it's been ages.'

'Ah, I was going to ask you to let me come in with you this afternoon.' Mary looked disappointed. 'I've even bought some grapes to take in with me.'

Eileen laid the iron down and folded one of Bill's shirts. 'I was goin' to get stuck into the bedrooms, kid, they look as though a bomb's hit them.' She saw the downcast look on Mary's face, and tutted. 'Okay, we'll go in. But they only allow two visitors at a time, so we'll get there ten minutes late to give our Edna a chance to talk to her nan.'

'I'll go and get me coat.' Mary was already on her way down the hall. 'Be back in two ticks.'

'Remember when we used to come in an' see your mam?' Eileen asked, as they made their way up the long path to the hospital. Half-way up, she stopped for breath. 'This ruddy path gets longer every day.'

'I remember very well,' Mary said, linking arms to urge Eileen forward. 'I was as worried as you are, but it turned out all right in the end, just like it will for your Mam.'

'This way, kid.' Eileen steered Mary towards the ward door. 'Come in with me an' I'll send our Edna out.'

Maggie was in the fourth bed down, and Eileen's eyes went straight to her. 'Oh, my God!'

Mary followed Eileen's eyes and gasped. Edna was sitting one side of the bed and Joan opposite. She held tight on to her friend's arm. 'Take it easy, Eileen, don't do anything to upset Maggie.'

As they neared the bed, Joan glanced up and the colour drained from her face. She looked around as though seeking a means of escape, then felt Maggie's hand on her coat.

'Sit down, love.' Maggie had seen Eileen and Mary before Joan had, and her initial sense of shock was soon replaced by one of happiness and a strange feeling of calm. 'Everything will be all right, I promise.'

Eileen neared the bed, her mind in a whirl. This was the last thing she expected, but oh, it was lovely to see her daughter. She bent and kissed her mother, then looked across at Joan. 'Hello, sunshine.'

'Oh, Mam.' Tears squeezed between Joan's closed lids. She wiped the back of her hands across her eyes, and her voice choked with emotion, she said, 'I'll wait outside.'

Eileen watched her daughter flee down the ward before turning her gaze to Edna. 'How did this come about?'

'She wanted to come, Mam.' Then Edna blurted out, 'She wants to come home, too, but she's frightened you don't want her.'

'Go out to her, lass,' Maggie said, her voice sounding tired. 'And make your peace with her. Life's too short for arguments and anger. She's a young girl who made a mistake and is sorry, so don't be hard on her.'

'Go on, Eileen, it's what you want,' Mary said. 'I'll just stay a few minutes because Maggie looks tired.'

'I am, lass, very tired,' Maggie admitted. 'All I want to do is sleep.'

'I'll be in tonight, Mam.' When Eileen bent to kiss her cheek she whispered softly, 'I love you, Mam.'

'And I love you, lass.' Maggie smiled. 'Go now and see your daughter before she runs away.'

Eileen sat up in bed, her elbow leaning on the pillow. She watched as Bill undid the knot in his tie and pulled it from his collar. 'Honest, yer could 'ave knocked me over with a feather when I saw our Joan. I didn't know whether to laugh or cry, belt 'er one, or kiss 'er. And to think I wouldn't 'ave seen 'er if Mary hadn't wanted to go to the 'ospital.'

'She's been a very silly girl and I hope it's taught her a lesson.' Bill was standing on one leg, leaning against the wardrobe taking his trousers off. 'That girl had no right to take her in, especially living the life she does.'

'It was the Yank who did it.' Eileen pinched at the fat on her arms leaving hollows that took a second to fill out again. 'He probably thought he was on a good thing with our Joan, but 'e didn't get anywhere with 'er. At least that's what she says, an' I believe 'er.'

'Well she's home now, thank God, so that's one worry off our minds.' Bill tied the cord in his pyjama trousers before throwing the bedclothes back and climbing into bed. 'And Ma looked a lot brighter tonight. I think seeing Joan bucked her up a lot.'

Eileen nestled into his body. 'I asked 'er if she wanted our Billy's room but she said she'd rather share with Edna. And yer should 'ave seen our Edna's face when she said that, she was as pleased as Punch.'

'I was going to mention that to you, chick.' Bill slid his arm under Eileen's shoulder and drew her close. Her body was so warm and comfortable it always relaxed him. Made him feel he was at home and all was right with the world. 'I hope you don't start making a fuss of Joan and leaving Edna out. That wouldn't be fair.'

'As though I'd do that! They're both my daughters and I wouldn't make fish of one and flesh of the other.' Bill felt the bed shake when Eileen began to chuckle. 'Anyway, our Edna wouldn't let me. She can stick up for 'erself, that one, so yer've no need to worry about her.'

Bill took his arm away and pulled the sheet over his shoulder. 'Anyway, you had all your family together tonight when Billy and Mavis turned up, so perhaps we'll see a smile back on your face.'

'Yeah, all back together again, just as it should be,' Eileen said. 'And yer don't 'ave to come to the hossie with me termorrer, 'cos Billy an' Mavis want to come. So yer can put yer feet up an' read the *Echo* to yer heart's content.'

Eileen listened to Bill's gentle breathing, and when she was sure he was fast asleep she turned on her back, her face to the ceiling. In a low voice, she said, 'Thank You, God, You've turned up trumps today. You 'ave given me my daughter back, and me mam's on the mend. You really are me best friend and I'll never forget You. I'm goin' to be so good in future, You won't know I'm the same person.'

Chapter Twenty Two

'Where are you two off to?' Eileen gave a little skip as she followed her daughters down the hall. 'Off flyin' yer kite, are yez?'

Edna opened the door and stepped into the path. 'I'm calling in to our Billy's, then going to Janet's.' A mischievous grin crossed her face as her sister joined her on the path. 'Our Joan's pretending she's going to see our Billy and Mavis, but I don't know who she's trying to kid. She's hoping to see Leslie Maddox, she's got her eye on him.'

'Go way!' Eileen folded her arms and leaned back against the door. 'Well I never . . . Leslie Maddox!'

Joan shot her sister a dirty look. 'Take no notice of her, Mam, she's pulling your leg.'

'Oh, aye? I suppose it's just coincidence that he's standing outside their door every time we go? And if you don't fancy him, why d'you go the colour of beetroot every time he speaks to you?'

'Oh, stop acting daft and let's go.' Joan linked her arm through Edna's and pulled her away. 'We won't be late, Mam, ta-ra.'

Eileen watched as they walked up the road arm in arm. Since Joan had come back home a month ago they'd become very close, and it did Eileen the world of good to see them so friendly. Now she only needed her mam home to make her happiness complete.

Eileen heard a door bang, then saw Mary coming towards her. 'Hi-ya, kid! Are yer comin' in for a cuppa? Bill's gettin' changed to go to the 'ospital but it'll be another ten minutes before he's ready.' She closed the door after Mary and followed her into the living room. 'Have yer ever noticed, kid, that men are more vain than women? All I've got to do is run a comb through me hair and I'm ready, but Bill takes ages. Mind you, with my tatty 'ead it doesn't look any different after I've combed it.' Eileen gazed at Mary's thick, curly blond hair and grunted in disgust. 'Every time I look at you I go green with envy.'

Mary pulled one of the dining chairs out and sat down. 'Harry asked if you and Bill would like to come for a run to Southport tomorrow night? We could stop at the Morris Dancers in Scarisbrick for a drink.'

'We don't get back from the 'ospital till half eight, kid, so it'd be too late.'

'One of the others could go in for you, Billy or one of the girls. Come on, Eileen, the weather's lovely and it would do you good. If your mam comes home next week you won't get a chance to go out, not for a while, anyway.'

'It's not certain she will be comin' out, we've got to wait till Monday to see if the doctor gives her the okay.' Eileen straightened the runner on the dining table and gazed at it with a critical eye, making sure the ends that overlapped the table were even. 'I'm keepin' me fingers crossed, kid, and everything else that'll cross. Except me eyes, of course, 'cos I don't want to go around lookin' like Ben Turpin.'

They could hear Bill's feet running down the stairs and Mary decided that she wasn't going to give Eileen time to make excuses. 'I'll tell Harry you'll be ready for seven tomorrow night.'

Harry took the country route to Southport. It was a bit longer than going down the dock road, but the scenery was lovely. Especially when the sun was shining, as it was now.

'It's lovely down these country lanes, isn't it kid?' Eileen gazed out of the window at horses grazing in the field. 'That cottage we passed before 'ad 1819 over the door, and this one,' Eileen pointed as Harry slowed down, 'was built in 1921. Yer'd 'ave a long way to walk to yer neighbours to borrow a cup of sugar, wouldn't yer?'

'An even longer walk to the nearest pub,' Harry laughed. 'We don't know we're born.'

When they neared the Morris Dancers, Harry was about to turn into the car park when Mary tapped him on the shoulder. 'Let's go to Southport first and call here on the way back. There's a smashing pianist plays here on Friday and Saturday nights, but he doesn't start till about nine.'

The fine weather had brought everybody out and Southport was crowded. Lord Street's fine Victorian arcades were bright with flower baskets hanging at intervals the full length of the wide street, and summer dresses, that had been brought out of wardrobes at the sight of the sun, added colour to the scene.

'Yer'd need plenty of money to live 'ere, wouldn't yer, kid?' Eileen paused to look in one of the high-class shop windows. 'Look at the price of that dress . . . nine pounds nineteen and eleven! Blimey, I'd get a full rig-out for that sort of money in T.J.'s, including knickers.'

They strolled up Nevill Street to the promenade and Eileen took a deep breath. She turned to Bill, who was walking behind, deep in conversation with Harry. 'Fill yer lungs with that air, Bill, it'll blow the cobwebs away.' They walked slowly along to the marine lake and Eileen nodded at an empty bench. 'Can we sit down for a while, me feet are killin' me?' She held out one of her legs. 'Just look at me ankles, swollen up like balloons. The warm weather's nice for some, but it sure don't agree with me.'

'You stay here and watch the sailing boats while I go and get the car,' Harry said. 'It'll save you walking all the way back.'

'He's not a bad old stick, your feller,' Eileen said to Mary when Harry had left. 'Nearly as good as my Bill.'

Bill was leaning on the railings around the marina. 'Come and see the swans, there's a whole family of them.'

'Ah, aren't they lovely!' Mary joined him at the rails. 'Come and see, Eileen, the little ones are gorgeous.'

'I'll 'ave to take yer word for it, kid. The spirit is willin' but the flesh is weak. I'm knackered.'

'It's crowded, isn't it?' Bill looked over his shoulder as he pushed his way through the mass of bodies. 'Is it always like this?'

'Every time we've been it's been choc-a-block,' Harry said. 'When you hear the pianist, you'll know why. He can't half tickle those ivories.' He spotted two empty seats and pointed. 'Grab those seats, quick. The girls can sit, we'll have to stand.'

The pianist was a man in his thirties, very ordinary to look at, but there was nothing ordinary about his playing. He could make the piano talk, and he knew which songs to play to get the crowd singing. After one sherry, Eileen was belting it out with the rest. 'Smoke gets in your eyes', 'Talk of the town', 'Who's sorry now', all her favourites.

'Someone's enjoying themselves,' Harry bent down to whisper in Mary's ear. 'It's a long time since I saw Eileen let herself go like this.'

'She's really enjoying herself.' Mary grinned, watching her friend's mouth doing contortions as she sang with might and main, 'My old man, said follow the van.'

When it was time to leave, Eileen did so reluctantly. 'I was just gettin' into me stride.' And as they made their way to the car she had them in stitches as she swayed from side to side, like a drunk, and slurred the words to 'Show me the way to go 'ome'.

'Woman, you're drunk,' Bill said, trying to keep the smile off his face. 'And there's nothing worse than a drunken woman.'

Eileen threw her arm round his neck. 'Yer've got that wrong, Bill Gillmoss. What yer mean is, there's no one better in bed than a drunken woman.'

Bill spread his hands out. 'What would you do with her?'

Harry scratched his chin. 'Take her home to bed.'

Maggie came home on the Tuesday. She was as white as a sheet, and so thin her clothes hung loosely, miles too big for her. But she was glad to be home and her relief brought the tears to her eyes.

Eileen was hopping from one foot to the other, her heart bursting with happiness. 'Come on, Mam, don't cry or yer'll 'ave me at it.' She'd missed her mother more than words could describe, but they were both too emotional to tell her now. She would tell her one day, but not until she'd got some flesh back on her bones and some colour in her cheeks. 'You're gettin' in that bed for a few hours' rest before the gang come in. And we'll 'ave a house full tonight, everyone's comin' to see yer.' Eileen slipped her mother's shoes off, then reached under her dress for the top of her stockings.

'I'll do that!' Maggie slapped her daughter's hand away, her face flushed with embarrassment. 'I'm quite capable of seeing to meself.'

'Oh, yer 'ome, are yer?' Eileen grinned. 'Gettin' yer knickers in a twist, as usual. Pity yer didn't leave yer paddy in the 'ossie.'

Maggie smiled. Oh, it was so good to be home with this daughter of hers. 'Just leave me, lass, and I'll get meself into bed. But I would like a cup of tea if you don't mind. The tea in the hospital was terrible.'

'Like maiden's water, was it?' Eileen threw her head back and roared. 'I 'aven't changed while yer've been away, Mam, either.'

Eileen popped her head around the door of Maggie's room to see Joan and Edna sitting on the side of her bed, both talking at the same time. 'Come on, you two, dinner's on the table.' She walked over and put another pillow behind Maggie's head. 'They'd talk the hind leg off a donkey, wouldn't they? I wonder who they take after?'

'Not their dad, that's for sure.' Maggie waved her hand at her granddaughters. 'Go and get your dinner, there's good girls. I'll see you later.'

'I've made some barley broth for you.' Eileen smoothed the counterpane where the girls had been sitting. 'Put a lining on yer tummy and some flesh on yer bones.'

'The girls seem to get on well together,' Maggie said, looking up into Eileen's face. 'Are you happy now you've got all your family together again?'

'They get on like a house on fire. Better than they ever did. And our Joan's not 'alf changed, she even washes dishes and helps with the cleaning.' Eileen put her hands on her hips and smiled down in to her mother's face. 'An' now I've got you 'ome, missus, me family's complete.'

'I'm happy for you, lass.'

'An' I'll be happy if yer eat the broth I'm bringin' in.' Eileen swayed to the door. 'Mary an' Harry will be down later, an' our Billy an' Mavis, so I'd better get me skates on.' She turned and smiled. 'They're all comin' to see you, yer know, missus, not me! What it is to be popular, eh!'

The first visitor that night was Martha Bradshaw, Mary's mother. Harry brought her down in the wheelchair, pushed her to the side of the bed, then left the two old friends to talk in peace and quiet. They'd missed each other so much and had lots to talk about. 'It's grand to have you back, Maggie,' Martha said. 'The days haven't been the same without you dropping in for a chat.'

'I'll soon be up and about, then you'll be fed up with the sight of me,' Maggie answered. 'Give it a week or two, and I'll be trotting up for me afternoon cup of tea.'

'Nan, can we come in?' Edna's head popped round the door. 'Me and Joan are going out, so we want to say ta-ra.'

Martha watched with a smile on her face as the girls kissed and hugged their grandmother, noting how gentle they were, careful not to hold her too tight. And her smile widened when she in turn received a kiss from each of them.

'Ta-ra, Nan!' they chorused. 'Ta-ra, Mrs B.'

'What it is to be young, eh, Martha? Still, we've had our time, haven't we? A lot to look back on.'

Martha looked pensive. 'Good and bad times, Maggie.'

'I'm sorry to break this up.' Eileen bustled in. 'But I've got a room full of people waiting to see her ladyship.'

Maggie raised her brows. 'Who's here?'

'Well, let me see.' Eileen held her hand out and started ticking off on her fingers. 'There's Mary and Harry, Vera and Arthur with Carol, and our Billy and Mavis.'

'It's good of them to come, and I do appreciate it, lass. But you won't let them stay too long, will you? I get tired very quickly.'

'Don't worry, they've been given strict instructions to be in an' out in five minutes. I'm keeping me eye on yer, so 'ave no fear, Eileen's here.'

True to her word, Eileen did keep an eye on her mother. She fussed over her like a mother hen, wouldn't let her lift a cup or make her own bed. Until Maggie put her foot down. 'For heaven's sake, lass, will you let me be? As long as you treat me like an invalid, I'll stay so.'

So Eileen stopped fussing and allowed her mother to move at her own pace. Maggie's progress was slow but sure. After two weeks of good food and plenty of rest, her cheeks and body were filling out. There was still a long way to go, but she was getting there. And when she asked Eileen one afternoon to walk her up to see Martha, Eileen was over the moon. Then a few days later it was a trip to the corner shop. After that they walked a little further afield each day, and both looked better for it. The pallor left Maggie's face and Eileen's chubby cheeks were a rosy red.

The only day they missed their daily walk was when the heavens opened and it poured with rain. 'Never mind, lass,' Maggie said. 'The farmers will be glad of it.'

Eileen set a tray with tea and biscuits, and when they settled she wracked her brains for something to keep her mother amused. 'Did you know our Joan's goin' out with Cissie Maddox's son, Leslie? Seems struck on 'im, too.'

'Doesn't the time fly?' Maggie said, shaking her head. 'It seems like only yesterday that Leslie was in short trousers and his face full of spots.'

'He's as old as our Billy. Done well for 'imself, too. Got a collar and tie job in Liverpool, which suits our Joan 'cos she's always been a bit of a snob.'

'Doesn't take after his dad for the gee-gees, then?' Maggie asked. 'His dad was always fond of a flutter on the horses. Lost more money on them than soft Joe. It's a mug's game, backing horses.'

'I never thought the day would come when me an' Cissie would be related.' Eileen chuckled. 'Remember the way me an' 'er used to fight? Many's the time we've rolled our sleeves up, stood eyeball to eyeball, threatenin' to knock the livin' daylights out of each other.' Her tummy shaking with laughter, Eileen spluttered, 'I'd 'ave died if she'd laid a finger on me. I couldn't fight me way out of a paper bag.'

'What about Edna?' Maggie asked. 'Hasn't she got a boyfriend yet?'

'She never says anythin', but I've got a feelin' she doesn't go to Janet's so often just to see 'er friend. I think Janet's brother is the attraction there. Edna's been sweet on John since she was a little girl.'

'You still miss the old street, don't you, lass?'

'Yeah, I miss all the old neighbours, like Cissie and Milly Knight. But we can't 'ave everything we want in life, can we? As long as I've got Bill, and you and the kids, I'm 'appy with me lot.' Eileen gave a cheeky grin, 'We did 'ave some good times, though, didn't we, Mam? Never short of a bit of gossip to make life interestin'.'

Maggie huffed. 'You were the one that gossiped, not me!'

'Oh, come off yer high 'orse, Mam, yer couldn't wait for me to tell yer all the news. Yer used to tut-tut, pretendin' yer weren't interested, but yer eyes an' yer lug 'oles were stickin' out a mile.'

The football season had started again, and one Friday night when Billy and Mavis called, Billy asked his dad if he was going to the match the next day. Bill nodded his head vigorously. 'Yeah, wouldn't miss it. It should be a good game.'

'You an' yer ruddy football! Like father, like son.' Eileen turned to wink at Mavis. 'Yer'll be a grass widow every Saturday, like me.'

'I don't mind.' Mavis gazed at the husband she idolised. 'It's his only hobby.'

'I'll meet you outside, Dad,' Billy said. 'Then we can stand together.' His handsome face creased in a smile. 'You wouldn't

209

enjoy the match without me standing beside you singing me heart out.'

When Bill came back from the match he found his wife sitting in Maggie's room with Mary. 'How did Liverpool get on?' Eileen asked. Then she added, 'It doesn't matter, I can see it on yer face. Liverpool won.'

'What about Everton?' Mary asked, rising from her chair. 'I hope they won because Harry always buys me a slab of Cadbury's on the way home. If they lose I only get a commentary on the game. How they could have won if the referee hadn't given a penalty when he shouldn't have done, or a goal had been allowed when anyone with half an eye could see the player had been off-side.'

Bill grinned. 'They were drawing at half time, but I haven't heard the final result.' He scratched his ear. 'What happens when it's a draw? Do you get a small slab of chocolate?'

'Yes, and all the excuses.' Mary patted Maggie's head before making for the door. 'I'll see you folks, ta-ra.'

'Yer half-an-hour later than usual, Bill Gillmoss, where've yer been?'

Bill opened the *Echo* he'd brought in with him, avoiding Eileen's eyes. 'I stood talking to Billy for a while. He's having a party for Mavis's birthday next week and wanted to know how to go about getting some beer in.'

Eileen screwed her eyes up. 'Funny he never mentioned it while he was 'ere. And surely he knows 'ow to get a few pints in, the daft article.'

Bill rustled the paper. 'Mavis's birthday is on Thursday, but he thinks they might have the party on Saturday, so everyone can have a lie-in the next day. Anyway, he's calling on Monday night to let us know.'

'I wonder what to buy Mavis? What d'yer think, Mam, somethin' personal or somethin' for the 'ouse?'

'Ask her on Monday. It's better to do that than buy her something she doesn't want.'

Eileen rested her chin on her hands. 'Will yer put the paper down a minute, Bill, an' listen to me? Did yer ask Billy if they wanted to 'ave the party 'ere? We've got a lot more room than them.'

'Eileen, they're married now, with a place of their own. They probably want to show off their house, so let them be, and mind your own business.'

210

Eileen's chins moved in the opposite direction to the shaking of her head. 'That's telling me, isn't it, Mam? Mind me own business indeed! I've a good mind to clock yer one, Bill Gillmoss.'

'If you do, don't be surprised if you get one back.' Bill let out a hearty chuckle. 'You'll get the one I felt like giving the goalkeeper when he let a goal in that even a child could have saved.'

'My God! No matter what subject we're on about, he always manages to get back to his ruddy football! I give up on you, Bill Gillmoss, yer past the post.' Eileen chuckled. 'Like that ruddy goal yer were on about.'

The following Saturday night Eileen was putting the finishing touches to her hair when Mary and Harry called to take them up to Billy's for the party. Mary looked more beautiful than ever, her long hair bouncing on her shoulders in a page boy bob, her lilac dress fitting her to perfection and her blue eyes shining.

Eileen plucked the loose hairs from the comb and threw them in the grate as she viewed Mary through the mirror. 'Yer lookin' pleased with yerself tonight, kid! Harry come up on the pools, 'as he?'

Mary shook her head, sending her hair swaying across her face. 'No, we're just looking forward to the party.' She held up a small parcel wrapped in coloured paper and tied with silver string. 'We've bought Mavis a link of pearls, I hope she likes them.'

'She'll be made up, kid.' After a last check on her appearance, Eileen spun round. 'What the 'ell's goin' on? You look as pleased as punch, an' Harry's got a grin on 'is mug like a Cheshire cat. am I missin' somethin'?'

Bill came in then, dressed in his best grey suit, white shirt and dark blue tie. 'Are we all ready? I promised Billy we'd be there for seven.'

'Where's our Billy?'

Mavis took their coats. 'He's just nipped down to the pub for a few more bottles of beer. We were frightened of running short.'

Eileen looked around. 'Are we the first? Our Joan an' Edna should be 'ere, they left the 'ouse ages before us.'

'You're the first.' Mavis patted the coats over her arm. 'I'll take these up and put them on the bed.'

'While we're waiting, chick, would you like to come over and see

Mrs Kenny?' Bill asked. 'When Billy told her about the party, she said she'd like to see you.'

Bill had a strange look in his eyes that Eileen couldn't fathom. 'Yer mean Mrs Kenny who lives in our old 'house?' When Bill nodded, Eileen grunted, 'I'm not going in there! What the 'ell does she want to see me for?'

'Come on, chick, she's an old lady. It won't hurt you to see her, just for five minutes.'

'Go on,' Mary coaxed. 'She can't eat you.'

Eileen allowed herself to be led along the hall, dreading the thought of going back into her old house, but afraid to refuse in case they thought she was being churlish.

Halfway across the road Bill took a key from his pocket. 'She gave Billy the key to save her opening the door.'

Eileen pulled her arm free, a startled look on her face. 'We can't just walk in someone's 'ouse, it wouldn't be right.'

But Bill ignored her and unlocked the door. There wasn't a sound as he led her down the familiar hallway. Eileen stopped at the foot of the stairs and refused to move as her eyes took in all the things she remembered. 'She's still got the same paper on the walls,' she whispered. 'It looks exactly as we left it.'

'She's an old lady, chick, she couldn't decorate herself and probably can't afford to pay anyone else to do it.'

Eileen took a deep breath. She shouldn't have let Bill talk her into coming. Didn't he have any idea what it would do to her? She made to turn to walk back out, but Bill was expecting it and in one movement opened the living room door and pushed her inside.

Eileen gaped and fell back against the wall. The room was full to overflowing and at first her mind wouldn't take it in. What was Billy doing here when he was supposed to be out buying beer? And surely Mrs Kenny wouldn't have invited Joan and Edna, or Arthur, Vera and Carol? And where was Mrs Kenny?

It was Carol who broke the silence. She freed herself from Vera's grip and rushed to throw her arms around Eileen. 'Hello, Auntie Eileen. We're having a party.'

Eileen absent-mindedly stroked the girl's hair, her mind in a whirl. She cleared her throat. 'Will someone tell me what's goin' on? If this is supposed to be a joke, then I'm not amused.'

Mary and Harry pushed her gently to one side to make room for

Maggie. Eileen stared at her mother open mouthed. 'Mam, what are you doin' 'ere? Yer said yer didn't want to come to the party.'

'I don't, lass, but I wasn't going to miss this.'

Eileen gazed at the faces watching her. 'Will someone tell me what's goin' on, please?'

No one spoke as Bill stood in front of her, a key lying in his open hand. 'The key to your new home, Eileen Gillmoss. Or should I say the home your heart has never left?'

Tears sprang to Eileen's eyes. 'Don't do this to me, Bill, please. It's not funny, it's cruel.'

Young Billy couldn't bear to see his mother cry and he rushed forward to put his arms around her. 'Me dad's not pulling your leg, Mam, he wouldn't do that to you.' He looked over her head and saw Mavis standing just outside the door with a glass in her hand. He motioned for her to pass it over. 'Take a drink of this, Mam, then me Dad'll tell you all about it.'

Eileen pulled a face as she swallowed the whisky, bringing a smile to those who were watching in silence. Bill waited till the glass was empty and Eileen calmed down enough to take in what he was telling her.

Mrs Kenny had reached the stage where she could no longer cope with living on her own, and had finally agreed to live with her son and his wife in Wallasey.

'That's what all the secrecy has been about, chick. She told Billy she was leaving, because she wanted him to tell you how much she'd loved living here, and this put Billy in a quandary because, like everyone else, he knew how you felt about this house. So he told me, and we took it from there.'

When it slowly registered in Eileen's mind that what was happening was true, the corners of her mouth curled upwards. She nodded knowingly as her gaze swept the room. 'An' yer were all in on the secret? That's why our Joan an' Edna were gigglin' when they left the 'ouse, an' why Mary an' Harry looked as though they'd won the ruddy pools!'

'Are you happy now you've got what you've always wanted?' Bill asked. 'Don't I even get a kiss?'

'We 'aven't got the 'ouse yet.' Eileen's grin was getting broader by the second. 'We'll 'ave to wait an' see what the landlord 'as to say.' Eileen heard the titters and giggles her remark brought forth, and her eyes narrowed. Pointing a chubby finger, she asked,

'What's so flamin' funny, Arthur Kennedy?'

Arthur put his arm across Vera's shoulder before shaking his head. 'Let Bill tell you.'

'There's no landlord, chick, I've bought the house.'

Eileen looked for somewhere to hang on to, and her son's arm was the nearest thing. 'What yer talkin' about, Bill Gillmoss? Yer couldn't buy the 'ouse. We've got no money.'

Bill took her hand, forced it open and laid the key in the palm. 'I took a couple of hours off work, went down to the building society and put down a deposit. The landlord wasn't going to rent it again, he wanted to sell.'

'Oh, my God, we'll end up in the work-house.'

Bill explained that the mortgage wouldn't be any more than the rent they were paying in Orrell Park. And with the girls' wages coming into the house, they could pay it off quickly. He closed Eileen's hand over the key and smiled into her eyes. 'By the time the two girls get married, we'll own our own house.'

It took a few seconds for Eileen to sort her thoughts out, then she began to chuckle. 'Oh, you lovely man, Bill Gillmoss, I love the bones of yer. I love all of yez.' Her hand moved to include everyone. 'I've got the best family and the best mates in the whole world.'

Then Eileen saw Maggie standing in front of the fireplace. 'Oh, Mam, I'm forgettin' you! Do you want to come back 'ere?'

'I can't wait, lass.'

The advantages started to spring to Eileen's mind. 'I'll be livin' opposite me son, isn't that marvellous? Our Joan's feller is only two doors away, an' I think our Edna'll be made up livin' near 'er friend. Then there's Milly Knight, I'll be able to get tick when I'm a bit skint . . . ooh,' her hips swayed, 'we'll all be so happy.'

'Except me and Mary.' Harry gave a lopsided grin. 'We're used to having you near us, now we're losing you.'

'Go on, yer daft ha'porth. Yer couldn't lose me even if yer wanted to. Me and me mam will visit yer, won't we, Mam? An' yer've got the car, so yer can come down whenever yer feel like it.'

'We've got some news for you,' Vera said. 'I'll let Arthur tell you.'

With one arm around Vera and the other around Carol, Arthur's face was the picture of happiness. 'Mrs Kenny has done us all a favour. We've been down to see your landlord and he said we can have your house when you move out. So me and Vera have made arrangements to be married three weeks today and we want you to be matron of honour and Bill our best man.'

Eileen's mouth dropped open and her eyes rolled. 'Don't tell me any more, me 'ead won't take it in. What a day this 'as been!'

'Mam, can we go over to our house now?' Billy asked. 'We can talk while we've having something to eat and drink. And at least we'll be able to sit down.'

'Oh, Mavis, I'm sorry!' Eileen hugged her daughter-in-law. 'We've spoiled yer birthday party.'

'Oh, no you haven't,' Mavis said. 'This is the best birthday present I've ever had.'

'You all go across,' Eileen said. 'Me an' Bill won't be long, we just want to 'ave a look around.'

They stood in the kitchen and Bill explained what he had in mind. 'There's a bloke in work who lives in a house like this, and he's had an extension built on the back. You'd have a bigger kitchen, and an inside toilet.'

'Ay, money bags, don't be goin' overboard. I managed before, an' I'll manage again.'

'The building society said they'll lend us a couple of hundred pounds on top of the mortgage to carry out the improvements,' Bill said. 'And before you explode, I've gone into everything with a fine-toothed comb. We can meet the repayments without skinting ourselves. I'm determined you're going to have a decent place to do your washing. And we'll all feel the benefit of an inside lavatory, especially Ma.'

In the bedroom they stood with their arms around each other's waists. 'It looks just the same,' Eileen said, leaning into Bill's shoulder. 'This room 'as seen a lot of lovin', hasn't it, Bill?'

'It has, and it'll see plenty more.' Bill squeezed her before moving away. 'I think we'd better get over the road. Don't forget it's supposed to be Mavis's party.'

When they reached the bottom stair, Eileen caught his arm. 'Bill, are yer sure? Don't do this just for me. I love this 'ouse, an' I'd be made up to come back again, but not if it isn't what you want.'

'As long as I'm with you, chick, I don't care where we live. Be it a hovel or a palace, as long as you're there, that's my home.'

'I love you, Bill Gillmoss.' Eileen gave him a bear hug that threatened to cut off his air supply. 'Now if you'll hang on a tick, I want to go to the lavvy.'

215

'Can't you wait until we get to Billy's?'

'Uh, uh.' Eileen was halfway across the living room when Bill called after her.

'I've got to give the key back tomorrow, you know, chick. We can't have it until all the papers are signed.'

Eileen was pulling the bolts back on the kitchen door. 'I've waited five years, Bill, another few weeks won't kill me.'

As she went down the yard, Eileen's eyes drank in everything she saw. The broken drainpipe, the black marks on the wall made by Billy's football, and the lavatory door hanging open, its lock skew-whiff like it had always been. Eileen peeped in at the wooden bench-like seat, and her eyes strayed to the nail in the wall they used to hang cut up squares of the *Echo* on when they couldn't afford toilet paper.

The memories came flooding back as Eileen stood in the middle of the yard with her hand on the old clothes line. She raised her eyes and whispered, 'You've been very good to me this year, God, and I want You to know how grateful I am. When I said I had the best mates in the world, well You come top of the list. I know people think I'm daft for wantin' to come back here to live, leaving a nice big 'ouse in Orrell Park. But part of my heart 'as always been in this little 'ouse because it holds so many happy memories for me. All me children were born in that front bedroom.'

Eileen heard Bill calling for her to hurry and she tugged on the line to let him know she'd heard. 'So You see, dear Friend, when we move back in, with all me family around me, this really will be the home where my heart is.'